The Gifted

Copyright © 2023 Mark A. Daniel

All rights reserved

The characters and events portrayed in this book are fictitious. Any similarities to real persons, living or dead, is coincidental and not intended by the author.

No part of this book may be reproduced, or stored in a retrieval system, or transmitted in any form or by any means, electronic, mechanical, photocopying, recording, or otherwise, without express written permission of the author.

Connie —
Welcome new reader!
I hope you enjoy —
Mark A Daniel

The Gifted

Mark A. Daniel

Mark A. Daniel

Chapter One
The Arrival

1

Taken as a whole the winter of 1955 was not any warmer or colder than most of the winters in Eastland. But for many years it was remembered as a cold winter in all of west Texas, due entirely to that one unusual week.

The cold air came barreling in on a Saturday afternoon. What had been a calm, warm Saturday good for yardwork and dove hunting turned into a blustery, cold Saturday evening which was suited only for staying indoors and getting close to the fire. Temperatures dropped from the upper sixties at noon to eighteen by nightfall. The arrival of this weather had been no surprise since it had been well documented, pushing its way down from Canada for the previous two days. What wasn't known was when it would go back to the north. No one had thought the storm would be as bad as it became.

As the sun declined into the west on Sunday night the snow began to fall. At nine o'clock Sunday evening Emily Robinson stood looking out the window of her living room at the fluffy flakes of snow which were illuminated by the back porch light as they descended. The next morning Emily stood looking out that same window at what seemed to be a foreign landscape. There were only a few mounds in the otherwise uniform white blanket which had been thrown over their land during the night. She could see a high mound where the garden tractor had been, and there was a slight dip where the old, dry creek bed ran across the field behind the house. The snowfall had been very heavy for this part of Texas. This was easily the thickest blanket of snow Emily Robinson had ever seen. Eighteen inches had landed during the night.

By Monday morning there was another twelve.

The town shut down for the entire week. No more snow fell, but what had fallen in those two blustery days still covered the roads and the cars and the homes belonging to the citizens of the small town. A few roofs had caved in under the weight of the snow, and Erma Keller had slipped and broken her hip. But aside from those events, and a few minor bruises, the snow and ice brought no real drama.

Schools closed. Businesses did not open. There were even two days when most of the mail was not delivered since Dell Johnson at the post office had only been able to dig up one set of chains for the three mail trucks.

For the most part the whole situation was a source of frustration for the residents of Eastland. There were many, though, who simply took it as a holiday and spent some time in their home with family.

Andy and Emily Robinson spent it alone. They had no children, though they had been married for five years, and had tried hard for four of those years. The doctors had been unable to find any real problem other than the fact that Emily didn't always release an egg, and Andy's sperm count was a little low. But it would happen if they just kept on trying.

This weather gave them the time and privacy they needed to give it a real good try.

It was three days after the snow began falling when Rebecca Robinson was conceived.

2

Nine months later there was a bumper crop of babies in the doctor's office in Eastland. Usually there were only one or two babies in the small room in the back of the office which now served as a nursery of sorts for the newborns. On this third week in September 1956, however, there was a total of seven babies, all delivered within thirty-six hours of each other. Doc Morgan had already figured out the week of conception for these children and had thus fondly named the entire group the 'snow babies' in honor of the snowstorm which had come nine months earlier and facilitated their almost simultaneous creation. There were not enough beds in the makeshift nursery and the Doctor had been forced to borrow cribs from some of the families in town. The word had been put out in the churches on Sunday, and the doctor ended up with two extras by the time the babies were delivered. Beds for the mothers were a different story, and the four healthiest were sent home to recover. Each of the four was distraught at having to leave her baby at the doctor's, but Doc Morgan had promised that their babies would be returned to them as soon as it was safe, which would probably be in just two days.

The Snow Babies were a happy lot. They were separated into different sides of the room, the three girls on one side, the four boys on the other. Nurse Verna Calloway stayed with them when the doctor was out, and she slept at the clinic in a room next to theirs, checking on them twice each night. She had been working with Doc Morgan for six years now, and had always lived in Eastland, except for the three years she had spent in Abilene training to be a nurse. In all of those six years she had never taken to a baby like she had to these. They were a special lot. She knew that she would watch them with particular interest as they grew, following their lives as they went to school together and became young adults. She felt tied to them somehow, and she knew they would always be special to her.

There was Timothy Watkins. He was the smallest and needed the most care. His little eyes didn't move like the others. He seemed to be concentrating on something very important, though sometimes the look seemed vacant.

Derek Lowrance cried the most. He also did a lot of kicking and moving. He was born with a head of jet-black hair, and his hands stayed constantly balled up into tiny little fists.

Steven Keith was quiet. He was the biggest baby of them all, just under eleven pounds at birth. He only cried occasionally, when the other babies were crying. Even then he was always the first to stop, and it seemed to calm them all.

Richard Hall was long and thin. His head seemed kind of smushed, and his eyes moved around the room as if he were always troubled. But then he would suddenly stop and grin as if he had just had the funniest thought. Verna called him her little grinner and mused that he might be the mischievous one of the lot.

Jennifer Summers glowed. Verna could never stop by her little crib without taking a peek. The little baby always cooed and seemed to enjoy the attention, though Verna knew this was scarcely possible. Verna felt drawn to Jennifer in a way that was different than the others, and the little gem was by far the most beautiful of the seven babies.

Samantha Chambers was the runt of the girls, though she was still bigger than Timothy. But her lungs were definitely the loudest. She was usually the second one to start crying, beaten to the punch every time by little Rebecca.

Rebecca Robinson was the most interesting little baby. She was always the one to start the group crying, but only by a second or two. It was as if she knew when the crying was about to begin, and the thought of it distressed her. She also turned her head when Verna walked by her crib, though she always did this a second or two before the nurse got to her. She would turn her head and stare at the wall, almost as if she were waiting for Verna to appear in her line of site at any moment, which is usually what followed. Verna thought the child was gifted, though she knew she gazed through biased eyes.

Verna loved these little children. She loved all the little children, but these little ones were somehow more special to her. It was as if she was being allowed to share in something great, something special. She checked on them more often than was normal, and she spent more time with them as well. Tomorrow all but two of them would go home. Then they would all be gone. It was like a small universe of time in which she was being allowed to experience true joy and wonder, a time she would never have again. It made her joyous. It made her sad.

3

The door had been opened a long, long time ago. It had been opened by a people who no longer existed, who had no descendants. They had chanted and sang and waited. Their land had become dry, their prey had moved away, and their enemies were killing them. They invited the strangers from far away to bring them power. Then they had left to journey south, their cries seemingly unanswered.

But the ancient ones had heard, and they were coming. As it was with the Christian God, a day was as a thousand years, and a thousand years were as a single day.

So they had come.

But their vessels, those who had been prepared to carry them into this new reality, had long since gone. In their place had come a new people with new beliefs and as time had passed the superstitions which had surrounded the ancient people remained only as tales now barely visible on the walls of dead caves.

But they had come.

Their power had arrived.

The terror had begun.

4

Verna awoke with a start.

Something was wrong.

She got out of bed quickly, stumbling over her shoes as she hurried to the door which separated her room from the nursery. She felt frantically for the knob, then threw the door open.

A quick glance told the nurse that the babies were all there, and that they were unharmed. Still, she felt uneasy, and she entered the room to take a closer look.

She had fed and changed them only an hour ago, and for now they all slept, all except little Rebecca. Her eyes were wide, and she was looking toward the wall, waiting for Verna to appear. Then the baby's head moved around almost frantically. Then Rebecca began to cry.

Verna's first thought was that this would wake the others, and she would have to hurry to the baby and discover if it was food or a change that she needed. But as she approached Rebecca's crib she could suddenly sense the danger. It was a smell, a feel, something like electricity or a smoldering fire.

Then there was a bright flash of light in the center of the room, just a few feet to Verna's left. It was followed by two more, then the sound of something tearing, like an old sheet or some clothing. The light filled the room, and the babies were coming awake.

But only little Rebecca was crying. The rest of them simply stared upward, toward the ceiling, their little arms moving about oddly as the smell of smoldering electricity filled the room.

Verna felt the panic. She had to get them out of here. She turned to grab Rebecca because she was the closest.

But instead she found herself turning toward the light. It flashed again, and she could not make her body do what she wished. Instead she walked to the spot where the light flashed and the tearing sound emanated, she walked next to the bed which held the black-haired little Derek whose bed was closest to the disturbance. Derek, too, was captured by the light, staring into it with his dark eyes. Verna could see into the flashing light, and she could see that it was not just light. There was something in there. She reached forward with her left hand.

Then she heard something like an explosion. Her ears hurt, and her head felt hot. New, terrible smells assaulted her, and the tearing sounds grew louder and louder. The light flashed brightly, but this time it did not go out. This time it burned its way into her brain. It fought past her will and her consciousness and buried itself deep within her mind.

And the lights went out.

Then the babies began to cry.

But Verna could not help them. Instead she lay a helpless mass on the floor of the nursery, a small line of blood seeping from her ear and marking the vinyl floor by her head.

5

She had found her vessel. She had found her place in the new reality. Now she would find Him. Then they would grow, they would multiply and spread themselves amongst the inhabitants of this world.

But she could sense that something was wrong. She could feel His presence. He had come, too. But He was not whole. Something had happened on the journey, something terrible. She tried to move, but her world was black. Her vessel was weak, and it would not rise. She could not see. She could not feel. It was dark

She would have to wait. It would take time to figure out how this vessel worked in her new reality. They had made the journey, and time had never worked against her before. But she understood that time had become real, and that in this reality it would work against them.

She could not fathom what had become of Him. But in time she would discover what had happened. Then she would repair Him. Then they would grow.

He was aware of his existence, but little more. This world seemed disjointed, and He knew something had gone wrong. He would not survive alone. He would not emerge in this form. Even now He fought with oblivion and felt himself losing the force that was his existence. He didn't even know if She had made it through or if She still existed.

His scrambled thoughts escaped as the darkness enveloped him. Losing the fight, He passed into his dormant state.

She would have to be his salvation now.

Chapter Two

1

January - 1957

Emily Robinson held her baby girl in her arms. Rebecca was a precious child. The most precious ever born. It had taken them five years to make her, and there would not be another. They had almost lost her in the hospital. They had almost lost all of the babies. Something had happened the night after Rebecca had been born. Emily had been in the small recovery room, asleep with two other new moms when she had awakened. She had been the first. Moments later came the sounds and the flashing lights which crept in through the window.

Emily had wanted to get out of her bed and run to her baby, but the surgery which had both saved her life and left her barren had also rendered her too weak. One of the other women, Myrna Watkins, had gone though. She had found the babies and the nurse in the nursery. The babies were all asleep. And they stayed that way, for too long.

The babies had slept for three days. The parents and those around them had all been frightened. The day Doc Morgan was going to send all of the babies to Fort Worth for the tests, the first one had awakened. It was Rebecca. The others followed.

The nurse was still "sleeping" in the hospital in Fort Worth they had moved her to after a week in Abilene. The doctors there called it a coma. Since the babies, too, appeared to have been similarly affected the small doctor's office had been checked thoroughly for chemicals and radiation. While the radiation levels had, in fact, been quite elevated, they were not sufficient to have caused whatever illness had stricken Verna and the babies. In addition to that, the babies now showed no obvious signs that they were still affected. The final piece that didn't fit was an old trinket of some kind which had been found by Deputy

Collins and had turned out to be literally thousands of years old, yet in mint condition, as if it had been recently fashioned. How it had come to be in the small nursery, almost exactly where they had found the nurse lying on the floor, was never understood.

It was the new year. 1957 was only a month old and had brought with it a new life for the Robinson's. The two of them had been reborn. Their love for each other had blossomed again with their love for the child.

Emily held her little girl close and fed her at her breast as she watched the child's mouth and eyes. Rebecca was a good baby. Emily knew that she was seeing through the eyes of a mother, but she remembered holding her younger brothers as well as her sister's three children, and she knew that Rebecca was truly different. At night Rebecca would cry when she was hungry. But she would almost always stop just before Emily got to her room. At first Emily thought that this might be a conditioned response to the hall light, but soon she came to realize that the little girl did the same thing in daylight. Emily also found herself waking up in the night sometimes and lying still for a few minutes before the crying started. It was as if she could sense that her baby needed something, or as if her little girl was calling to her with her silent voice. Emily wrote it off to mother's intuition. Inside she knew it was something more.

Emily rocked her baby gently and wondered again what had almost taken her jewel away from her. Nobody knew. The final declaration was that there had been an electrical disturbance, something like a lightning strike, only it had been September and the skies had been clear. But the babies had come through the ordeal seemingly unharmed, and the stories and rumors had been relegated to lore. Maybe someday they would have the answers. Emily didn't really care. All she knew was that it had passed, and that her baby was in her arms.

Rebecca released her mother's breast and cooed gently as her mother smiled down at her.

2
April - 1957

Ima Lowrance awoke again to the cries of her child. He always waited. He waited until she had just drifted to sleep before he started his crying. It was a routine he had started soon after they had brought him home from the doctor's office and had carried on for almost seven months now. The time of night was irrelevant. No matter how late she stayed awake, Derek was always able to catch Ima just after she had fallen asleep.

Ima rose from bed and made her way to the kitchen to warm the milk. She had wanted to breast feed the boy, but he had been too rough with her, biting down with his gums and squeezing too hard with his little fingers. He was a strong baby, and the pain was too much. So he was already on the bottle. When the formula was ready she took it to him and picked him up out of his crib. Tonight she had forgotten to pull her hair back and he grabbed a handful and pulled. When her face was close enough he slapped out and his little nails drew a small line of blood across her face. He always went for her hair. Jim thought it was funny and laughed whenever it happened. Derek never did it to him. It was just one of the secrets which had seemed to form between the boy and his father.

She tugged her hair loose, leaving a few strands of it in his little hands, then pushed the bottle into his mouth. He sucked for a while, then spit it all up. She was ready for this, and she turned his head toward the cloth diaper she carried over her arm. He always spit up at first, as if he wanted something else to eat. Then he would settle in and finish off whatever she gave him. At first she had fed Derek until he stopped. But she had become concerned at the amount he was eating and had consulted the doctor. Now she gave him only a certain amount with each feeding. He was still growing fast, but he was messing in his diaper much less.

Ima loved her baby, but she was concerned. At six months he seemed too hard to handle. She knew babies could be work, Derek was actually her second, but Gerald had never been like this. She thought it had something to do with that night at the doctor's office when all of the babies had gone to sleep for three days, and the nurse had gone out for good. At least it seemed as if she had gone out for good. The last Ima had heard, nurse Calloway was still in that Coma over in Fort Worth where they had sent her in February. Sleeping like a baby. Ima had talked to Nancy Hall, the preacher's wife, at church a couple of times about her baby. But Nancy had said that Richard Jr. was doing fine. Yes, he got her up at all hours. No, he didn't seem grouchy all of the time. Yes, he smiled and cooed like most babies. Derek had made his own baby sounds, but in Ima's opinion he had never cooed.

The bottle emptied and Derek let out a baby burp, followed immediately by a baby fart. His father had mastered the adult versions well and would have been proud of the little boy.

Ima put Derek back into his crib. He was asleep before she even turned his light out.

But he would awaken for another feeding in a couple of hours. About when Ima was finally dozing off.

3
July - 1957

Verna Calloway's body sat up in her hospital bed and stared ahead at the wall. The entity that had taken Verna's body also possessed the woman's thoughts, her feelings and memories. But it was not Verna inside. Verna was gone forever.

She had awakened a month ago after nine months of blackness. She had tried many different things before finally stumbling upon the ones which finally brought this vessel to consciousness. Yet She had been conscious the entire time. Only this body had been asleep.

And now it was awake.

The doctors had come and gone. She listed to them talk. She tried to mimic their speech. At first they had been pleased that Verna was talking. Then they had realized she was only repeating what she heard.

Their looks of anticipation had turned into looks of dismay. She was not coming along. The tests all said her body was okay and her brain was okay, but something had happened inside her brain, and they feared she would never be herself. They had no idea how right they were.

Hal had come. He had been Verna's husband. Hal had come to see her, to ask the doctors how long before he could take her home. Now there was new talk, talk of how he could not care for her, and where she would be most comfortable.

But now She listened and waited. He was here somewhere, She was sure of that much. But He had changed. He was broken. She would find Him and fix Him.

But for now She would wait and get used to this vessel. It was not at all the way it had been before. There were new rules and new constraints. But in time She would overcome these things. She would leave this place and search Him out.

They would propagate.

They would thrive.

She stared ahead as she had for the entire day at the television. She watched the images and listened to the words that made the language that constituted their communication. She would master it soon. Already She had made progress. But it was not like learning something new, it was like being born all over again, born again but remembering She had existed before and that She was not alone.

Two hours later She closed her eyes as the mysterious thing called sleep crept up and overtook her.

4
July - 1959

Myrna Watkins washed the morning dishes as Timothy played in the living room. He was almost three years old now, and she felt comfortable letting him play on his own for a few hours each morning. She didn't worry any more about "the problem." Timothy was mentally challenged. The doctor had broken the news to her on their second visit. Timothy wasn't hard of hearing, he didn't have a nerve disorder, what he had was brain damage. It had happened in the womb, a slight misinterpretation of the genetic code.

Timothy was her third and final child. The first had died while it was still inside her. The second had lived a healthy life for two months to the day, then it was over. She had prayed and cried from the day she found out she was pregnant with Timothy to the day she delivered. She had hovered over him as he had slowly developed. Then the doctor had declared that the dangers had passed. The boy would live. But he would not be "normal."

Myrna didn't care for that word, 'normal.' She did not cry when the doctor gave her the news. Timothy was alive, and he was hers, and she loved him. Her husband David had been distressed, but he, too, loved this child. Timothy was a gleeful child. His face smiled even when his lips did not. Even though there would be times when his eyes seemed distant, there were others when something clicked, and they lit up so brightly. He was a good little boy, and Myrna had the time it would take to prepare him for the world. She would do it a day at a time.

Timothy's eyes lit up their brightest when the music was on. He had reacted to music almost instantly, and they had made it a point to keep the music around him. During the day Myrna played either jazz or classical music, and at night she played the piano for him and for David for an hour. Timothy always stared at the piano keys as his mother played and he rocked back and forth. His eyes were bright and intent, as if he were studying her hands and those keys. He listened for as long as she would play, and he smiled from time to time when he heard something he particularly liked. Even though he was two months from his third birthday, even though he was slow, he knew when it was almost seven o'clock and he made his way to the living room to wait for his mother to appear at the piano bench.

Myrna knew her child was special. But she could never have guessed at the significance of those evenings by the piano and her child's rapt attention. Today she would find out.

Timothy played in the living room every morning while Myrna performed the morning cleaning. He had learned what he could touch, and what he could not, and he was good at following the rules. He was not mischievous, and it was not hard to tell what was on his mind. He would scribble with crayons or build with blocks while his mother cleaned. The small square blocks his father had made him were good for hours of amusement, and every day they seemed like new toys to him. Myrna knew he was trying. The boy's brain wanted to learn so badly, and she knew this would be a source of much joy, and of much pain.

That morning the radio sang Chopin while Myrna washed the dishes. It was a lovely piece, but a short one. It lifted her soul and made her feel light. But as it came to an end there was a loud 'pop', and then silence. She hurried into the living room, afraid that her son had decided to break something. Timothy was just sitting in the middle of the floor in the midst of his blocks, staring at the dead radio. Myrna walked over and tried to get it to work, but it was quite broken. She would find out later that it was just a tube that had gone bad. But for now she just shrugged her shoulders and apologized to her son. Then she returned to her work.

She whistled that short, beautiful song she had heard as she put away the last of the plates.

Then she heard the music.

It was a little choppy, and there were notes missing, but it was that same song that had just been playing on the radio. She stopped and stood still. Her eyes grew wide, and her heart began to race. The song continued, note after note, until it was over. Then it began again.

She walked slowly to the living room and looked around the corner.

Timothy was sitting on the piano bench. His little fingers were moving around the keys as he tried to make the music for his mother. He could not reach all of the keys for all of the music, but he knew how to make the sounds and he rocked back and forth as he played.

Myrna dropped the plate which split in two when it hit the carpet.

The noise startled Timothy and he turned to see his mother. Her hand was over her mouth. Her eyes were wet and she was shaking.

Was it bad? Did he do a bad thing? Was he not supposed to come up here without Mom?

Timothy was sorry, and he began to cry.

But his mother came to him, and she comforted him. She held him and she rocked him, but she was crying. She told him it was okay, that he was not doing a bad thing. Then she put his hands back on the keys so he would know it was okay.

He looked up at her and smiled. He tried to understand her tears.

Then he played another song for her.

5
September - 1960

Amanda Keith and Nancy Chambers sat at one of the park benches and watched their children play. They talked about the fall fashions, new recipes, Elvis, and the president. They reminisced on what the fifties had been and speculated about what the rest of the relatively new decade might bring.

There were a dozen children in the park, but Steven Keith stayed close to Samantha Chambers and her little sister, Sabrina. Steven got along with most of the children in the park, most of the time. But he always kept an eye on Samantha. She was his special friend. His mom had told him the story of how the two of them were born at the same place and shared a room, and she also gave him a special feeling, almost like family. Rebecca Robinson also made him feel this way, but her mom didn't bring her to the park on the same days, and her mom and his mom didn't spend as much time together as his mom spent with Manda, Samantha and Sabrina's mom. There were other special children, too. His mom had told him who they were. They all gave him special feelings, though not always good ones. Derek Lowrance gave him very bad feelings. Derek knew something too, because he always stuck his tongue out or made faces when their eyes met at the grocery store or when he saw him while riding in the car down the road.

Samantha Chambers was making something with the sand in the sandbox. It had deep valleys and small hills, and it was winding and pretty. Steven played on the merry-go-round but looked back to the sand box from time to time, until Samantha seemed to be finished. He got off the merry-go-round and stood, a little dizzy, at its edge. He looked at the sandbox and tried to tell what she had made. But she was standing on the other side, so he imagined it upside down.

Then he could see it. He had been expecting something like a city, or mountains and rivers (that's what he liked to make), but then he saw that she had made the head of a horse. It was like a picture. There were holes for the nostrils, and hills for the flowing mane. There were eyes and ears, and he could almost see the wind pass by as the great beast ran.

Samantha was good at making things. She always had good ideas, and she could make wonderful pictures. Steven smiled. Samantha looked up and saw him, and she was happy that he liked it.

But Sammy Hamilton didn't like it. He didn't like Samantha either because she was a girl and because she always made sissy pictures. He glanced around the swings and the sandbox once to be sure Steven was not in the park, then he ran across the field and leapt into the sandbox. He landed on the horses neck and shuffled his feet until its mane and face were obliterated.

Samantha started to cry. It had taken her over an hour to make the horse, and she hadn't gotten to show it to her mother yet. She wanted to show her friends, too. But Sammy was two years older, and much bigger. He stood and laughed at her, then kicked some of the sand in her little sister's eyes. Samantha was sad, mad, and scared. Her little sister began bawling, and that made it even worse.

Then Sammy felt a little hand push his back.

Sammy Hamilton was big for a six-year-old. Steven was going to be four in two weeks. Although Steven was also big for his age, Sammy was a head and shoulders taller. Still, Steven was a little rock. Sammy couldn't back down now, some of his friends were watching. He tried to push Steven down, but Steven just took two steps back. This made Sammy nervous.

"You messed up her horse," was all Steven said.

"It was a stupid horse. It was a sissy picture, and it was ugly." As he said this he threw a glance at Samantha. The insults to her artwork hurt her more, and the crying continued.

By the time he had turned back to Steven, Steven's hands were already on his chest. Steven pushed, and Sammy went down on his butt. He landed in the sandbox, which was soft and didn't hurt as badly as the ground. Then Sammy stood up and fought like his dad had taught him. Sammy balled up his hand into a fist and hit Steven once in the face. Steven had never been struck like this, and he had never fought like this. He had never had to. His face stung, and Sammy was standing there like he was waiting for something.

Steven balled up his fists and hit back, first with his left, then his right.

Sammy fell down again, and everything looked funny. Then his face burned, and he started to cry. Sammy's older brother was watching from the jungle gym, and he laughed loudly.

Then big hands grabbed Steven's arm from behind and pulled him away from the boy. It was Mom. Steven was scared that he was in trouble, but Mom just led him away from the sand and the other kids and walked him toward her table. Manda came too, and she carried Sabrina while Samantha ran along side.

When they got to the table they had a talk about big mean boys and fighting with fists. Steven listened and realized that he was not going to get a spanking. He would remember that thing about fighting with fists. It worked good.

Samantha wasn't crying anymore, and that was good too. He looked across the table to her and she was smiling at him.

"I liked your horse," he said.

"Did you see it?"

Steven nodded.

Samantha beamed.

They sat with their mothers for a few more minutes before leaving the park and each other. They would always be special friends.

6
October - 1962

At the age of six, Richard Hall seemed troubled beyond his years. He was not a joyful child. His forehead was almost always wrinkled in a frown of concern. But he had memorized over fifty versus of the bible, and he knew most of the hymns they sang on Sunday by heart.

Richard Senior had been the leader of the Eastland Baptist Church for fifteen years. While Richard Junior had both a younger brother and a younger sister, the bulk of the discipline fell to Richard Junior. His mom had told him he would always be the oldest son, and that this was special. He was to be an example to his siblings as well as to all of the other children that he came into contact with. He was being groomed to take his father's place someday, though not necessarily in Eastland. Nancy Hall had plans for all of her children. Matthew was going to be a missionary. Sarah was going to be the wife of a preacher. Richard was going to preach.

Richard had visions. His mother had caught on to them at an early age. At first he wouldn't talk about them much, but she finally convinced him that it was best for him if he did tell his mother so that they could interpret them together. He told her about the good visions. But sometimes he had bad visions, too. When these came he usually made up something else. Otherwise his mother would accuse him of having sin in his heart which brought out the evil visions.

But they could be awful; and sometimes just bad.

Last night he had seen the monster vision again. This vision had plagued him for as long as he could remember. Now he didn't cry when it came, so his mother wouldn't know. The monster wasn't after him, it was after his friends. He watched as it ate them and made blood everywhere. Then the monster looked at him and laughed and said, 'you made me do it, Richard.'

The good visions were usually about such things as colorful flowers or flowing rivers. They were never very concrete, and his mother said they had to do with the spiritual airplane, whatever that was. Richard had seen planes before, but he didn't know the difference between a regular plane and a spiritual one.

7
April - 1963

At six Jennifer was still the charmer. She was spoiled rotten by her parents, her grandparents, and just about everyone else she could manage to wrap around her petite little fingers.

She was a beautiful little girl and her gentle pout and lively eyes demanded attention. When she entered a room she soon became the center of attention. Her mother knew it was a gift. Even strangers always wanted to come up and talk about her adorable little girl. Jennifer was charismatic. Something about her grabbed people's attention and held it for as long as she wished. Already Jennifer had won two pageants put on by the city. She had been allowed to enter the category for the first graders two years before she had entered the first grade, and had one both years. Now that she was in the first grade there was really no reason for any of the other little girls to enter, except to glory in taking second place to Jennifer Summers. From her first pageant to her last, which was many years later, she always took the crown, even this year when her two front teeth were missing.

And she always would.

She was gifted.

8
November - 1963

Rebecca Robinson was seven years old when the incident which would shape her life took place.

It was a cool November night when Emily was awakened from her bed by the cries of her daughter. Rebecca was not given to needless crying, and she normally slept soundly, so Emily got up and went to Rebecca.

Emily entered the room and switched on the light. Rebecca was lying on her bed, looking toward the ceiling. Tears were rolling down the sides of her face and wetting her pillow. Emily went to her daughter and sat on the edge of her bed.

"What's wrong, honey?"

"They killed the nice man," she sobbed. Her eyes remained on the ceiling.

"What nice man?" Emily asked.

"I don't know."

"Who killed him?"

"I don't know."

Rebecca finally looked at her mother. The image had come to her in her sleep, as many of them did. There had been blood, and flesh, and a black car. Most of the time Rebecca kept these visions to herself. Tonight she could not.

Emily had learned not to discount her daughter's strange talk. Often times this strange talk meant something. Emily knew that her daughter seemed to have a dose of precognition. She seemed to know when relatives were coming to visit, and she always won at 'go fish.' Emily believed that her daughter was gifted, that she was in possession of an ability which most people did not have, so she tried to understand why her daughter was crying.

But even Rebecca didn't know why she was crying. She didn't know who the nice man was, but she was very sad that he had to die. It was very real to her, and she knew that it had happened. Or that it would happen.

Her mom held her as she cried until she fell to sleep almost an hour later.

Emily heard her daughter cry two more times that night.

The next morning Emily sent Andy off to work and her daughter to the school. It was a cool November day. Rebecca was unusually quiet. Mrs. Childers scolded her for not paying attention in math.

Finally, during writing practice, she started crying again. This time she could not stop. Her sobs became so loud that all of the children turned to look.

Mrs. Childers walked to her desk to ask her what was wrong.

But before she could get the question out the public address system popped on and the principal interrupted her.

Apparently something serious had happened.

Principal McKinley announced that President Kennedy had been shot. They didn't know yet how serious it was, but it did not look good.

Rebecca knew that he was dead already. She remembered the images of the blood and other things she had seen on the woman's jacket in the big car.

Mrs. Childers just looked at Rebecca as the shock of the event overtook her.

Back in her home Emily Robinson cried tears of her own not only for the fallen president but for her daughter as well.

2
January - 1967

It was a cold winter morning the first time Derek killed.

It was late January. A cold snap swept over west Texas. An even colder one had hit the southeast, and below zero temperatures were popping up all over the Midwest and northeast.

Derek was at home by himself. His mother had gone to the store and had left him home. It was what he had insisted on, and he could be plenty of trouble if he didn't get what he wanted. His older brother, Gerald, was playing next door with Tommy Matson. Derek played over there sometimes too, but today he wanted to stay home, by himself.

Derek sat in his room and watched Wilbur, the pet gerbil he had gotten for Christmas. At first he had thought it was a pretty neat present.

But then he discovered that Wilbur pooped and peed a lot, and that he was expected to regularly clean up the small fish tank that was Wilbur's home. Derek's dad insisted, so there wasn't much leeway here. He overheard his parents discussing Wilbur and how he was going to teach their little boy about 'responsibility.' Derek wasn't sure what responsibility meant, but if it meant cleaning up gerbil poop, he'd had enough.

He took the lid off the gerbil cage and put his hand inside. Wilbur didn't seem to mind, he'd grown used to being handled. Derek wrapped his hand around the little rodent and pulled him out of his tank. Derek smiled at the little creature. "I've got something in mind for you," he said. Then he headed to the kitchen

He got out one of his mother's clear glass bowls and threw Wilbur inside. Then he covered the top of it with foil. He placed the bowl into the preheated oven, then turned the light on so he could watch.

At first Wilbur didn't seem to notice the heat. Then a few minutes later he started darting around the bowl. He would run for a second, then stop, then run, then stop. Derek grinned as he watched the animal try to figure out what was going on.

It took ten minutes for it to get really hot inside the bowl. Then the Gerbil was jumping and dancing around. It bounced off the tin foil as it leapt, and the foil became loose. Then it jumped for the lip of the bowl and got hold. Derek watched the Gerbil as it pushed its way through the foil and leapt onto the oven's grill. Then the show got really exciting.

Wilbur the gerbil danced and leapt and flew around inside the oven until it fell through the gap where the grill met the side of the oven and landed next to the heating element. One of its left legs burned and stuck to the element. As Wilbur tried to get away his fur melted on his left side. Smoke was coming from his body. Derek watched and grinned.

Then he thought about the mess. He didn't want them to know, and they might see the mess. He pulled open the oven door and reached for the Gerbil, but it was too hot inside. He got the long fork out of a drawer and used it to pop the smoking animal off the element. Then he picked it up by its smoldering tail and looked at its twisted body.

It was still moving

His eyes wandered to the gerbil's eyes. They were deep and black.

Wilbur twitched once more. Then he died.

Something happened then. Derek felt something tingling in his head. It moved through his brain and then his whole body. It was difficult to stand up as his legs weakened. It was the most pleasurable feeling he had ever felt. It lasted for just a second, then was gone.

What was this? What had happened? This had to be like one of those 'happy drugs' that Pep Barton at school had talked about. It felt so good.

When the feeling wore off he closed the oven door and carried the dead animal back to his room. He was going to put it back into the aquarium and claim a natural death, but the tiny pet was too damaged now from the heating element. There would have to be another, better story.

He called Butch, their big, black tomcat. Butch had been eyeing Wilbur since Christmas. Now he would get his chance.

It only took the cat a minute to take care of Derek's little problem.

Derek petted the purring cat as it devoured his well-done Christmas gerbil.

Derek wondered what it would be like looking into Butch's dying eyes.

It took him two months to figure out how to get away with it.

Chapter Three
1
1997

He was taking a big chance. He had taken big chances before, but this was different. In the past he had taken easy opportunities and made convenient plans around them. That's how he had gotten away with killing his own sister. That's how he had gotten away with killing Tommy Matson, his brother's friend and next-door neighbor. He had also killed some nameless faces, faces which no one would miss. Always for the rush. The rush was better than sex. The rush was better than life. He spent his waking hours trying to carefully plan how he was going to get that rush again. He was careful because if he did get caught and sent to prison then he might never experience that rush again, and so his true life would be over. Not that his life had turned out to be anything worth bragging about. The only thing about his life that made it worth living was the planning and scheming, and finally the rush of the kill.

But tonight he was taking a very big chance. He had been lured by the woman, the crazy woman who had been dogging him for years. She had finally come to him with the revelation that she knew his secret, that she knew he had killed, and she named names. He thought about just killing her too. Nobody would care. They all knew she was crazy. But she was crafty, too, and she had hidden notes that would be found if she died. Notes which would mean the end of the ecstasy. So he had listened.

At first he supposed that she would want money. He had money. Not enough to be considered rich, but enough. But she did not want money. She simply wanted him to kill someone for her. She said that the killing was really for him too, that he could not possibly comprehend what awaited him. If he would just kill the person she wanted him to kill, then he would understand. He would evolve into something new that understood death and transcended it. He would take the first step in healing the cosmic tear which had shattered her lover into so many little pieces.

He had heard this ranting before, but it had been a very long time ago. The woman went on about the terror of the transcendental transformation, about the rending of universes and other such things. She had been uttering this nonsense for as long as he could remember. They used to make such fun of her. She was the town nut. She had been crazy before she had gotten old, and none of that had changed. But none of that really mattered now. What mattered was that she had gotten him into a corner, so now he was taking a big risk.

He had refused to kill anyone in Eastland in twenty years. There were already too many questions after the death of his sister. His brother Gerald was doing time somewhere in Alabama for killing a man in a bar fight. Gerald had spouted off from time to time about Derek, but never if he thought word would get back to his younger brother. Gerald was afraid of him. That was good, it helped keep him in line. But now Gerald was far away, and that was even better.

The old woman had given Derek a name, one he remembered from years past. It was one of the girls he had gone to school with, the pretty one. He remembered that she had been the head cheerleader, and that she had run with the crowd he could never have been a part of. She was a self-centered bitch. When Verna had uttered the girl's name a grin had crept across Derek's face. The kill would indeed be a pleasure, though the risk pretty high considering what Jennifer had become.

Jennifer had left Eastland twenty-three years ago. She and all of her friends. Her parents had moved on almost ten years ago. It would be impossible even to find her, much less kill her. But the old woman had a city, and an address, and even the woman's new last name, though that wasn't much of a secret considering the popularity of the football player she had married. The old woman had done all the research. Now it was time for Derek to execute, in more ways than one.

| 25 |

So here he was, in the middle of the night, scaling the outside of a large home in Alpharetta, Georgia, a trendy upscale suburb north of Atlanta. Verna had even paid for the plane ticket and given him some fake identification. Apparently the old woman had been planning this for some time and had been certain that he would accept. Verna had also mentioned a reward several times, though would not explain what she meant when he asked for the details, which made him suspicious. But it was not the reward which motivated him, it was the threat of incarceration combined with the thrill of the challenge and scope of his own personal reward.

Verna had given Derek some strange instructions on how to do the job. The one thing she kept stressing was the eyes. She explained that it was very, very important that he be looking into Jennifer's eyes as her life left her. She said she would know if he did not, and that she would tell the police about him if he failed to do this. There was no way she would be able to know. But he would do it anyway. That always made the rush the best, seeing the life drain from the eyes, feeling the electricity of the fleeing soul. He had felt that rush perhaps two dozen times in his life and had never been able live without it for more than one year.

Derek climbed over the railing and onto the balcony of the master bedroom. He stopped for a moment and looked down from the balcony to the yard he had crossed. It was a huge yard with elegantly sculpted shrubbery and well-groomed rose gardens. The yard was surrounded by a wrought-iron fence which was anchored to stone pillars. It looked secure. It was designed to keep people like him away, people who weren't good enough to stand in the presence of Jennifer and her famous husband Jack. Jack Cassidy had only last fall retired after twelve years of those fall and winter Sunday afternoon battles which captivated millions. The man had two rings from two trips to the Super Bowl, and a wife who had given up the beauty pageant circuit years earlier and now had her own evening entertainment show which was getting bigger by the year. Derek had even seen that show once or twice. It stank. It was a bad rip-off of Entertainment Tonight, only with more interviews. But he had to admit that Jennifer's legs did look better than Mary Hart's, which had been a point of controversy for the tabloids when Jennifer had started her new show.

The air was cold on his face. The adrenaline was flowing through his veins. He had killed before, but not like this. Before it had been something like opportunism, an artificial accident. This was more like murder. This was stalking and hiding and leaping out in surprise. He had a knife because it was silent. There were guards here, but they sat in the living room awaiting a frontal assault which they knew would never come. Jack was out of town working on a television deal of his own. Jennifer was sleeping. They were supposed to be taping next week's shows early the following morning.

But Jennifer would not be on time for the taping. In fact, she would not be there at all. She would probably be mentioned in passing on that competitive show this very evening, its hosts no doubt sporting ample amounts of false dismay, eagerly awaiting the bump in ratings that would come from the weakening of the competition.

French doors led from the balcony to the bedroom. They were elegant, but not sturdy. Derek turned the knob silently and pulled. They were locked. He would have to hope that Jennifer was a heavy sleeper, because he was going to have to make some noise. Derek made sure he would be able to reach the knife quickly once he got inside. Then he took a deep breath and closed his eyes.

He wouldn't do this again, it was simply too dangerous. He would kill the crazy old woman and leave Eastland. There probably weren't even any notes.

He pulled suddenly and firmly on the French doors. He had done this to many such doors before, they were really nice to look at, but ineffective for security. The wood frame popped as the shaft of the dead-bolt lock tore through. The curtains which draped the length of the doors fluttered as the doors flew open.

In an instant he could see where the bed was. The moment he looked he knew she was in it. He could feel it. It was a feeling which pulled at him inside. It always had. It was a feeling which begged him to come closer, and since he never could it had made him bitter. But now he would come closer, he would come very close indeed, then he would deliver a gift to her and look into her dying eyes.

She stirred.

Derek leapt into the room and crossed the oriental rug which covered the floor. In a moment he was next to the bed, looking down. He could have driven the knife home in that instant. There would be no sound. She wouldn't have any idea what had happened.

But instead he waited. He wanted to look into her eyes.

They opened slowly. For just a moment they looked up in puzzlement, but then recognition flashed into them.

"I knew you would come," she said quietly.

He waited for her terror, but it did not come. Her eyes remained calm. She did not move.

She was beautiful, even like this. Her soft porcelain skin reflected the moonlight, her lips were full and inviting, and her eyes, oh her eyes were so deep.

Before she could work her charms on him he drew the knife. Still she did not move. She lay helpless, and this truly made it harder. He had to know more.

"What do you mean?" he asked her.

Jennifer only smiled.

His rage burned inside. He would never know the answer to that question. It was a puzzle that would haunt him for eternity.

He raised his voice. "What do you mean?"

Her eyes remained calm and resigned. "I won't scream."

Her beauty and calmness infuriated him all the more. Derek looked at her one last time, furious that she would not give him the answer he sought, then brought the gleaming blade down upon her.

It entered her body swiftly and silently. It cut cleanly through her flesh and pierced her heart in an instant. A rush of air escaped from her mouth, and it sounded almost like a sigh of ecstasy.

Her chest heaved, but she did not cry out. Her eyes squinted from the pain, but they did not close. Instead her eyes remained on his. She would not look away. And he began to understand what Verna had meant.

Then it came. It was unlike anything he had ever felt. Jennifer's eyes pulled at him, he felt something deep inside himself stir.

Then the fire leapt out of her eyes and consumed him. His body burned and all of his nerves cried out first in pain, then in total ecstasy. He tried to look away, to close his eyes, but he was captivated. His body continued to burn as something forced its way into his head, then nested somewhere deep within him.

He felt the warmth then, inside. It wound its way through his body and aroused him. It made him feel strong. It made him feel invincible.

The old woman had been right. Perhaps she was not so crazy after all.

But if she was not crazy, then what was she? He would have to find out when he returned to Eastland.

The fire subsided, but the warmth remained. Derek realized that he was holding her now lifeless head in his right hand. He lowered her head back to the pillow, then closed her eyes. She was still beautiful, and it still infuriated him. He considered taking that from her, slashing her flawless face into oblivion.

But he already had something which had been hers. He felt it inside. And suddenly he knew that there was much more.

He knew in that instant that he had changed. He knew that as time passed he would better learn what he had become, or what he was becoming. Tonight it was a beginning, though of exactly what he could never fathom.

He looked away from Jennifer and leapt back to the balcony, only now he seemed to fly, touching the floor only once as he crossed the bedroom. He began to climb down the wall, his hands were strong, and his feet were sure. He leapt the final ten feet, and it was like jumping off a curb. His feet landed firmly on the grass and it was like landing on the softest sand.

This was wonderful.

He would go home and find the old woman. She would tell him what this all meant.

But first he would hunt.

Derek fled across the yard, scaling the fence in one fluid movement, disappearing into the night so quickly it was as if he could fly.

2

Rebecca Robinson was the first to know. Even before Jennifer's maid found the body in the morning, Rebecca knew.

Rebecca was sitting at her desk in the back of her small apartment in San Francisco, rummaging through photographs and personal effects of a missing little girl when it hit her. She had opened herself to her gift, and answers to what had happened to the little girl and where she might now be were beginning to come to her in indistinct images.

Then it leapt out at her. It was like the day the president had been killed, or the day the space shuttle had exploded. It hit her suddenly and ran though her like a deep chill, and Rebecca knew that Jennifer was dead.

They had been close friends in high school. They had written each other letters in college. Even now they spoke several times during the year. They had spoken just a few weeks before, during the Christmas holidays. Jennifer's show was going well, her son was doing well in school, and her husband was working on a new, exciting project with a studio in New York.

But now that was all gone.

Rebecca also knew that something terrible had happened. It hadn't just been death that had come for Jennifer. Something else had come, and it had taken a part of her with it. Rebecca could still feel that part. It was still alive, and the killer was carrying it with him.

It was a man. She could tell nothing more. It was a shock to her system. It was sad, disorienting and terrifying. Her first instinct was to pick up the phone and call Steven Keith, another friend that she kept in touch with from time to time. She also kept in touch with Samantha Chambers. Rebecca kept in touch with them, though they did not speak much with each other. In 1986 they had gotten together for a reunion, and it had been almost like days had passed instead of years. Rebecca kept in touch with each of them, and she passed their stories around the circle. She felt this was important. She knew this like she knew many things, though like many things she was not sure why.

But the circle had been broken, and Jennifer was dead.

Rebecca pushed the pile of evidence away. These images of the little girl were gone now, and they would not return. For now Rebecca would be consumed with the death of her friend, and nothing else would come to her. She prayed that it would not cost the life of the little girl she had been paid to find. San Francisco was a large city, and without her help the little girl might disappear into one of its dark alleys or the deep, cold bay. She would try again later. How much later she didn't know.

Rebecca laid her head down on her desk and began to cry.

3

Steven was in the mountains when he felt the pain. It was a sharp pain in the center of his chest. He put a large right hand on top of the pain for a moment, but then the pain passed. It was all that dried food. It had to be. But there was also a sense of loss which he could not place.

Steven rolled over in his big sleeping bag and patted his golden retriever, Pat. Pat moaned once and shifted, then went back to sleep. It was cold, but Steven's bag was good down to ten degrees, and it wasn't quite that cold. He'd ordered it special since the bags in the stores didn't fit his six-foot seven-inch frame. The tent was a two-man tent, which was perfect for him and his dog. Pat had a sleeping bag too, which was opened and laid over him like a blanket. Pat wasn't a puppy anymore and Steven could tell that the cold hurt her joints. At night she rarely got out from under her bag. On cold days she just kept moving.

Steven had come here two days ago to be alone and to fish the great frozen lake. The days had been bright and almost warm, though the nights were frigid. He would also be attending to some business here, taking readings off some of the elevation markers which had been placed in the area by his employer, the United States Geological Survey, twenty years ago. There had been an unusual change in elevation of some of the markers in the San Gabriel Mountains near Pearblossom, so he had come further north to see if this was an isolated incident, or if a greater geological event was happening, or preparing to happen.

He loved his work. It meant hours and hours of driving federal green trucks and climbing over rocks and fallen trees. But it was what he loved best. At times he would intentionally take the harder route, doing a bit of rock climbing on the way to his goal. On the real tough routes, he would leave Pat in the vehicle. Pat had fallen once while trying to follow him up a steep pile of rocks, and he didn't want to take that chance again.

The next morning Steven fished for an hour before packing up and heading back to the valley. His home was at the edge of that valley, in Redlands. It was a small spread, somewhat isolated. Within thirty minutes he could be in the middle of the desert, or deep in the rolling terrain of the San Gabriels. The drive home was a pleasant one, full of trees and wildlife. On arrival he unpacked his bags while Pat reestablished her link with home by chasing the cat and barking at a few of the Palm trees.

Steven threw his pack in the garage and walked into the kitchen to check the contents of his refrigerator. He had been in the hills for three days, and the taste of freeze-dried food had coated his tongue. He settled on a ham sandwich, then checked his phone messages while he waited for the ham to warm up in the microwave.

It was the third message.

He knew in an instant who it was, and he knew what had happened just before Rebecca's recorded voice actually said the words. Still it brought the pain back to his chest and he dropped the mayonnaise covered knife. Steven opened his book of telephone numbers which he kept in a drawer under the phone and looked up Rebecca's number. Today was Sunday and he wasn't sure how old the message was. It had been the second to last one, so hopefully it wasn't too old. As he dialed her number he remembered the pain in his chest which had come to him in the night, and he knew now what it had meant. This knowledge frightened him. He knew that there was something special between him and his childhood friends, something that went beyond the shared delivery room and common brush with death. But this something had never been concrete. It had meant shared dreams, common thoughts, a certain unspoken communication which only the best of friends and the closest of families ever catch a glimpse of. It was more than this, too. It was the success that had come to them, it was the gifts that each of them had found. Even the simple boy, Timothy Watkins, was gifted in his own way. There were others too, others which had shared the experience but who had never been a part of the circle.

But the circle was broken now.

Rebecca answered on the third ring. He instantly recognized her soft and questioning voice.

"It's Steven, Rebecca."

"She's gone, Steven."

He could feel the loss in her voice. He knew she could sense it in his, even though no one else could have. "I know. I got your message." He was silent for a moment. "What happened?"

"I didn't know until this morning. The police weren't very helpful because of her celebrity status, but I got some information from a few reporters I know down there. It was murder."

The statement shocked him. He had known she was dead from the moment he had heard Rebecca's voice on his answering machine. But he had thought that there had been an accident, perhaps a car wreck. Murder had not even crossed his mind.

"Steven?"

"I'm here Rebecca." The shock ran through his body. "Why would anyone want to kill Jennifer?"

"There aren't any leads yet, at least not any that my friends have heard of. They found a knife, but it's a common kitchen knife that could have been bought at any Wal-Mart, and there aren't any prints. There are some deep footprints outside the window since the killer apparently jumped from her balcony, but there's nothing else. Nothing more than a shoe size."

"That's it?" Steven was still in shock.

"That's all I can find out."

Steven had known Rebecca all his life. He knew of her gift, and he wondered what it told her now. "What else?" he asked. "What do you feel?"

Rebecca was silent for a moment. "I don't know," she answered. "It's all jumbled and confusing. It was a man. He was angry." A Pause. "I can't see anything more."

"Are you going down there? Are you going to work with the police on this?"

"I am going down there. The funeral is tomorrow. Her dad will be coming in from Colorado and I've told him I would be there. She's going to be buried in Atlanta. She's lived there for over twenty years, and she considered it home more than anywhere else. As for working with the police, I haven't decided yet. I want to see where they get on their own first. But if there aren't some answers soon, then I will get involved either with them or on my own."

"I'll be coming too," Steven offered.

"Samantha will be there," Rebecca explained.

The news made Steven feel warm inside. The three of them would be there for their special friend. It would be one last time to share what they had been. It had all changed forever now.

Steven and Rebecca shared sorrows and then made their plans. Then Steven hung up the phone and closed his eyes for a moment. Pat nudged his hand to comfort her ailing master. Steven opened his eyes, and a single tear ran down his face. He looked at his faithful Pat and patted her head. His dog's tail wagged gently.

"You're a good dog, Pat." Steven got down on his knee and hugged his dog's neck.

And he tried his best not to cry.

4

Samantha snaked her way through the crowd at LaGuardia on the way to her gate. The airport was crowded. The city was crowded. It was a long way from Eastland, Texas, but it was where her work had taken her. She was an artist, making paintings that actually sold and designing sets for Broadway plays. She wrote and choreographed and sang with a lovely voice. She had made the most of her talents, and she knew it was still just beginning.

But now she was racing for a flight which was going to fly her to see two living friends and one dead one. It was terrible. She had awakened in the night to dreams of fire and of deep blackness. She had seen Rebecca's face for an instant and at first she thought it was she to whom something terrible had happened. But then Rebecca had called, and Samantha had not slept the rest of the night.

That was two days ago. Samantha had been forced to put a few things on hold and had passed up on an offer to oversee the painting of the Bussman Center, which had to start immediately. Those things would be replaced. She had lost something which could not.

She stood at the gate staring at the card which had been placed next to the departure time. She wasn't going to miss her flight after all. The bad weather had delayed all flights, and it would be another two hours before she would be in the air.

Two hours to sit in the airport and think tortured thoughts about her friend and about death.

Who had done this thing? Rebecca had shared only vague ideas. But they felt right to Samantha. There was something more than murder here, something much darker. But what it could possibly be was beyond Samantha's imagination. She would have to wait and see.

She tossed her long blond hair over her right shoulder and brushed it back with her hand. A man to her right smiled when she caught his gaze. On another day she might have smiled back. He was not from here. His smile was too warm. He was going home, back to Atlanta. His eyes turned away and she knew he was thinking that she was from this place, that she was just another hardened New York soul. But she knew better. Her spirit had remained free. She had seen to that.

But tonight the weight of her friend's death was heavy on her soul, and she could not shine. Instead she sat and watched the people as she waited for the flight that would take her south, to her friends.

Chapter Four
1

He had made the news, and it had been a secondary thrill for him. Four murders in one night in Atlanta, all women. They were calling him things like "mysterious killer" and "unknown assailant." He liked this. He had never thought he would like the attention like this, but he did. It was like having your picture in the paper without the name and wanting to shout, 'hey, that's me' to everyone who read it. But more than that, he knew that across Atlanta, across Georgia, even across the country women by the hundreds or perhaps thousands now feared him. Many of them probably even dreamt about the faceless killer. That was the biggest thrill. Maybe someday he would reach out and touch a few of them, too.

But now Derek sat in a dark, musty room across from the old woman. He had come to her this time. He wanted answers. He wanted to know what had happened to him in Atlanta. He was different today than he had been before that trip. He felt more complete, as if something which had been missing all of his life had been found there. But he also felt a new hunger. He had tried to feed that hunger in the suburbs of Atlanta, but there had only been the rush in those deaths, no growth, no change. He had thought that the killing of Jennifer Summers had caused a transformation in him, that each new death would take him further down that road until he became something bigger than he was now. But that was not what had happened. Instead he was left with this new level of being combined with this terrible hunger.

Verna Calloway just looked at him and smiled. Her eyes had always looked crazy to him. But now he saw more. Part of it excited him. A greater part of it terrified him. She had dogged him all her life. He remembered the day she had come back to Eastland from the loony bin.

She had still been loony, but the state had decided that she was going to get no better, and that despite her ranting and raving she was not a threat. So she was medicated and released. In the thirty years since her release she had approached each of the children who had been struck down on that same fateful night in 1956. She had been waiting to come to them. She made strange suggestions to them until she had realized that it was their life forces which kept her beloved torn apart. They could not join together as she wished, this was not a part of their reality. But there was a way. So she had begun to torment Derek because he was the most likely to understand, and because her beloved had forced the greatest change in that boy.

She had been patient. Now her time had come. Derek sat before her, hungry and confused. He was still very human, and he was still dangerous. But there was more of her beloved here now, and that would only help her. It would soften Derek's mind, it would make him understand more of the bizarre things which she told him. He would listen. Perhaps now he would believe.

Derek stared at the old woman who was dressed in rags and who had apparently decided that bathing was too carnal a concern. "What the fuck is going on?"

She smiled at him again. This made him furious. "I want some answers."

"What are the questions?" Where before her voice had seemed harsh and grating it now seemed almost melodious. Had her voice changed, or was it only his perception?

"What is going on?"

"The world is turning," she replied.

"I don't want to listen to your crazy shit," Derek spit out. "You know what I mean. What's going on?"

"Ask me a question." She had to get him to look within himself before she could reach her beloved.

Derek was getting angry and impatient. He thought again about killing the old bitch. Only now he had too many questions, and she held the answers. This hunger was a terrible thing, and if she had given it to him, then she knew how to satisfy it.

"You would never have the knowledge if you killed me," she replied. She could not read his mind, but now she could sense his strongest emotions.

But Derek didn't know this. He thought she could read his mind, and this frightened him.

Verna sat back on the couch, her dirty night shirt slipping down around her left shoulder. "Why did you come here?"

"Because something's not right. Because you sent me to kill someone I knew, and when I did it, something happened to me. I think you knew it would happen, and I want to know what it's all about."

"Ask me a question," she whispered.

He felt a stirring inside of him. For a moment he was attracted to her. But this lasted only a moment, then he was repulsed by the thought. He tried to clear his mind, to think of a question she would answer.

"What happened to me in Georgia?""You killed one of the vessels."

"What do you mean?" Derek had heard her ranting about "the vessels" since the first day she had approached him, on his walk home from grade school.

"Ask me a question."

He closed his eyes and tried to keep the anger away. There were answers here, he just had to know how to ask the questions.

"Why do I feel like this?"

"Like what?"

He tried to think of the words. "Like I need to kill."

"You've always felt the need to kill," she replied.

The statement burned inside. It was true. It was his darkest secret. She spoke of it as if she had always known. "It's worse now," he explained. "It's like I can't put it out of my mind."

"You are driven," she explained.

"Why?"

"Your journey has just begun."

"What do you mean?"

"Ask me a question."

He closed his eyes again and made a note to himself not to ask her again what she meant. "What journey?"

"The journey to completeness."

Another term he had heard coming from what he had always considered her crazed mind. "Where am I going?"

She just smiled again. "You need to kill."

The statement and something else caused something inside him to stir. His fear subsided. "Yes."

"You need to feed the hunger."

"Yes." He could feel something inside, as if his soul were salivating, preparing for the ephemeral feast.

"I will give you a name and a place."

Something inside stirred. "Will I have to travel again?"

"Yes."

This he did not care for.

When she gave him the name he understood something more. This was another of those kids, now adults, who had shared something with his past. Then he thought of the others, the ones who were still in Eastland. They would feed his hunger, and they were close by.

"You must not feed on those that are nearby until the end."

"Why not?" he asked. She was denying him his feast. The hunger drove him to frustration, and he already was planning the kill.

"Think on that yourself. You will understand. You did before."

Derek did remember. He could not cast suspicion on himself and killing people in Eastland would do just that. Connections would be made. Sheriff Sharp would make them. But couldn't he defeat the sheriff? Couldn't he run like the wind now? Couldn't he attack like lightning?

"You are not invincible," Verna reminded him. "Not yet. And your power comes and goes." The woman stood and raised her hand toward the door. "You will go now, go and harvest. When you return you will be fulfilled." She looked into his eyes. "Your journey is nearing its end, my beloved."

He felt the thing inside of him stir again. Then he felt the electricity course through his arms and legs. It tickled his brain, and his eyes began to burn.

She saw these things within him and she knew that what little there was of her beloved had heard her, and she was filled with the pleasure of that knowledge.

"Go," she said.

He wanted to know more. He had come here to learn. She was sending him away with no answers.

"When you have killed, then you will know more. Then you will be ready for more."

It was over for now. He would go out and get his own answers. Then he would return.

He willed himself to go and found himself at her door. Then he was outside, breathing the cool night air. He looked up into the stars and tonight they did not seem so vast. He looked to be sure no one was watching, then he headed for his home. In the darkness of the night he seemed no more than a misty image and he could not feel the ground beneath his feet. He did not know where this power had come from, but it was wonderful, and it would grow within him as he continued on his quest.

From the bushes of the house next to Verna's a pair of terrified eyes watched Derek as he emerged from the house, then transformed into the misty monster from his dreams.

2

Richard Hall Jr. had, in fact, become the minister at the same church where his father had preached. His father had passed the mantle to him three years ago, then had taken a less stressful job at the small congregation in Cisco, ten miles to the west. His father would still come to his old church from time to time, just to make sure that his son was tending his old flock as he himself would have done. Most of the time he was not disappointed.

It was early on Monday morning. The sun was not up yet, but Richard was. He sat at the old oak desk in the room he used for an office, his head in his hands, his old bible he had used since college in front of him. The pages were folded, torn, and heavily marked, but he had invested so much of himself, his soul, in that book that he would use it until the binding dissolved and the pages scattered.

He still had his visions. They were both a blessing and a curse. Over the years he had come to understand that they were glimpses into the lives of those around him. He had not understood this in his youth, and this had caused him endless torment and suffering. One night he would dream of moving north to the mountains of Colorado, the next he would be caught in terrible fantasies of molesting small children. Often the visions would even come in the daytime. He would be trying to prepare a sermon when suddenly he would see the coming of loved ones he had never known, or a nude woman who was performing the most hideous sexual acts. He had gotten beyond the guilt of the evil visions which came as frequently as the good. Sometimes he saw enough to know who they were about. Sometimes this was a good thing. It had helped him to finally discover who was molesting the children in Eastland, and he had confronted that man. There had been denial, but Richard knew too many details, and the man was now in jail. From time to time it had helped him to counsel those in his flock. For the most part the visions came from close by. They were from the people of Eastland, they came from Cisco too, and sometimes the most joyous and most violent came from even farther away.

The past two days had been the worst. Saturday night he had experienced the most vivid and most horrible vision ever. In that vision he was a terrible, dark creature. He found himself climbing the outside of a palatial home with the darkest of intentions. Moments later he was in a woman's room, staring into her eyes as he drove a knife into her heart. He had known this woman. She had left Eastland long ago. That

Sunday, after services, he had discovered that Jennifer Summers had in fact been murdered. He knew that he had seen it happen, not as a vision of what might be, but he had been there. He had actually witnessed the death. This time he could not fight off the guilt.

He found out that Jennifer had moved to Atlanta, and this is where she had died. Could this vision have come from so far? And what about those visions which had come to him since then? They were confusing images. They were pictures of more death, of vast empty space, and of a terrible, evil hunger. He knew that these visions were coming from the same monster that had killed Jennifer. But was the monster still in Atlanta? Did the monster know he was watching? Would it come for him?

There had been no killing on Sunday. There had been glimpses of the monster's world which had distracted him during both the morning and evening services, and his sleep during the night had been restless, filled with incoherent dreams. There had been no killing. But there would be. He could sense it. The time was getting closer, and the monster would kill. There was nothing he could do about it. He could not keep the guilt away this time.

Bonnie stuck her head through the door. "Are you all right, honey?"

Richard looked up to his loving wife. She knew about the visions, though not everything about them. "I'm having some troubles, but I'm working my way through them."

She came into his office and sat down in the chair across the desk from him. "Are you having bad dreams again?"

"Yes," he answered her. He placed his hand on the bible in front of him.

"Do you want to talk about it?"

He thought for a moment. Was this a burden he should share with his wife, or one he should bear on his own? His wife's questioning gaze remained across his desk. He decided to share just a little. He told her about the new visions, about how he had known Jennifer Summers had been killed. He didn't say he knew that she hadn't screamed, and that the killer had taken something from her soul.

"Do you know who it might be?" she asked her husband.

"No. Not yet."

"What do you mean, yet?"

Too late, he realized he had said too much. "He killed someone else too, someone I don't know." Actually he had seen four deaths through the monster's eyes. The first had been Jennifer. The next three had been indistinct images in dark places.

"Do you know enough to go to the police?" she asked.

"No."

Bonnie sat silently, watching her husband grapple with his feelings. "Do you think it will go away?"

"I'm not sure." It was a small lie. Inside he knew that this was just the beginning.

"Is there anything I can do to help?" she asked.

He looked up from his desk and smiled at her. "You help me by just being here." Her eyes were soft. They were what had first drawn him to her. "I know I can count on you, and I'll let you know if there's anything you can do."

Bonnie walked around the desk and kissed her husband softly. He was a strong man. He was also a tormented man. She left him alone in the room. Their boys would be getting up soon, and she had to help them prepare for a school day.

Richard thought briefly about the blessing his wife was to his life. He prayed that this darkness would not touch her or his boys. Inside he feared this and more.

Richard opened his bible and sought inspiration, hope against whatever it was that had broken into the secret spaces of his mind.

3

The sky was overcast, and a light drizzle blanketed the grass and the headstones. Family and friends gathered around the ornate casket of Jennifer Summers. Outside the main tent were hundreds more who had come to know her. Beyond that were those who had not known her well but wanted to be seen in the right places.

Rebecca, Steven, and Samantha stood at the edge of the tent, listening to the preacher as he committed her body to the earth and her soul to God. Each of them could feel the emptiness inside. Something that they had taken for granted had changed suddenly and drastically, and life would never again be as it had been. Their special friendship would continue, but now there would be a hole where Jennifer had been. The preacher seemed inadequate. His words were from a script. He had not known Jennifer well, and his words could have been used in a thousand places to describe many other people. So inside each of the three said their own eulogy.

Steven saw the famous Jack Cassidy sobbing. It was something he would never have wanted to see. Jack was still a big man, and Steven remembered watching him rumble down the field on Sunday afternoons. Now Steven saw that Jack was not, in fact, superhuman.

When it was over the three of them went to a quiet restaurant on the north end of town. It was a homey place with wooden chairs and wooden tables. The walls were covered with pictures and artifacts of another, simpler time. The colors were natural and quiet, appropriate for the somber mood. It was three o'clock, so they were the only customers. Still, they asked for a table upstairs, away from the counter and the kitchen. There they sat and talked of their past and their friend.

Rebecca, Samantha and Jennifer had spent many nights sleeping over at one house or the other. When they had gotten older they had covered for each other once in a while when there really was no sleep over. Rebecca was remembering these times.

"She was always a peaceful girl," Rebecca offered. "We certainly didn't agree on everything, but I don't think I remember ever really having a fight with her."

Samantha was about to agree, when she remembered the one time they had, in fact, fought. Jennifer hadn't been forceful or loud, but some of her comments had cut, and they hadn't spoken for several months. And it had been over a boy. But not just any boy. Samantha looked across the table to Steven. She remembered back to the times they had spent together in his dad's Blazer. They had broken up weeks before he ever went out with Jennifer, but it had still hurt, and she had still been furious. Now it was all irrelevant, the musings of children from another time.

"I didn't send her a Christmas card this year," Steven said. This had been bothering him on and off all day.

"You didn't send me one either," Samantha reminded him.

"I know, but it's different. It's like I wonder if it mattered to her, and what she thought of me. I wonder if she still considered me a good friend, or just one of the thousands of people she had met in her life who still clung to her."

Rebecca looked to Steven with surprise in her eyes. "You've got to be kidding." Steven looked back to her with puzzlement, wondering what was coming. "Jennifer was a better person than that. She cared for us all. She never forgot the ties we had. She never thought any of us were trying to keep in touch with her because she was becoming a celebrity. We were her true friends, and she knew that. No matter how famous she might have become, we were there before all of that. We were the only ones she could really trust, the only ones she knew for sure cared for her just for what she was, not for who she had become or what she had gained in life."

Steven bit his lip. He hadn't thought of it like that, but it made perfect sense, and he was embarrassed for not giving Jennifer the credit she was due.

The waitress appeared, but no one was ready to order. They hadn't even looked at their menus. The young girl refilled their coffee cups and told them to take their time, though she did not seem sincere.

Samantha stared at her menu but did not read it. Instead she thought about Jennifer, as they all did. She looked up and spoke to Rebecca.

More was on her mind than she had shared so far, as was true of each of them. "What do you think the police are doing?"

They had already discussed all of this the previous evening at the hotel, but it was not resting well with Samantha. It was not resting well with any of them, but Samantha seemed the most agitated by it all.

Rebecca had already made a few calls over the weekend. "I think they're following leads and looking for more leads. They don't have much physical evidence to go on, so I suppose they're trying to find out if she had any life insurance, or if she'd made a producer mad, or if someone had lost a job because of her. Heck, they're probably even checking the Nielsens for the past month."

"But is it enough?" Samantha asked.

"It'll have to be."

"Why?"

"What else can be done?" Rebecca pointed out.

Samantha sat silent for a moment, wondering why her two friends didn't understand how important this particular case was.

Steven put down his menu. "I know it's frustrating, Samantha, but they're giving it as much attention as they would any other case, probably more because she was so well known. And you can bet the press is digging around for answers too."

Samantha looked past Steven to the window behind him, and beyond. The clouds remained. Rain gathered in small bubbles and ran down the window in random patterns. There was something else that was bothering her, something more than just the questions which remained around the death of her friend. "I don't feel safe."

Rebecca understood. It was an understanding which had come from years of working the terrible cases of missing people and dying friends. "Whenever anyone close to you goes like this it shakes up your whole world. You begin to consider possibilities that you had never thought of before. There are always these little things gnawing at the back of your mind, things which you never gave much thought because to dwell on them would drive you crazy. What if my plane crashes? What if I get hit by a car crossing the street? What if someone breaks into my house to kill me?"

"You're saying it'll pass?" Samantha asked.

"No," Rebecca replied. "I'm just saying that your feelings of insecurity come from your world being rearranged. The death of Jennifer has forced you to consider death in general. Not just yours, but ours and that of your loved ones."

It seemed to make sense, but there also seemed to be more here. There was a feeling of impending disaster, but nothing substantial with which to support it. She let it pass and relied on Rebecca's intuition. It was always a safe bet.

Steven had felt these very things himself, and hearing Rebecca explain it to Samantha set his mind at ease some.

But Rebecca felt more than this. She had used her best skills to set her friend at ease. But Rebecca, too, had experienced these dark feelings. For her it was more than a rearranging of reality. She had seen death many times in the faces of her clients and of those whom she helped from time to time. She had seen death up close once or twice. She had already gone through her period of introspection and new understanding. This danger was something else. Whatever had killed Jennifer was a danger to them all. She did not know what kind of danger, and she certainly didn't think that someone was after all of them. Until she figured out something more she was not going to alarm her friends. She had learned that often her own feelings of doom were misplaced. More than once she had caused severe alarm in people she knew by sharing these feelings before she understood them. This time she was going to wait until there was more, or at least until she was more certain.

Samantha spoke again. "Did Jennifer ever talk to you about her dream?"

Both Rebecca and Steven looked up to her. Jennifer had told them both but had asked them not to talk to anyone about it. They had all thought of that dream at least once in the past few days, but no one had mentioned it until now.

Samantha could see that they both knew what she was talking about. "Do you think it had anything to do with this? I mean, how she saw death coming for her and she just smiled and passed through the evil and into a great light. Do you think it was some kind of precognition?"

Steven spoke first. "I'd thought about that once or twice myself. They say the guards downstairs didn't hear a thing." He looked at Rebecca. "And you said that there were no signs of a struggle."

"They say it's because she died in her sleep."

Samantha spoke up, "Do you believe that?"

"There were no signs of a struggle. She was a strong woman; she would have put up a fight."

Steven objected. "But she had to hear him come in. You said the killer had forced his way in through a locked balcony door, there had to be a lot of noise."

These things had also bothered Rebecca. But again, she had kept these questions to herself. She had also thought about the dream.

Steven could see the struggle Rebecca was having with herself. "Look, Rebecca. We're all adults here. We know more about each other than you typically know about the people you work with. You can tell us what you're thinking and feeling. Don't worry about frightening us, or giving us ideas. We're both probably doing just fine frightening ourselves."

Rebecca fidgeted. Samantha looked at her as if to agree with Steven.

Steven continued. "We've known you since we were children. We know that the things you see and feel are sketchy, that your biggest job is understanding and translating these feelings. But we're being open with you, and we'd like the same in return. We've all lost a dear friend. We're all looking for answers. Anything you can share will help us to deal with this."

It was against Rebecca's better judgment, but Steven was right. These were her friends. She owed them more than to treat them like she did the masses of people she worked with.

She waited until the waitress came and went, this time with their orders. Then she told them what was in her heart.

4

He had never been to New York but had always hated it. Being here now only reinforced that hatred. But this town had something to offer him, and he was here to collect.

Derek walked down the alley behind the apartments. The front of the complex was tall and majestic. The area behind it, however, was dirty and rotten. Garbage filled the dumpsters and flowed out of them. Stinking men in rotten clothes lay in and around the garbage, many of them hugging a brown paper sack which held the bottle that was their only friend in this world. It was cold and misty. Night had fallen about an hour before.

He had arrived in New York as the sun had begun to set. The name on the plane ticket had not been his own, and he did not understand the reasoning behind this. No one would possibly suspect him. Still, the crazy woman had thought it to be a good precaution, and it certainly didn't hurt anything. He had taken a cab to a street about a mile away, then walked to this alley. It looked familiar to him, even though he had never been to New York before. It was from a distant part of his memory, something not quite him, yet not completely anything else.

He put his hand into his pocket and felt the knife inside. He had stolen the knife from a store just a few blocks away. There were mirrors everywhere, so it had been very difficult. He had waited outside until someone else had wandered in, a black man with worn out clothes. He knew they would be watching him closely, and they had. So Derek had made off with the knife. He'd wanted to bring one of his own, but didn't want to take the chance of being questioned at the airport. Nothing would come of it, but someone might remember his face.

Suddenly there was a tug at his arm. He swung around quickly, drawing the knife part way out of his pocket. An old man stood looking at him with wide eyes, his hand held out and his mouth open. But the question never came. The look in Derek's eyes terrified the old bum and he turned to run. Derek could have no witnesses, and the small feast would feel good after the long day. The old bum was easy to catch, and his already dulled eyes rolled back into his head as Derek slid the blade into his heart.

Derek set the body against the brick wall. No one would notice the slumping figure for days, not until it emanated an odor worse that could be accounted for by poor hygiene alone. Then Derek made his way to the fire escape on the west end of the building. The steel ladder was too far from the ground. He rolled one of the dumpsters until it was under the ladder, then climbed up on the big container. From its top he was able to leap up and grab hold of one of the rungs and pull himself onto the retracted ladder. The metal was wet with the mist, but his grip was tight and he did not slip. Moments later he was working his way up the series of ladders which wound back and forth. He stepped off the ladder at the fifth floor and onto the ledge. The window to the apartment he needed to get into was still a hundred feet away.

Derek made his way along the slick ledge, gripping the stones which made up the building's exterior. He held onto the spaces between the stones with his strong fingers, his grip never in question. When he came to a window he would peer in first to be sure no one was looking, then he would work his way quickly across. Only twice did he have to wait for a few minutes until a room emptied, or until its occupant looked away. Most of the people here did not even have their curtains opened since the view into the alley was an unattractive one, and the rent on these units was quite high. The units were occupied by doctors, lawyers, bankers and several successful artists. It was one of these artists he was here to visit.

He found her window and tried it. It was locked. He removed a small glass cutting tool from his pocket and began to cut a circle in the glass near its center. He cut freehand and moments later the imperfect circle fell into the room, shattering on the floor. It didn't matter. She wasn't here now. He didn't know when she would be back, but he felt it would be soon. The funeral had been earlier that same day. She had work to get back to. She would be back soon. Even now he felt as if she were in the air, heading northward toward him. Toward death. A thousand miles away, thirty thousand feet in the air she felt something too. But she brushed it away as another strange emotion which had come with the death of her friend.

Derek reached through the window and unlocked it. The window slid upward too easily and hit the top of the frame with a loud 'whack.' He looked around instinctively, then realized he was still five stories up, and that he was in New York. No one would notice. If they did, they certainly wouldn't check it out, not before he was able to slip inside.

Derek climbed into the warm apartment and found himself in a dark room. He could see outlines of objects, more than he could have seen before the transformation, but he could not tell what they were, and he could not turn on the light. He closed the window and the curtains, then pulled a flashlight from his jacket.

The room was filled with clay pieces, wood sculptures and paintings. There were bronze art pieces and other types of art with which he was totally unfamiliar. There were images of nature, of man, of science. There were paintings of strange cities in vast wildernesses, and bright stars in the palm of a child's hand. Some of these pictures struck a chord inside him. There were paintings which were totally abstract, symbols and colors which meant nothing, yet which meant something. It was not as if he were looking at the sketchings and objects which had come from a woman's imagination, it was more like looking at a picture of a place he had been but could not remember. It was like seeing a book written in another language, knowing that there was meaning here, but having no clue at what that meaning was.

A fiery anger rose up within him and he struck out at one of the sculptures. It flew across the dark room and crashed into an unfinished painting which rested on an easel. He stormed across the room to its door, unsure of where this anger had come from.

When he reached the door he stopped. What if she came in here first? She would know something was wrong. He would still be able to overpower her. And he knew she would yield willingly. But there was no sense in taking this risk. He walked over to the sculpture and picked it up. One of its edges was broken off, but surely she would not look closely at this one object and make any sense of it before he had gotten the opportunity to drive his blade into her. He returned then to the downed painting. It was in much worse shape. He picked it up from the floor and set it back on the easel.

The picture jumped out at him suddenly. It was a swirl of colors and indistinct images. There was nothing here of substance, just a misty blend of color and false light. But it pulled at him. The image evoked a feeling in him that was something like 'home.' He also knew that it was a painting of him, though this, as well, made no sense. What did she know? Was she waiting for him too? Did she know he would be coming?

The anger rose within him again. He grabbed the painting and threw it to the ground, shattering the backing. Then he picked up the canvas and began tearing it to shreds. He felt the fire within him cooling as he destroyed the painting and with it the images which taunted him and made him feel the strange and awful feelings.

When it was done he laughed out loud. She would notice this for sure, but only if she came in this room first. But even then it would not matter. He knew, now, that she was waiting for him. She would see salvation in his eyes, and there would be no struggle. Now he knew why the first one had not fought him, why none of them would. He laughed again, then he left the dark room.

Derek opened doors until he found the one which led to her room. He looked it over quickly and again saw reminders of himself. Then he found a closet which looked as if it saw infrequent use. There were old empty moving boxes which had been folded and stored here, as well as screws and pieces of broken appliances. He moved the boxes to one side and found he could fit. He pulled the door shut and could see through the slats in the door. That would be useful. Then he leaned back against a shelf and relaxed his muscles. The relaxation ran through him and he slipped slowly into a restful state. He would sense when she was here. Even now he could feel her coming closer. In a few hours she would be in this room with him. Then he would reveal himself to her. She would come to him. He would take her soul.

Then the power would grow within him. He would transform once again. He would be one step closer to his destiny.

Derek closed his eyes and waited.

Chapter Five
Eastland, Texas - 1974

1

It was Prom Night.

Steven held Jennifer's hand as they entered the big room together. They had come with their friends in Steven's car, but now it was as if the two of them were entering the room by themselves. All eyes turned toward them. There were eyes of envy, eyes of jealousy, and eyes of admiration. Most were the eyes of friends, friends they had known since grade school, friends they would soon separate from in that ceremony called graduation. But that was still a month away. Tonight they were amongst their friends. They all wore clothes they had just bought, made or rented. The room was dark, reflections from the big mirrored ball in the center of the room danced about the decorated walls and the white table cloths.

It was prom night.

Jennifer was queen, of course. Kristin and Heidi had only been on the ballot as acknowledgment of their accomplishments and popularity. But even they had known it would be Jennifer. They had both even voted for her. Jennifer was beautiful, and smart, and she had the best boy in school. But she was also friendly and kind, and those who would be her rival quickly found that it was easier to be her friend.

Steven was the biggest boy in school, and he had a football scholarship to Texas A&M waiting for him. His father was hoping Steven would forget about rocks and study something useful, but Steven had developed an interest in geology two years earlier, and it had grown to a passion. There was money to be made by a good geologist in the field of oil and gas exploration, and this was the only consolation for Steven's father. Steven's good looks and physical prowess combined with his affable nature had assured his place by Jennifer's side. They had only started dating about a week earlier, though they had gone out a few other times in the past four years. He had always liked Jennifer, but so had everybody else. Steven had wanted to be different, to be the one who didn't feel like he had to possess the best girl in school. He had always fought his attraction to her, and had told himself that it was all a front, no one that pretty could really be that nice. But after just a week he could see he had been wrong. She really was very nice, and he could talk to her like he could talk to no one else. He wished he had done this sooner, when there had been more time. When summer came they could be together for a few months. But then it would be time for college. He would be heading two hundred and fifty miles to the southeast, she would be going even farther, to a college in Atlanta. There would be talk of keeping in touch and visiting on holidays, but he knew it would really be over. He had seen it before.

But tonight none of that mattered. Tonight was its own time, a time they both knew would be special forever.

"Hey, Steven!" It was Frank Sharp, his best friend. They had run in the same group since junior high. Sometimes the group had been big, sometimes small. Boys had entered and left it. But Steven and Frank had always been at its core. Frank was on the football team too, but he played an unglamorous position on defense. Frank's dad was a cop for the city. Frank thought he wanted to get into law enforcement too, but hadn't decided yet just what that meant.

Steven and Jennifer took a seat at the table with Frank and Heidi. Karl and Kristin were there too. After the girls had all complemented each other on their outfits, the talk turned to plans for the summer and beyond.

After a few minutes of talk the music began, then the dancing. Steven looked at the faces that looked back at him. They were admiring him, they were admiring her, too. These were faces he had grown accustomed to over the years, many since childhood, but they had never gathered in a place like this and the feelings were overpowering.

Samantha was here. His eyes met hers only for a second. There was hurt in those eyes, but there was forgiveness, too. She had been the one to change things between them. He knew the hurt would heal. She was one of the special group of friends who shared the same birthday and the story of how they had all escaped death together. They all had gifts, even Timmy Watkins, the simple boy who could play the piano like no one else Steven had known or heard of. The town knew who they were, and they had been treated just a little differently than the rest of the young men and women who had grown up in this small west Texas town. His eyes met with Richard's. Richard's father had relented and allowed him to attend the prom with the promise from his son that he would not dance. Rebecca was here too. He couldn't see her, but he knew she was here. They were all tied together in a way none of them understood, but each of them accepted.

Just as he knew that somewhere out there, not here in the building but somewhere in town, was Derek Lowrance. He was like an ever present dark cloud which hung on the periphery of Steven's special vision. He had never spoken of this to the others, but he suspected it was the same with them. Derek's name had rarely been spoken over the years and had always been accompanied by an air of disgust. Tonight that cloud seemed closer and darker. Steven just wrote it off as part of the whole experience of the evening.

But Rebecca could not write it off.

Her date, a boy she had been seeing for just two weeks, squeezed her hand and asked her again what was on her mind. She searched again for her friends and found them. And with them she found the dark cloud. It had grown larger just these past two days, and inside of it was death. She knew. She had seen many faces of death and she knew that it was showing itself again. She did not know who would die, or when. But she knew death was coming.

Then she turned her attention to her date. He wanted to go to the dance floor, now that the music had started in earnest. As she stood she saw Steven and Jennifer. They had always been her friends, and they had seemed very happy together. But Rebecca knew that it would not last. Their lives would go separate ways, and both would find joy in their own worlds. It was just something Rebecca felt, something she knew. She could see it more clearly in her special friends than in most others.

"Where's your mind now?" Rebecca's date asked.

Rebecca looked at Tom and just smiled. "Let's dance," she exclaimed. Then she grabbed his hand and lead him to the floor.

Moments later she stopped suddenly. She looked around the room frantically for Principal Baker. But she could not find him. She ran off the floor, pushing friends and classmates aside as she ran. She found a nervous looking Mrs. Stovall and grabbed the woman's arm.

"Where's Mr. Baker?" Rebecca asked frantically.

Mrs. Stovall looked at Rebecca. "He's taking care of a small problem. He'll be right back."

Rebecca felt the tug of her date's hand on her sleeve, but she pulled away. She headed for the front door where Mrs. Carey stood, looking in her direction.

Then she began screaming.

2

Everyone was at the prom. Everyone he knew, even the only kid in town that would hang around with him was there with that fat Miller bitch. Derek wasn't going to ask some social reject out just so he could go to the prom. It was a stupid event for the pretentious and the blind. It was a show for those who still looked forward to Christmas and believed that human nature was inherently good.

The only Christmas Derek had ever really enjoyed was the one three years ago. He had gotten the best Christmas present ever when the black and white had pulled up to the curb and Tom Sharp had told his mother that Mr. Lowrance wouldn't be coming home, that his days of driving home drunk on the wrong side of the road were over. It had actually been a couple of days before Christmas. Derek remembered it well. It had been cold, and late. He had crawled from bed when the police knocked on the door, and he had sat around the corner of the entry giggling as Mr. Sharp broke the news to his hysterical mother. She should have been glad too. The scars from the last beating which had drawn blood were still fresh on her chin. But she had gone totally nuts.

It wasn't Christmas, but Derek was ready for another such present. He spun the chamber of the snub nose .38 and grinned. He had paid Tommy Runnels to steal this gun for him from a very special place. Derek knew it would be there. He had found out simply by paying attention on one of his visits to the principal's office.

It had been almost a year since his last human kill, and the hunger was tearing him apart. At night he dreamt of the kill. In his nightmares he was stranded on an island in the middle of the ocean with nothing but food and water to sustain him for as long as he could live, but with no people. He did not crave their contact beyond the exhilaration of imagining their deaths. He had imagined many deaths. From time to time his imagination gave him something that would work, something foolproof. He could not afford to be caught, ever. That would be worse that being on that island. He would not be locked away. So he would only kill when he knew beyond a shadow of a doubt he could not be caught. Tonight was one of those times.

Three weeks ago Budd Campbell had been expelled for writing death threats to the principal. Budd had been suspended at least three times every year since he had moved to Eastland in '71. Once he had been suspended for making crank calls to the young English teacher and describing what he wanted to do to her in graphic detail. From the way Budd told it, she always waited until he was finished making his suggestions before hanging up on him. But Budd had been stupid, and he had been caught. The death threats to the principal had begun after Budd's second suspension in as many months. Derek had actually given him the idea, even the part about the dead possum on the doorstep. Budd admired Derek's darkness, and Derek knew this and used it to his own advantage. Tonight Budd would be at the prom, but he would not be inside the building. Budd was going to get the principal back in a big way, in front of everyone. In the end Mr. Baker was supposed to end up naked and debased in front of all those who were supposed to either respect or fear him. But this was not how it would actually end. Although there were those who had a bad feeling about this evening, only Derek knew exactly what was in store.

3

Stew Baker stood in one corner of the big building that had been donated for the evening by the Kiwanis. They had provided the location for the prom for the last twenty years, for the last three it had been in this building which also served as a community center. Stew was a Kiwanis member himself; it was an unspoken requirement for the position of principal of the only high school in Eastland.

The kids seemed to be having a wonderful time. This was a special class. They had come in as freshmen at the end of 1970 and shown a lot of spirit and potential. As seniors they had done well in sports and agricultural competitions, and three of the boys from the football team had gotten scholarships to Texas colleges. It was a happy occasion and a sad one as well. Soon this class would move on and another would take its place. He did not think he would be so fond of a class for many years to come

Stew was brought out of his contemplative state by a tug on his left sleeve. It was Wanda Stovall, a math teacher. Her eyes were wider than usual, and they looked even more alarming as they were magnified through her thick spectacles.

"You'd better go outside, Mr. Baker."

Wanda was excitable, so it was impossible to tell how much of an emergency there might be. "What's the matter?"

"There's a terrible fracas going on out there, something you should take care of."

Stew looked past the agitated woman to the doors which led outside. Standing by the doors was another teacher, Jean Carey. She was signaling him to come over. Jean was much more levelheaded, but there was an air of urgency in her motions, so he knew this was something more than a stink bomb or cigarette smoking rebel.

He stayed near the wall, in the shadows, as he circled the dancing youth and made his way to the doors. When he reached them Mrs. Carey said nothing, she just opened the door and led him out.

Stew had parked his 1972 Lincoln at the end of the lot, away from where the students would be walking. He may have been fond of the class in general, but there were always a few students in any class who didn't care for him. This class was no exception. Parking at the end of the lot was a simply way to help these students avoid the temptation of running a key down the length of the car or spitting quickly and unnoticed on the windshield. But apparently one of these students had disregarded this precaution and went out of his way (and he was sure it was a he, and almost as sure *which* he) to have his revenge.

Black smoke billowed from the front of the car. At first it looked as if the smoke was coming from under the hood. Then he saw the yellow flames dancing near the ground and realized that it was only his tires which were ablaze. If he stopped the fire now he would only need to replace the tires and clean the car's body. If he waited another five minutes the car would be gone.

Stew ran across the parking lot to his car as Mrs. Carey shouted at him to be careful. He ran to the trunk where he kept his fire extinguisher. When he got to it he saw that there was nowhere to insert his key, the keyhole had been drilled out and the trunk was already partially open. Hadn't anybody seen this? Then again, how long would it take to pop up and drill the hole, then slip back down and crawl to the front of the car. There was no lighting in this corner of the lot, and the light which normally burned in the lot by the barber shop was curiously out tonight.

Stew threw open the trunk, knowing that the extinguisher would not be there. But as it opened he saw that the fire extinguisher was not only in its place, but the pin was also pulled and it was ready to use. On top of it was a piece of paper with writing on its front. The author had been trying to disguise his handwriting, but he had seen two similarly styled notes in the past six weeks, and he knew in an instant who the author was.

The writing was large, in big red crayon. There were three or four words to a line, seven lines on the page. He read them all in a couple of seconds.

"Put out the fire. Come to the back. Signal no one. Bring this note. I have a gun. I see you now. Do it or die."

Stew paused only briefly to read the note, then he grabbed the fire extinguisher and ran to the front of his car, to the side where the smoke was the worst. The flames had already seared the paint on the fender. The breeze was from the north, so the smoke billowed up and away, toward the barber shop. Stew aimed the extinguisher at the top of the tire and began shooting the white powder on it. The smoke billowed away from the spray, then some of it puffed back in his direction. He sprayed the whole tire, spraying in a circular motion as the flame fought to live. Slowly Stew won the battle. Eventually there was no more yellow glow, and the smoke was no more than residual. He took a step back and looked over the damage. He had completely emptied the extinguisher, which was probably more than he had needed to do, but this certainly had done no damage, and he had to be sure the fire was out for good.

"Is everything okay?" It was Mrs. Carey, still standing at the door. He thought about saying nothing, or letting her know there was indeed a problem. He was silent for too long. Then he heard a whisper from the darkness.

"Tell her everything's fine. Tell her to get back inside." At first Stew said nothing. Then he heard a sound he knew to be the hammer of a gun being cocked.

"Everything's okay here," he called back to Jean in a strained tone. "Go back in and keep the kids in the building. Tell Wanda that everything's taken care of out here."

Mrs. Carey stood for a moment looking at Stew and his smoldering car. "Are you sure?" she called.

The whisper came again. "Get the bitch back in the building, then get to the back of it. Now."

"It's fine. Keep those kid's inside, I'll be inside in a few minutes."

She hesitated a moment longer, then decided it would be best to do as her boss requested. She left the parking lot and reentered the building just as one of the boys she'd had in her eleventh-grade class was trying to exit. She told him he would need to stay inside for a few moments, and this didn't seem to be a problem for him.

Stew looked into the darkness but could not make out a form. He looked back to his car. It would be okay now. The damage was repairable. Now he had to decide whether or not to go to the back of the building. It was dark there. Many things could happen. Would Budd shoot him if he turned and ran? Stew didn't think so, but he could not be sure. He thought he might be able to dive back behind his car, but then what? He had no weapon. Budd could come around and shoot him anyway, or hit him with a tire iron, or any number of things.

"Move it," came the voice. "Or I'll do you where you stand."

"What are you going to do?" Stew's voice wavered more than he thought it would. He had meant to sound in control. Instead he had sounded scared, which he was.

"I'm going to shoot your ass if you don't do what I say, and now."

Stew could see a dark mass now, but nothing more. He tried to think of something else to say, but nothing came to mind, and he began to wonder if what awaited him behind the building would be worse or not than what would happen here if he continued to stand his ground.

He decided he would take his chances behind the building. Perhaps between here and there he could think of something that would save him any humiliation or worse. Perhaps.

Stew walked across the gravel to the end of the parking lot and the building's edge. Then he walked into the grass which grew along the side of the building. There were no windows here, and only one around back. He could hear heavy steps behind him.

Stew tried to reason with the boy. "If you stop this now, Budd, the worst that will happen is that you'll spend a little time in the juvenile hall. Push this any farther and you're going to spend a lot of time there, and you'll spend time working the paving crews in the summer."

Paving the city roads in the summer was one of the worst jobs in all of west Texas. Most often there were one or two youths working with this crew, youths who had been assigned the job by the county judge who thought that hard work was still the best way to correct a wandering young soul. But this threat evoked no response. The footsteps continued behind his. He tried to think of something more, but there was nothing.

"You'd better think hard about this, Budd."

"I've been thinking hard about it for days."

More walking. More heavy steps.

"You're throwing away your future here."

"No, Mr. Baker, you sonofabitch I'm throwing away yours."

A few more steps.

"Stop there," came the command from the darkness.

Stew stopped. The building was still just a few feet to his left. Ahead and to the right was a big mesquite tree which the Kiwanis had decided to let stand when they had put the building up. Behind him the voice snickered.

"Take off your pants."

The command confused him. "I will not."

"Listen, shit for brains, I'm very serious here. I have a little amusement in mind. If you follow my directions carefully all that will be hurt is your pride. If you give me a bunch of shit, I'll fill you with holes. I've thought about this a lot. I'm ready to get it over with. You make it hard on me and I'll blow your nuts off. Now take off your pants."

Stew was beginning to get the picture. He thought there was a good chance Budd was bluffing, but it wasn't a chance worth taking, not if all that was supposed to happen here was a little embarrassment. He chose to follow Budd's directions and piece by piece he removed all of his clothes.

Budd snickered as the principal removed his clothing. He could hardly wait. This was going to be great. At this moment he was happier than ever that he had met Derek Lowrance. "Oh, Jesus, Mr. Baker," he said as the underwear came off. "I guess it's true what all the kids say about you having such a little pecker." He burst out laughing, then caught himself. He didn't want anyone to hear them, not yet. First he was going to take all of Mr. Baker's clothes, then he was going to put a cloth over the big jerk's mouth and render him unconscious, then he was going to drag him around to the back of the building and drop him through the only window. A moment later he would yell out his victory cry which would draw everyone's attention. The only way out would be the front door. Everyone would be watching. All of the kids would see him naked. It would be the best. He only wished he could be on the inside to see it all. But two of his buddies were inside. They had made sure the window was unlocked, and they would tell him later what had happened. Budd had wanted to tell them about his plan, but Derek had said to trust no one until it was all over, and Derek seemed to know a lot about these kinds of things.

"Step back to the building," Budd commanded the principal. Mr. Baker stepped back. "Turn around and put your nose to the metal."

"I thought this wasn't going to be painful."

"Shut up and do it or I will make it painful."

Stew turned around and faced the wall.

Budd picked up the clothes and threw them by the tree. He would grab them on his way back, as he fled toward home. He pulled the small bottle of chloroform out of his pocket, and the rag he had brought to soak with it. For this he had to put the gun down, so he watched the principal closely as he uncapped the bottle and poured some of its contents onto the old pair of underwear he had grabbed out of the dirty laundry.

Mr. Baker just stood, his face to the building, his mind racing, running into walls. There was no way out of this without taking a risk that was too big. If it were just him he would turn around and try to take the boy down, hoping the gun was a bluff or that Budd would be too wrapped up in what he was doing to react quickly enough. But there was a wife. And there were two little girls to consider as well. Where would they be if Budd wasn't bluffing?

Before he could reason it all out there was another voice which came from the darkness behind him. It was one he recognized but could not place.

"You done good, Budd."

Budd turned around, the bottle and rag still in his hands. "Derek! What are you doing here?" He could only see the outline of the boy against the tree. Mr. Baker's heart sank into his stomach when he heard Derek's name. Things had just gotten much worse.

"I wanted to make sure you didn't fuck it all up. And I wanted to be here."

"I'm glad you came," Budd exclaimed. "I've been thinking, it's going to be kind of hard getting this tub of lard through that back window." Budd was pointing to the back of the building.

Derek looked to the building, then back to Budd. "Put the lid back on the chloroform and hand it to me." He looked at Mr. Baker. "I have a better idea."

Budd was confused, but this was Derek's idea to start with. If he had a better one now, then Budd was willing to go along. He walked to Derek to hand him the bottle when he noticed something was already in Derek's hand. Just as he realized what it was two shots rang out from the snub nose .38 that had days ago rested in Mr. Baker's dresser drawer. Budd's eyes grew big, and Derek felt the thrill run through him. Budd's eyes would not turn away as he stared in surprise at the boy who he thought had been his friend. Derek just smiled as the electricity ran through him. Then Budd fell forward to the ground and writhed as the pain ran through his gut.

"Sorry, Budd, but it had to be a close shot."

Derek looked up to see the principal who was standing naked against the metal building, his back against the outside wall. At the sound of the shots he had finally turned around to see what had happened.

"I've been thinking about this one since February," Derek said quietly, as if the gunshots had gone unheard. He would have to be quick now, there was no time to delay. The timing of the shots was crucial. Yet it was exhilarating to watch this man who had once been so in control as he stood naked and totally frightened.

"Don't you wish you'd been just a little more tolerant of me over the years, Stew?" Derek knelt down and picked up the gun which Budd had set down. He stood and quickly walked up to Stew Baker. Then he placed the barrel of the gun against his chest and looked into his eyes.

Images of wife and kids ran through Stew's mind. He had known Derek for years, and he knew he was capable of pulling that trigger. "Please don't."

"No more detention?" Derek asked.

"No more, I promise."

Derek grinned. Then he fired two shots. No one would know which gun had fired first, so the number of shots had to be the same. The man's eyes ballooned as his heart burst. His death was almost instantaneous, and Derek reveled in the thrill of it.

Stew slid to his knees, then fell to his face on the hard ground. Derek quickly slid the .38 into Mr. Baker's left hand, he had remembered that he was left-handed and knew this would be important. Then he returned Budd's gun to Budd's side. Budd had stopped moving and the blood was still flowing. He would be dead soon. But Derek would not be able to hang around for that. Already he had stayed too long.

Derek gathered the chloroform and ran westward, heading across the field which stretched for a mile behind the big building before coming to an old gravel road. It had all worked as planned. He had no fear. He knew he would not be caught. Everyone would know Budd had finally decided to kill the principal. Everyone would know that the principal was scared enough to carry his gun. It would be an easy case, one that old drunk Sheriff Thompson would be more than happy to close quickly.

Derek ran and ran until he came to the paved road. The electricity ran through his body as he breathed in the warm night air. He felt alive. It was the best feeling that there could possibly be. And he looked forward to the time that he could feel it again.

Chapter Six
1

Steven Keith sat on his old leather couch near the western wall of his den. His dog, Pat, lay on the couch with him, her head in Steven's lap. It was after midnight. His plane had landed in Ontario only a few hours earlier. His bags were sitting in the middle of the den, still full of used and wrinkled clothes. On the coffee table in front of him was a stack of old yearbooks from junior-high and high-school. He had flipped through their pages, looking closely at the images of himself and those of his friends. Jennifer had always been beautiful. Though he never would have said so while she was still living, her eyes now seemed somehow sad. He remembered her dream of death that she had shared with him in that final summer before college, the dream she had shared with Rebecca and Samantha as well. Had it been a premonition? Had she known it was time? Her eyes seemed so sad. It was hard not to cry.

But he had done his crying, and now he just stared at the old images of his friends while that heavy knot rested in the pit of his stomach. Pat shifted and let out a sign, Steven patted her on the side. She was a good dog. She had waited patiently for his return and had lifted his spirits when he let her in and she had greeted him heartily. But she knew something wasn't right with her master. She could sense the sadness, and so she had stayed close to him while he looked at the pictures and remembered.

There was something terribly wrong with it all, something beyond the obvious. There were new and strange feelings. He didn't know if they were a part of the grief, or if it was something else. There was a connection he was missing, an obvious answer which eluded him. The feeling had become stronger as he had perused the pages of his past. The answer was buried in his mind and in these books. But he could not find it. His eyes were beginning to burn from all of the looking and searching, and his head was beginning to hurt. He looked through the final pages of his senior yearbook. It had been a good year, one of the best ever.

Steven turned the page and then saw the picture which shook him. It was a picture of him and Jennifer at the senior prom. It had been a magical night, and a terrible one. Her sad eyes pierced his soul and he took a deep breath to hold back the threatening tears. He had been in love many times but had never married. Had he ever been in love more than he had been with Jennifer? Now it seemed as if he had not. But now it did not matter. He thought again of Samantha and Rebecca. They were probably his best friends and probably always would be.

But as he looked at the picture and thought about that night back in '74 he wondered if a shadow had fallen over them all.

The night crept by slowly as he waited.

2

Timothy Watkins lay awake in his bed. He had his own bed in his own room in a house which was his own. He worked at the grocery store by day, bagging groceries for the residents of Eastland, Texas who had come to know and respect the hardworking man. On the evenings and weekends he played his piano. He played for the churches, and he played for the old people in the retirement home, and he played for the college when they needed him for their shows. From time to time he would travel to Abilene and play at one of the big colleges, and once he had even performed with the Dallas Symphony Orchestra when they had come to Abilene Christian University. But he never traveled far from home, and he never left Eastland by himself. It was scary to him in other places, even after all these years. His mom would go with him most of the time, but when she couldn't go usually Bob Marston or Jake Wallace from the church would go with him. He loved to play. He loved how it made people smile and how it made them cry. When he was playing it felt like he was floating outside of his body and his brain was growing bigger than his head.

His house rested on one corner of the property which belonged to his mom. His dad had died five years ago of a heart attack. That had crushed his mother. Timothy had been depressed for months, but mostly because he feared that his mom would go away too. His mom's house was about a hundred feet away. It was close enough that he wasn't scared most of the time, and far enough away that he didn't feel like a child. But tonight he wanted to go to his mom's house and crawl through the window that lead to his old bedroom. She had kept it like he had left it, and sometimes he would stay there, usually on a Saturday night before church day. But during the week he tried very hard to stay in his own house. He knew it was part of being grown up, though he still didn't really understand why. But his mom wanted him to be grown up, so he tried his best for her. Tonight he wanted to cheat. Last night had been bad too. There was a monster out there, and it was a real one. All his life he had believed in such monsters. He had seen them vividly in his dreams from time to time. These monsters didn't eat you like the ones in the movies, they sucked out you, and what was you, and you became them until you weren't anymore. They didn't have sharp teeth, but they had invisible claws which reached into your eyes and pulled you out and then put you inside them. His mom had told him over and over that there were no monsters. Years ago he had finally agreed, but only so she would be proud and so she would quit worrying. But he knew they were real, and now one was here, in this town. It was already eating people, but nobody seemed to know. Last night he had seen it. Something had made him wake up and go outside. He had walked the six blocks to the house with the scary old woman in it. He knew she was bad, but he hadn't known she had one of the monsters in her house. At first he thought that the monster had gotten her and he had seen it run away fast like lightning. But no ambulances had come, and this morning he saw her on her front porch. She had smiled and pointed a knowing finger at him, and he knew then that she would send the monster after him. But he could not tell Mom. He knew she would just tell him that it was his "magnation" and that the monsters were only on the TV. So he kept it to himself, and he kept an eye out. He tried to think of how he could fight the monster, but the only thing he could think of was to carry a knife, so he kept one with him all of the time. He wanted to carry a gun because he could kill it from farther away, but he didn't know where to get one, and he was afraid that he might shoot himself. Right now the knife was on the stand by his bed. He stared at it as the minutes ticked by. Maybe the police would find who the monster had killed, then he could tell them. He knew that there was no chance he could beat the monster by himself. He didn't even know how much the police could help. But he would have to wait. If he told them now they would smile at him and pat his head and call his mom. He had been through all of that before. He would have to wait.

The night crept by slowly as he waited.

3

Another chill ran through Samantha's body from head to toe. She had tried to sleep on the plane ride home but was not able to. The ride had been smooth despite the weather delay, and the cabin lights had been turned off, but her memories and this chill kept her from sleep. She could not shake the sense of dread, and it only grew stronger as she approached her dwelling.

The cab ride home was uneventful. This driver did not feel the need to discuss his hard luck, which was usually the talk she got on her cab rides to or from the airport but left her to ponder her feelings. She could think of nothing but Jennifer and her friends. There was anticipation mixed with the dread, as if something terrible loomed ahead, yet something which would make her more complete.

She paid the driver and lugged her travel bag out of the trunk and into her apartment building. The security guard saw her coming and opened the front door for her, greeting her as she entered. Phil was from a small town near Birmingham, and there was a special friendliness in his eyes which was always refreshing. It was as if the two of them had a little secret which the 'Yankees' who occupied the remainder of the building would not understand anyway. It had something to do with lazy afternoons resting in the shade of an old oak tree while chicken roasted on the grill. Or something very like that anyway.

Phil carried her bag to the elevator and held the door open for her as she got in. They exchanged pleasantries and the doors closed, leaving Samantha to herself and her dread once more. Her heart began to race as the elevator rose. Once, just before the opening of her first big gallery showing, she had experienced her first and only panic attack. This was very much like that. The doors opened and she stepped onto her floor. The familiar surroundings now seemed foreign, and she had to hold firmly to the handle of her bag lest it slip out of her sweat covered palm. Samantha paused for a moment and closed her eyes, but this did not help. She needed to get inside. She needed a glass of water, or perhaps something stronger. She hurried to her door and unlocked it, then stepped inside and closed her door.

The darkness enveloped her. It was cold too, yet she could feel the sweat beading on her forehead. She reached over and flipped on the light. As she did her heart leapt, as if something was supposed to happen.

But nothing did. The familiarity of her apartment began to soothe her, and she headed straight for the kitchen where she poured herself a Crown and Seven. Not the drink of the jet set, but her favorite nonetheless. She downed the first one quickly and made herself another. Then she carried it to her living room where she sat on the couch and looked to the wall she had turned into a mural of nature defeating modernization, the irony of its being painted on the fifth floor of a high-rise apartment which had been built on what once had been tribal hunting grounds fully intended.

As she sat and stared at her wall her body finally began to relax. Both it and her mind were exhausted from the day's events. It had all happened so fast, now her life was supposed to return to normal, as if it had not been shaken. She did not think it could. It would be a while before she could push the dread and depression from her mind so that it would not affect her work.

She would go upstate. She would visit the falls and stay in Brett Munchard's cabin for a few days, by herself. She would have to cancel some important appointments and delay her work on the Bussman Center, but it had to be done, and she knew that she would be forgiven.

Her pulse softened and her eyelids crept down over her eyes. That terribly elusive sleep was now pouncing upon her. She would have to get a shower, then jump into bed. Or perhaps she would just jump in bed so that the shower wouldn't wake her.

Calmness settled over her.

She knew she needed to get up, but she would in just a minute or two. Right now she was so tired.

So sleepy.

Her head lolled gently to her shoulder as sleep conquered.

In the closet thirty feet behind her there was a rustling which caused her eyes to flutter open for just an instant, then she dismissed it as her mind slipped finally into sleep.

4

Rebecca saw the terrible monster. It was not her monster, of this much she was sure. This was someone else's monster, someone else's fears which had made their way to her sleep. The image was dark and unclear. It undulated and changed shapes as it floated through a dark room. There was a man here too. It was a man who looked familiar, but her dream-mind could not recognize him. It was he who feared the monster, but the monster did not turn on him. Instead it flew out of a window and disappeared into darkness.

Then she saw an image of a woman. Her dream-mind knew this woman. It was Samantha. She was floating in another strange room. Rebecca called to her, but Samantha did not respond. She was not asleep. Rebecca knew that Samantha was dead even before her body rolled slowly toward her, revealing the torn clothing and swaths of blood across her neck and arms.

Rebecca did not turn away. She had seen much worse than this in her dreams and in reality. She had learned not to turn away because she knew that no matter how awful it was, she would learn more if she stayed.

Then Samantha's eyes opened, but they were not Samantha's. These were the eyes of the monster. They were deep, and black, and they tugged at her soul.

"Your time will come. And so will theirs." Its lips did not move, yet its voice came from everywhere.

Rebecca knew. She knew that her friend was dead, or soon would be. She knew who had killed Jennifer now, it was this monster. It would come for her too, of this she was sure.

Why them? Was Steven in danger too? This was hidden from her, but she believed that it was true. What was this monster? Why did it want them all dead?

Samantha's body began to float. Her skin bubbled and melted as she became something different, something that did not belong. Her head grew long and thin, darkness began to shoot out of her body where the skin had fallen away.

Then there was a flash of light and a loud sound.

Rebecca awoke in a terrified state. Her Atlanta hotel room was dark, too dark. The vision lingered in her mind, the malevolence of the monster pervading the darkness and the miles.

The miles.

Samantha.

Rebecca felt for her lamp and turned it on. She grabbed the phone and dialed quickly, but carefully. If Samantha was still alive then every second counted. If not...

Rebecca tried not to think of what might come next. Instead she sat and waited for an eternity for the call to go through.

5

Derek emerged from the closet quietly, the knife still gripped firmly in his hand. She had not gone into her gallery. Instead she had come to her couch and drank herself to sleep. The sleep was deep. He could tell by the silent but deep breaths. He could also feel it. He knew moments before she had entered the room that she had arrived. And in a few moments more she would be even closer. He would thrive on her death. This time he was ready for her submission if she awoke. He would not be disappointed by the way she smiled and accepted the shiny blade he had brought for her.

He walked silently across the wood floor to the small step which led to the sunken living room. She sat at an angle; her head lolled to the right. He would approach her from behind and drive the knife into her chest, holding her head back by her hair so that she could not look away. But he knew that she, like Jennifer, would not try to look away. He had the same feeling. This was just a part of some awesome plan that he was only beginning to understand.

He reached the back of the couch and looked down at the side of her face. She was pretty, but not like Jennifer had been. But this made no difference. In moments her body would be nothing more than an empty shell.

Derek grabbed her hair and gently pulled her head back, exposing her neck. She stirred but did not awaken. He looked one last time at her chest, rising and falling with the rhythm of her breaths. He studied it and memorized the spot where the blade would enter to pierce her beating heart. She would not scream. She would not resist.

He raised the blade.

The shrill ringing caused him to jump. He looked quickly to his right before realizing it was just the phone. He looked back down at Samantha whose eyes had come open and stared upward into his face. He smiled. She didn't move.

"I have come for you," he whispered.

The phone rang again.

Samantha pulled her head forward.

Derek did not expect the move and he lost his grip on her hair. In a moment she was up, standing across the couch and facing him. She did not recognize this man. Derek had grown heavier over the years, and he now sported a goatee. But still there was something familiar about him. Even something inviting. Regardless of the knife he held in his hand she felt no fear. She saw something in his eyes though, something which reminded her of Jennifer. The phone continued to ring.

Though this was a deadly situation, she felt an odd calmness. "What do you want?" she asked him.

"Come to me."

She felt drawn to him. His voice seemed melodious. She stood her ground nonetheless.

Derek could see that she was not going to be as willing as Jennifer, but she wasn't going to be any trouble either. He walked around the couch and toward her. Samantha backed slowly away, trying to understand why there was no fear. Her mind raced. The ringing phone helped hold her in the world of sane thoughts like a slap in the face. She fought against the placid feelings. She closed her eyes for a moment, and in that moment she saw her dear friend, Jennifer Summers, lying dead in a pool of blood.

Then she knew that this was Jennifer's killer, and that he had come now for her.

As Derek closed the distance between them Samantha opened her eyes and darted suddenly for the kitchen.

Derek could have reached out and grabbed Samantha, but her sudden movement had been totally unexpected. This was not supposed to be how it went. Where was the submission? Where was her eagerness to join with him? He turned and watched as she disappeared around a corner. Then he shook himself of his surprise and went after her.

Samantha knocked the phone from the wall as she ran. Then she screamed out. Whoever was calling would have to hear her. The kitchen was dark, but enough light came through from the living room that she could make out the counters. He was coming for her. There was no way out of here. Why hadn't she run for the door? Her reflex had been to go for the phone, now she was trapped. She could hear his heavy steps coming up behind her. He knew that the only way out was the window, and it was a long way down.

She turned and faced him as he entered the dark kitchen.

"What do you want?" she yelled at him.

"I'm here to help you." She was being too loud. He would have to hurry. He stared at her outline in the darkness, his new eyes telling him just where her heart was.

She could feel him pulling at something inside her. She backed away nonetheless, back to the sink. She reached back and felt inside of it. At that moment she was glad she hadn't done the dishes before her trip. The water was cold and the soap had collected on the bottom, the grease on the top. The afternoon before her flight she had made a ham sandwich. Real ham, smoked in a smoker and shipped here from Arkansas overnight in a refrigerated trailer. Bought the next day by a young artist with a hankering for a meal her mom used to make back in west Texas. Real smoked ham. The knife she had used to cut the small thin strips lay at the bottom of the water, pieces of pork still clinging to its serrated edge. She gripped the handle of it firmly in her hand as the madman who seemed so familiar approached.

Derek could see her heart and he focused upon it. Her will was fading. She was facing him, her eyes were wide, but she was waiting, nonetheless. She was terrified. It was time.

She tried to cry out, but her voice left when the terror took hold. He crossed the white and gray ceramic tile in a single tremendous leap and was instantly before her, his shining blade held out in front of him. In the same instant she brought her own blade around, aiming for the blackness which leapt at her.

He had wanted to look into her eyes. He had wanted to see the terror and the fear which came before the yielding then the dying. But as he readied the blade he felt a hot fire in his side. Her eyes were not yielding, they were defiant. He lashed out with his blade nonetheless, eager to have the kill. But the woman moved suddenly, and he missed the beating heart.

Samantha felt her knife sink into the man's side, then she turned to run. As she did she felt his own blade as it entered her shoulder. She screamed out in pain. He withdrew the blade and slashed out again, but Samantha went for the floor and the blade just grazed her face. She tried to crawl away, but the pain in her shoulder was tremendous. Derek slashed out again but missed her completely this time.

Someone knocked on the door. A distant voice. It was Eddie, her next-door neighbor. "Are you all right in there, Samantha?"

Derek went to his knee and held Samantha's left leg as she tried to scoot away. She screamed out again as he leapt up the length of her body and poised his knife carefully. "Help me, Eddie!" she cried, but her voice seemed too silent and feeble to have made it to his ears.

Derek drove the knife into her back, sinking the blade two inches into her body, piercing her upper intestine and her left lung.

Eddie did hear the cry, followed by a scream of pain. He had lived in New York long enough to know that he had to act now and fast. He didn't have a weapon, but maybe he could frighten the man away. He lifted his foot and kicked once, but the door didn't give in. He tried with his shoulder and this time he heard the frame splinter.

Derek pulled the knife out of Samantha's body and grabbed her hair. He had stabbed her in the back to wound her but had aimed carefully so that she would not die from the wound. He wanted to look into her eyes as death came for her. He wanted to see the power as it leapt from her body and joined with his. He stood upright and lifted her head, turning it to look at him. As he did this something tore through his side. He let out an exclamation of pain as he dropped Samantha back to the floor. His side burned, and something was wrong with his vision. He could no longer make out the shadows of the kitchen, and Samantha's outline was only barely visible as it scooted away from him. He reached down and felt for the pain. It was warm and wet. Wetness had soaked into his shirt and was running down the leg of his pants. Blood was coming out of him in streams, streams too fast and too hot. He held his hand on his wound and looked again for Samantha. He felt weak and his legs were shaking. He had to get away from here. He had to get help.

He heard the door to the apartment explode inward. Samantha's outline disappeared around the corner of the kitchen entry, toward the door. He ran toward her, but the pain tore at him. He had to kill her before he left. Perhaps her death would heal him.

As he rounded the corner he met the surprised gaze of a tall, thin man. Samantha had regained her feet and was disappearing out the front door. The man stood in the way; his hands held out as if to halt Derek. Derek rushed forward and drove his blade into the man's stomach. The man doubled over, and Derek withdrew his blade, letting the man fall to the floor with a moan. Samantha was gone, out the door. A voice in his head told him to flee. He could not be identified. He could not be captured. And there was his wound. But Samantha was so close.

Derek ran out the door after her and saw her disappear into the next apartment. He rushed to the door, but she managed to close it and lock it before he got to it. He hit it once with his shoulder, then doubled over as the pain in his side shot through him.

Another door opened somewhere behind him. Someone else had decided to check on the commotion.

He could not get into this apartment. Samantha was lying just on the other side of this door, bleeding to death. Could he feel the rush of power from this distance, without even seeing her face?

But how long could she hold on?

The door which had opened was closed again. They had not seen his face. If he stayed, someone would, someone who would live to describe it to the police. And the blood was coming from his wound too quickly.

He kicked the door in fury, then turned and headed for the stairwell at the end of the hall. As he entered it he heard another door open. Soon there would be sirens. Then the police would begin asking if anyone had gotten a good look at the attacker. He fled down the stairs, though his pace was barely human. The pain in his side screamed out as he descended the stairs. He would have to go to a hospital. It should be safe. It would have to be. The wound felt deep.

Finally he emerged from the apartment and walked casually for three blocks before getting a taxi. He dropped his blade outside the door and told the driver to take him quickly to the emergency room of the nearest hospital

A mile down the road they passed the first rushing police car.

Derek held his side and stared into the night.

<u>6</u>

Samantha sat on the floor of Eddie's apartment, her back against the door. Was he gone? He had to be. There was pain on her face and in her back. There was a burning inside her. It hurt to sit, so she lay down on the floor.

Samantha lay still. She could hear her heart faintly beating in her ears. It was hard to breath. She coughed, and the blood which had gotten into her lung dribbled down her chin. More of it simply oozed out her back and soaked into her sweater.

She knew that if she had the energy she would be able to name the man who had just tried to kill her. Or perhaps he had succeeded. But her energy was waning, and dark edges were creeping into her vision.

She lay there for a few more moments, praying for help and waiting for the sirens. But before she could hear them she passed into unconsciousness, slipping slowly toward death.

Chapter Seven
1

Richard awoke in a sweat, his body shaking from the adrenaline which had been pumped into it. It had happened again. Another murder. Even though it had been over twenty years since he had seen the woman, he knew who it was. Samantha Chambers. This could not be a coincidence. Two women from the group of seven children who had been born in Eastland in September of 1956. Samantha Chambers and Jennifer Summers. He knew now that the rest of them were in danger too, himself included.

He got out of bed and went to the closet to put on some clothes.

His wife stirred. "What is it, Richard?"

"It's something important, honey. I've got to go out for a little while, but I'll be back before morning."

Bonnie got out of the bed and walked to her husband. She put her hands on his shoulders as he pulled on his pants. "Where are you going? What's wrong?"

Richard turned and faced his wife. "I've had another dream. I think it's something the sheriff should know about."

Bonnie looked at her husband's face. He had gone to Sheriff Sharp a few times over the years, when his dreams had been strong and he had known whom to accuse. It had made a difference more than once. He would only go if he knew who to name and what terrible act had been done. She could see in his face that this was something which disturbed him deeply, like the dreams of the child molester had disturbed him. He hadn't told her the specifics of that until after the arrest. She could see that he didn't want to talk about this one yet. She stood back and let him dress.

"You be careful. And I'll be here if you want to talk when you get back."

He kissed her on the forehead. "You go back to bed and get some sleep."

She grabbed his jacket out of the closet and handed it to him. "Don't forget this."

He kissed her again and headed for the door.

Bonnie went back to bed and lay awake, wondering what new horror had invaded her husband's sleep.

2

The lights were on in the sheriff's house when Richard got there, despite the late hour. He walked to the front door and knocked loudly. Moments later the door opened, and the sheriff stood looking out at him.

"Well, good evening, Mr. Hall. What brings you here at this hour?" Sharp could see the lines in Richard's face, and he knew that the man was under stress. He also knew why he was here.

"May I come in, Frank?"

"Of course, Richard." The sheriff stepped back and let the preacher into his home. "Would you like some coffee?"

"That sounds good."

The sheriff went to the kitchen where the fresh pot of coffee sat. He was still a single man, though last year he'd come close to changing his status. Now she was married, and he was still single. As Frank poured the coffee he asked Richard what was on his mind.

"I think someone's killing the snow babies."

Most of the people in town wouldn't have known what Richard was talking about. But Frank Sharp had gone to school with the seven children who had come out of that 1955 winter storm. He had been best friends with one of them, and still saw Steven from time to time when he came to visit his parents. Frank took two cups of coffee into the kitchen and joined Richard at the table.

Frank took a sip of his coffee, then spoke to Richard. "Steven called a little while ago. That's why I'm up. He said someone's tried to kill Samantha Chambers in her apartment in New York. He thinks it more than a coincidence, too."

Richard looked up from his cup. "Tried to kill? What do you mean?"

Frank looked at Richard closely. "Why are you here tonight? Did you know about Samantha?"

"I saw it, Frank. I saw her running, and I saw the knife. I saw it with Jennifer, too."

"Why didn't you say something then?"

"I didn't think it had anything to do with us. I just thought it was something else I'd dreamed about. Nothing I saw in my dream could have helped anyone." He took a sip. "Besides, I don't want word to get out about these dreams. I don't want people looking me up to find their dogs or solve their brother's murder. I have that right, Frank. Besides, I'm here now."

Frank knew Richard was right, but it bothered him nonetheless. "You know me better than that, Richard. You know you could have told me and the press wouldn't be on your doorstep the next day."

"There was nothing that would have helped."

"You can't know that Richard. I'm a police officer, I've been trained to see significance in things you might discard. You never know what will help and what won't until you tell me." Frank relaxed a little, not meaning to preach to the preacher. He asked a pointed question. "Do you know who's doing this?"

"I have no idea."

Frank was familiar with the details of Richard's strange gift. "Did you see Samantha's face? Did she seem to recognize the attacker?"

"It was dark. And it was misty. It wasn't so much her face as her, her, well her spirit, if you know what I mean."

Frank looked a little puzzled.

"I just knew it was her." Richard sipped his coffee. It was still too hot. "New York is a long way away. Until the dream about Jennifer, I've never dreamt about anything so far away. That's another reason I think it has to do with the snow babies. Someone's after us."

"But why? Is there some reason someone would want to do this?"

Richard hadn't given that much thought. "I can't think of a sane reason. It's got to be some crazy person, someone who remembers us."

The first crazy person Sharp thought of was the old nurse. She still lived in town. He would pay her a visit first thing in the morning. He didn't think she was capable of scaling walls or even figuring out how to get on the right plane, but it was a place to start, and that's all he needed for now. He would also visit a friend tomorrow, a friend whose wife had a very special talent. Perhaps she could help. Perhaps not.

Richard saw the sheriff's mind was working. That's why he had come here. If anyone would take him seriously and act upon it, Sheriff Frank Sharp was the man. Richard heard stories about what had happened to Frank in Cisco three years earlier, things which had changed his life and opened his mind. It had also made an opening in the position of county sheriff, an opening which Frank won with the next election.

The sheriff looked out the window into the darkness of the night. "I've got some ideas, but they'll have to wait until morning."

Richard stood. "I understand. Let me know if you need my help."

The sheriff stood with Richard. "I appreciate the offer. I'll let you know. Get in touch if you think of anything else, or if you see anything you think might be helpful."

Richard extended his hand and shook with Frank. "I'll be going. Thanks for the coffee."

Frank led the preacher to the door. "Don't mention it. I appreciate your help."

The men exchanged final pleasantries and Richard disappeared into the night. Frank closed the door, and his mind began to race. There was something strange about all of this, something that went beyond revenge or insanity. He could sense it. It had the feel that the case in Cisco had given him, too many unanswered questions, too many coincidences. He closed his eyes and said a short prayer that he would find the answers before it went too far this time.

3

Tim ran the morning paper route in Eastland. The small Eastland paper was actually sent by mail, but the Abilene Reporter News had fairly wide distribution throughout the area referred to as the Big Country. Abilene was also where all of the television broadcasts came from, aside from a few small independent stations and one network in San Angelo. There were only two paper boys in Eastland. Timothy had his route which had remained virtually unchanged since he had started it twenty years earlier. The other route changed names and faces every couple of years. At first the paper had been concerned about Timothy learning the route, and there had been several weeks of misdelivered papers, and he had gotten lost his first day on his own. But after he'd gotten past the hard part he became the most reliable paper boy the Abilene paper had ever known or would ever know. He never left town overnight, he never took vacation, and many of his customers had grown quite fond of him over the years. He made enough money in tips alone to cover his cable and electricity, and even had some left over for what his mom called "fluff money." Timothy always thought that was a funny word for it, and sometimes people looked at him funny when he called it that.

Despite his start as the runt of the group, Timothy had grown to be a very big man. He stood six foot four, and weighed over two hundred and thirty pounds, though his soft features and friendly demeanor left him anything but intimidating. This morning was cool, but not so cold that he had to wear his heavy coat. He peddled his bicycle which he had bought last spring toward his route, his basket and his carrying bags full of papers he had carefully wrapped in plastic since the forecast called for a chance of rain. His old bike rested inside his rickety old garage. It had served him well for ten years, but the rust and the road had finally worn the poor thing down to where it was too hard to ride and not reliable for the route. But it was still a good bike, and he couldn't bear to part with it. There was one other bike which had served in the early years. It had stood in the garage silently for two years as a sentimental reminder of the past. It had been his friend, and he would not throw his friend in the trash. But then he had given it to a boy who was a friend of his, a friend on the route who didn't have a dad and whose mom couldn't buy him a bike. From time-to-time Timothy would see the boy on his old bike riding through town too fast and grinning from ear to ear. That made Timothy happy.

Timothy saw The House from two blocks away. He always spotted The House and tried to ride past it as fast as he could, on the opposite side of the street. He had been doing this for five years. It was then that the state had set her up in that place. Originally a nice old lady had lived there for many years. After she died in the house it had stayed on the market for almost two years before they put the crazy woman in it. At first she would wait for him to come by every morning. She would shout crazy things at him, like he was her lover and she wanted him to come to her and stuff like that, but he stayed away because he knew she was crazy, and because her house smelled real bad. He knew she talked crazy a lot. He'd heard her shouting the same kinds of things at some of the kids. Once or twice he'd seen her being hauled away by the police from her hiding place near the school, and one time she had been naked. She would hide there from time to time, waiting to grab one of the kids and say crazy things. He'd seen it happen to a girl once, her name was Jennifer, he remembered her because she was so pretty and because when she saw him she would smile and wave, not turn and laugh like other kids. And he could see her light. He could see the light in some of the nice ones, at least he could back then. It followed them around and lit up their head and shoulders real funny. He remembered Steven and Rebecca and Samantha and Richard. But he didn't see the light on people anymore, even the nice ones. Sometimes he saw Richard, and he still had the light. He wondered if the other kids had grown up with their lights too, or if Richard got to keep his because he was a Man Of

God. Timothy wanted to me a Man Of God too, but he never saw a light on his own head.

Timothy delivered the last paper before the bad house, two doors away, when she came out. He had seen her peek through the curtains almost every day he came by, but she hadn't come out for years, and he was glad because it scared him when she did. This morning she came out. His fear caused him to miss the door of his last delivery, so he had to get off his bike and get the paper out of Mrs. Kenawick's flower bed. He tried not to look back at her, and she wasn't talking to him, so it wasn't hard. He laid the paper on the doorstep and headed back for his bike. But she had left her yard and was walking toward his bike too. Timothy ran, afraid she was going to steal his new bike. But she didn't run. She just kept walking, and he got there first.

"Hi, Timothy."

It was the first time she had said his name. Usually she would say 'lover' or something like that. He looked at the ground and got on his bike.

"My name is Verna Calloway. I'm getting better now. Will you talk to me? I want to say I'm sorry."

He looked up at her and was surprised that she did not look so bad today. She wasn't wearing any makeup, and her clothes were still torn, but she was smiling, and she seemed calm. Timothy was confused. But he didn't want to be rude. "It's okay," he replied. Then he tried to look away so he could leave, but his eyes wouldn't work right.

"I know where you are now," she said. "I know all of their names. Soon we will be together."

She was talking crazy again, only now there was something inside him that told him it wasn't crazy, that she was saying true things that he couldn't understand.

"I know who you are, Timothy Watkins. I've watched you come by my house almost every morning for five years now. I feel like you are my friend. Are you my friend?"

Timothy didn't like her at all, but if Timothy Watkins was anything besides simple, he was polite. "I guess, ma'am."

She smiled a wide, inviting smile. "I'm getting better. I know you want me to get better." She looked around quickly to see that no one was nearby. Timothy looked too out of reflex. Then she whispered to him. "Would you like to get well?"

Timothy thought, but he couldn't understand what she was saying. "I feel fine, ma'am." His eyes broke away. "I really need to get my papers done, or my customers are going to get mad."

"Timothy. Look at me."

He was frightened again, but he looked.

"You *are* sick. It's what makes you stupid. I know how to fix that."

Timothy's face flushed in embarrassment. She was making fun of him. He remembered the time the high school boys had given him something to eat because it would make him smart, but it was chocolate mixed with dog crap and they just laughed at him and made him cry.

"You're makin' fun. I gotta go."

He started to mount his bike, but then she grabbed his hand. He cried out and tried to pull away, but her grip was strong, and she was staring into his eyes. He felt an electric shock, then something deep inside of him stirred.

Timothy pulled hard and got his hand free. Frantically he pushed at the ground with his foot and began riding away on his bike.

"Come back!" she shouted at him. "I know you felt it. Come back tonight and we'll make you well."

He rode away without looking back. Tears began to stream down his face. She was right. He had felt it. When she had touched him it hurt for a second like a shock, then suddenly he understood more than he ever had before. He understood why people laughed at him, he understood why some people helped him and liked him. He understood why he could only deliver papers and sack groceries, and that despite what he had come to believe, there was much more to life than doing his daily chores, watching television at night, and playing his music. He understood what being simple meant, and he didn't want to go back to it. But this sensation had lasted only for a second and now he understood none of these things. He was scared, and he was sad. He rode to his next delivery, three houses away, and stopped. He was still scared, but he looked back anyway. She was in her yard now, walking to her door. Without looking at him she went inside. When he knew she would stay inside he threw his paper to the porch in front of him and went on to the next one.

As he threw his papers and rode fast to make up for lost time he rubbed the tears from his eyes and tried to remember what being smart had been like.

4

Rebecca stood by the bedside of her friend and held onto her cold hand. Rebecca had come up from Atlanta on the first available flight. She had decided to stay in Atlanta an extra day, just to look around and to see if she could be any help. Two of Samantha's New York friends were sitting in the waiting area, waiting for family to show. Samantha's parents were on their way and were expected by evening. Rebecca had spoken with Samantha's parents before the hospital had called. They had been happy to hear from her, at least at first. Steven was coming too.

Samantha was out of it. The weak beat of her heart was translated by a steady 'beep' on the monitor beside her bed. Surgery had taken six hours. She would live, but there had been a lot of damage inside. No one had said when she would come out of the coma. There had been a lot of blood loss. There might be brain damage. It would be some time before they knew. Samantha would need to open her eyes first, then they could go from there.

Rebecca had put her work back home in San Francisco on hold. She had called her clients to let them know that she was having a crisis of her own and that she would resume their cases as soon as she could. That was little consolation to the mother of the little girl who was still missing. Rebecca explained to the mother that even if she had stayed and worked on the case, her mind was so distracted that no progress would be made. It was true. Her mind was focused on Jennifer, and now on Samantha. The implications were too great, too much of a distraction. The girl's mother said she would wait, but Rebecca sensed her great pain and promised to hurry back.

Rebecca held Samantha's hand tightly and closed her eyes. There were images here, but they were dark and indistinct. She could not tell what they were, or even what they were supposed to be. Perhaps when Samantha awoke, coherent or not, she could learn something more.

She thought again about her dream, the one about the monster. Whose monster had it been? She was sure it was connected to the attempt on Samantha's life, the timing was more than mere coincidence. But this, too, was incomplete and virtually meaningless. She was once again frustrated that she did not have more control over this gift of hers, that she could not point and aim it as she would like. Instead she had to wait for it to feed her the pieces she needed, and even then it didn't always perform as she needed or wanted. And she needed answers badly now. They were all in danger. She had known that in Atlanta and she had shared it with her friends. But the demon had swept down on Samantha, nonetheless. Was there escape? Was there any way to prepare for the attack? Was the killer still in New York? The police had done a sweep of the hospitals and turned up nothing despite the blood which had trailed away from the apartment and down the stairs, blood that had come from the killer. This was the same killer who had taken Jennifer. Rebecca knew that for certain. Tomorrow she would go to the apartment to confirm this, and to feel around for any other clues. But she and Steven would have to be careful, because they were targets, too.

But targets of whom, or what?

The answer lay in the dream of the monster.

Rebecca opened her eyes and looked again at her unconscious friend. She prayed that she would come back soon, and that an end would come to this madness.

5

Frank Sharp walked into the feed store just south of Albany. Albany was in Shackelford County, not Eastland County, but he had business in Albany today, nonetheless. He was in uniform, but the big man behind the counter called him by his first name anyway.

"Hey, Frank, I haven't seen you in a while. Come on in here."

The rustic bell jingled on the door as it closed itself. This store was deceptively quaint. It's owner was a shrewd businessman who had finally gotten out of the hectic Dallas life five years ago and moved back to his home town where he'd opened a feed store and lived the life of his boyhood. He was a man at peace. Frank hoped that someday he would find the kind of peace Dean Curtis had found.

"How's business, Dean?"

"Well, the rain's wreaking havoc with the planting season. Jed Rawlins got his tractor stuck in his peanut patch again out your way. But everybody's livestock's still eatin' good."

"Jed gets stuck every spring. He always tries to plant too early, and he gets that old Minneapolis Moline dug in axle high. Has to pull it out with Ben's tractor when the ground finally dries up. Every spring."

"Like clockwork," Dean tossed in.

Dean and Frank were old friends. Their dads had worked together in the oil field, and the boys had seen each other at picnics and sometimes just visiting on Sundays growing up. Dean had left for college and hadn't come back. There wasn't much money to be made in these small towns anymore. But for Dean it was peace of mind that had finally brought him back. A successful feed store business had helped to keep him there, that and a good teaching job for his wife.

Frank had gone to school and come back, gone to work for Sheriff Pritchard in Eastland County straight out of school. Sheriff Pritchard had died badly in the mess in Cisco four years back. It was a shame. The Sheriff had been a good man, and a clean sheriff.

Dean looked the sheriff over. "I can see by your uniform that you're here on business."

"Well, I haven't got any cattle, Dean."

"I hear you're raising a couple of chickens, though. Ned Wascom was in here last week, said Ruth Jacoby was complaining about your rooster crowing at all hours of the night. Is that so?"

Frank laughed. For someone who had spent seven years in Big D, Dean had done a hell of a job keeping his perspective. "Yes. That stupid rooster of mine crows every time a set of headlights goes by the house. I've gotten used to it. Apparently not everybody has."

"Goes against ordinance, you know, Frank."

"That's city ordinance. I work for the county. Doesn't count."

Frank leaned on the counter. There was only one customer in the store. He was carefully reading the labels on the various brands of catfish food Dean had in stock.

Dean came up close to the counter and looked at his friend. "What's on your mind, Frank?"

"I've got some trouble in town. Kind of like my trouble four years back, only different."

Dean was familiar with what had happened in Cisco four years ago. It had all come down shortly after his feed store had opened. Julie, his wife, had known something was coming, but it had all happened so fast it had gotten by the both of them until it was all over.

"What's going on?"

"Do you remember Steven Keith?"

"You guys were pretty close in high school, weren't you?"

"Best pals. Still keep in touch."

"So, what's he up to?"

Frank shifted his weight. "He works for the U.S. Geological Survey in southern California. Checks the height of survey markers, takes rock samples, things like that."

"Sounds like a tough job."

Frank grinned. "Sounds like something you'd like."

"Probably so. So what's the deal? He in some trouble?"

"A couple of days ago a girl Steven and I went to high school with was killed in Atlanta."

"Sorry 'bout that, Frank."

"Me too, Dean. She was a great girl. Had made quite a career for herself, too. Finally got out of the small town, like she always said she would. Got her own television show and married Jack Cassidy."

Dean perked up. "The football player?"

"That's him."

"Who killed her?"

"Nobody knows yet."

"So you need some help with the case?"

"Not really, not like that, anyway. Atlanta's a little out of my jurisdiction."

"You mean we still haven't annexed Georgia yet?"

Frank chuckled. Dean was always the one for understatement and sarcasm, though never in a cutting way.

"So what's the problem?" Dean asked.

"Last night another girl we knew from school was attacked."

"Really?"

"Yes. She survived, but she's in a coma right now."

"Are the incidents related?"

There was a coughing sound and Dean realized that his customer had finally decided to save some money on the lower protein brand of catfish food and was waiting to pay for his purchase. Frank apologized and stepped out of the way while the man paid for the feed and explained that he'd haul it out himself.

"Much obliged," Dean called after the man. "Come back."

The man grunted his thanks and Dean turned his attention back to Frank. "So, are the attacks related?"

"I'm pretty sure that they are. And I have a feeling that there's something beyond the normal involved, but I'm not sure what."

"Why do you think that?"

"These two people not only went to school in the same small town, they were born on the same month of the same year, just a few days apart."

"That's certainly strange."

"There were seven children born about that time, about nine months after the town was shut down for a week for a winter storm. They were called the 'snow babies.' Steven Keith is one of the seven. Three of the others still live in town, one more lives in San Francisco. She's that Robinson girl, the psychic girl that knew about Kennedy getting shot."

"You never told me that story."

"I'll fill you in some day. Right now I'm concerned that Steven, as well as the other 'snow babies', is in danger. Right now I'm pretty sure it's just some crazy person."

"Not really, or you wouldn't be here."

Frank pushed his hat back. "That brings me to my point."

The store was silent for a moment as Frank prepared to say what Dean knew was coming.

"Do you think Julie can help?"

Dean looked down at the counter for a moment. When they moved out here they had talked about this. They wanted to live a normal life as normal people. They'd seen enough of the strange and supernatural in that terrifying week in New Orleans five years ago. Julie had special gifts, talents which had been passed down through the generations. But there were only a few close friends out here who knew. Frank was one of them. Frank had shared his bizarre stories about the spirits that had come to Cisco, and Dean had shared his story about the cult and the holocaust which had almost come. Julie had been Dean's salvation back then. When it had all come to an end they had married and moved out here. They decided that Julie would not become a psychic for the police, she had decided that in her youth. She wasn't really a psychic anyway, she simply knew what chants to sing and the herbs to use to open her eyes to the realms which most could never see. It was a gift passed to her by her grandmother almost forty years ago. It was a gift she would someday pass on to their little Chelsea's daughter. In the past she had let the idea that she could be using this gift to help people torment her. Now, after what had happened in New Orleans, she realized that she had her own life to live. Besides, together they had saved millions of people, though no one would ever know, enough to cover a lifetime of police work. So together they lived their own, peaceful lives.

The sheriff could see these thoughts running through Dean's head. "Look, Dean, I won't be put off if you say no. We talked about this when you told me about Julie. I wouldn't have come if I thought this was a normal case, but I don't think it is. I don't have any hard evidence yet, but I'm just getting this feeling, like four years ago. It's not right. This goes beyond some crazy person settling an old score or killing out of an old yearbook or something like that. I just want to get her feel for this. She doesn't have to come by the station or anything like that, just let me know what she thinks."

"I'll talk to her about it tonight. I'll tell her what you've said and see what she thinks."

Frank looked at his friend closely. "What do you think, Dean."

"Well, it's really up to her, but I don't think it's an unreasonable request. It's not like you're asking her to hold a seance in the courthouse or something. Of course, this would have to be kept strictly confidential."

"Of course."

Dean glanced around the store, then looked back to his friend. "I guess I'll put my vote in, but the final call is going to be hers."

"Sure."

"I think she'll go along. I'll let you know tonight."

Frank reached out and patted his friend's shoulder. "I appreciate it, Dean. And I'm sorry to intrude like this."

"Hey, it's no problem." Dean grinned again. "Just don't make a habit of it." His eyebrows came together slightly. "Have you thought about contacting that girl you said was psychic?"

"I've got Steven working on that. But I don't think she's in tune to all of the possibilities. I mean, she's been working with the police in San Francisco from time to time so she's certainly seen her share of mysterious crimes, but nothing like what you and Julie have seen. I don't think her mind is open to some of the options. Besides, she's just a mild psychic, and she's better at telling the short-term future than solving crimes from what Steven says."

"You don't have any resident psychics in Eastland County?" Dean chided.

"Had one, but she didn't survive that Cisco thing. I'll be trying to get you to move into the county after this. We need a good fortune teller."

Dean chuckled. Frank knew Dean would never leave this place. This feed store was his dream, and it was working. Julie was teaching at the grade school in Albany and was in love with her work. They had found their place. They were one of the few who had found true contentment, and nothing short of a catastrophe could shake that.

The two men settled on small talk for a minute or two, then Frank headed back to Eastland. He thanked his big friend and was pretty sure he would have the help he had come looking for.

Chapter Eight
1

It was dark when Derek came through the door. He was supposed to be back earlier than this, but he had missed his flight due to his short stay in the hospital. Actually, he was not supposed to have left the hospital, but had made his way out nonetheless. Not too many patients try to escape from a hospital, so it had really been quite easy work. Now he stood in Verna Calloway's den as she sat on the couch looking him over in disgust. He was dirty, and his clothes were torn, but these things did not bother her. He was wounded and wore cloth dressings over the wounds. Blood seeped through where the wound had not closed completely. But it would close. He would live. And he would heal faster than he would have before having killed Jennifer Summers.

"You failed."

"She did not yield."

She stood suddenly and struck him hard. He did not expect this, and he went to the floor. Derek looked up with defiance, ready to kill now, already planning how he would do it quickly.

She sat down. "You will not rise against me." She spoke with supreme confidence and utter arrogance. She smiled a wry smile. "There is something in you that will not allow it."

She was right. He rose again to his feet feeling both angry and ashamed. He didn't know what to make of these emotions. Regret was not normally in his repertoire, but he was sorry.

"You let a stupid girl get away from you. And so much of you was stored inside that vessel. You would have understood so much if you had taken her in. The things which make her creative and insightful are the same things which once made you these things. She holds one of your most important elements. Now you do not have these things, and we are no better off."

He no longer dismissed her speech as wild ravings. He knew that however odd it sounded, there was also knowledge and truth here. "I can go back. I know how to get into her room. I can make quick work of it this time."

"No."

Derek's eyes flared again. Who was this woman to tell him no? Nobody told him no. The anger did not flee this time.

"I tell you what is and what is not. You will heed, or you will not live."

Derek took a step toward her. "What makes you so sure you won't die first?" He leaned forward quickly and grabbed her neck in his hands. She did not flinch. Her expression did not change.

"You cannot."

"How do you know?"

She stared directly into his eyes. There was absolutely no fear there, nor was there defiance. Just pure unadulterated confidence and depth. "You cannot."

He was tempted. In seconds he could break her neck and be over with all of this. But there was something here for him. This power, this transformation. He didn't understand all of her talk about being made whole and his most important elements, but he understood the power. He had tasted it, and it was coursing through his veins.

He would gain the power first, then he would kill her. But not until then.

Derek released his hold and took a step back. "If it suits me, I will kill you."

She laughed out loud at Derek, and this surprised him. "You are such a fool, boy."

"I'm no boy."

She glared at him now, and this sent chills through his body. "You are a child. You know nothing. You are nothing." She spoke to him differently now, as if she spoke to the part of him that had nothing to do with her plan. "The thing which grows inside you is older than you are by centuries. You are an unworthy vessel, and if you fail, if you continue to fail, you will be killed and replaced. There are others who can do your work, others which are not as well suited, but who will do."

"There are no others."

She remained silent. Derek wondered for a moment who these others might be. Then he understood. "They won't kill for you."

"Do your work well and I won't have the chance to prove you wrong."

Her words haunted him. He looked down at his wound again. It still hurt, but it also tingled. It felt as if something was crawling around inside of him, and he knew that this was part of the healing. He wanted this power and more. "Where will I go next?"

"You will stay here."

Derek wondered who it would be. Would it be the retard? He would be an easy kill, but surely there wouldn't be much to gain from it. It had to be that preacher. Derek had hated that guy for as long as he could remember. Many years ago Derek had taken a key down the side of Richard senior's new Oldsmobile. Killing Richard junior would be a thrill. He would make it last. He would feast on the fear in the man's eyes and laugh. Maybe he would tie him up and rape his wife in front of him first. Maybe kill his kids. There was a lot of potential here.

"When the time comes," she warned him, "you will kill quickly. This is not a game. If you are captured or killed it's over for both of us."

"I will decide how I kill."

"You will kill as I say."

He did not know whether or not to believe her threats. His nature was to take control, and he did not have control here. It maddened him, but he yielded for the sake of the power.

"Who is next? Is it the preacher?"

She grinned. "He would be an easy target, but he has little to offer you. It is important that you become powerful quickly. With each killing our chances of being discovered increase. We will be discovered, that is a fact. If you are powerful enough when that happens, then it won't matter. You will be able to protect both of us until your task is complete."

"So who's next?" Derek waited anxiously for the new name.

"You need physical strength and power. Your mind needs improvement as well as your reflexes. The next logical kill would be Steven."

Derek grinned. He knew all of the names. Some had special meaning for him. Steven Keith, Mr. Football. Mr. Popularity. Derek had despised the boy in school. Killing him would be a pleasure. It could also be quite a challenge. But he did not live here.

"They will come to us," she explained to him. "They will all be in this place, except for the woman in the hospital. We will wait for them to come. While we wait you will find help. You will not kill Steven on your own. He is much faster and stronger than the woman who beat you. If he is not killed, he may wound you more seriously, perhaps even kill you. You will go out and find people who will help you."

"Someone to help me kill? I'm sorry, lady, but I don't have any friends who will help me kill, not just for fun anyway."

Verna grinned this time. She explained to him that there was an account in the bank in town which had lots of money, money the government had given to her over the years and which she had squirreled away. This money would convince his friends.

Derek agreed. He thought for a moment about the money. He could take the money and leave this crazy bitch. Leave this small town and go somewhere else, somewhere big where he could kill and not be noticed. But he also thought about the power he could already feel running through his veins, and what it would feel like if he let it grow and visions of Steven's death began playing in his head.

2

It was late Tuesday night. A spring storm was winding its way toward New York. Steven and Rebecca sat in a small diner which despite its cracked plaster and exposed electrical wires was full of people. The food was good too, though it tasted bland nonetheless to the two of them, their minds elsewhere.

"She hasn't gotten any better," Steven observed. He wondered if she would ever get better.

"I believe she'll come out of it. Her wounds will heal quickly. Her mind is just suffering from the trauma, mostly from the blood loss, the doctors say. But she'll come out of it. Physically she'll be fine."

"And mentally?"

"There's no way to know."

"But?" Steven could sense Rebecca's unspoken thoughts.

Rebecca sipped her coffee. Her eyes sparkled, even under the circumstances. Steven felt drawn to her as he had to Samantha in his youth, even as he had felt drawn to Jennifer. Something inside these women. Something about the experience they had shared as newborns tied them all together in a special way. He could see more than just her facial features. He could see beyond to what was inside. He could read her emotions like a book, something he could only have done with Jennifer and Samantha.

Rebecca put her coffee down. "But nothing. I've held her hand. I've tried to see what might be in store. But there's nothing to see, really. I do feel optimistic, though, and I think this comes from something inside which does know what will happen. She'll be okay. I think she'll be okay soon."

"And what if he comes back?"

Rebecca looked pensive. "I don't think he'll try anything in the hospital, not with so many people around, and not with someone constantly monitoring her. It would be too difficult. If he wants to get her he'll wait until she comes out of this and goes home. He'll wait until she's alone again. And he won't give her the chances he did this time."

"You think he underestimated her?"

"I think so. I think Jennifer didn't put up a fight, and I think he expected that Samantha would go gently into that awful night too. But she didn't."

Steven could sense something coming from Rebecca. It was a kind of confidence. She had figured something out, something important. "Do you know who's doing this?"

Rebecca paused. She looked out the window at the busy street and the liquid crowd. "I don't know who's doing the killing, but I have an idea who might be behind it."

Steven had thought long and hard about who might want to kill them all but had come up with nothing he thought was worth sharing. Rebecca apparently had. "Who is it?"

"I'm not sure, and I don't really have any special feelings about this one way or the other, but I believe that it might be that crazy nurse."

Electricity went off in Steven's head. He hadn't thought about the crazy old nurse in years. He instantly remembered her now, and the strange things she had said to him from time to time over the years. It was odd to think she might be behind all this, but something seemed right about it, too.

Rebecca looked intently at him. "Do you remember any of the times she approached you."

He laughed sarcastically. "Of course I do. The first time I was just eight. It scared the shit out of me. I told my mom and she called the police. They had a talk with her and she didn't do it again for a couple of years."

"It scared me too. Do you remember what she said?"

Steven thought about it. "I remember the first time really well, because it scared me so bad. She said something like, 'why won't you talk to me, my lover? Why won't you join with me? Have I done something to offend you? Where are the others? Why do you remain apart?' That was about the gist of it. It lasted about five minutes, and she grabbed me by the shoulders for the last minute and just stared into my eyes. Then she laughed her crazy laugh and ran away."

Rebecca remembered when the nurse had come after her. It had been that same year, late in the summer. The exchange had been a similar one. "I think she bothered all of us back then, but just us. I don't remember anyone else ever talking about that crazy woman approaching them, just the snow babies. Richard even mentioned it to me once when I was in the youth group at his church one summer. I never spoke much with Timmy or Derek, but I'll bet they went through the same thing."

"I wonder if they're okay. As far as I know all three of them are still in Eastland. It seems like that would be the best place for her to start."

"Not if you didn't want to get caught. Not if you wanted to keep any pattern a mystery until they were the only ones left."

It seemed obvious to Steven. "Of course." He thought for a moment. "So either you or me would be next."

"Right."

"Do you think the killer is still here in New York?"

"I think it's a good possibility. He'd have to know we'd be coming here."

"But what if she hadn't given him our names yet?"

"They could talk on the phone, or she could send him right back out here."

Steven cocked his head slightly to one side. "Do you think we should tell the police? Act like bait and lure him in?"

Rebecca shook her head no. "I don't like the idea of being bait, especially here in New York. He could get to us too quickly, before he could be stopped or caught."

"Obviously you've thought this over," Steven observed. "What do you think we should do?"

"I think I should go back to Eastland. I think you should do what you think is best."

It was quiet for a moment. Then Rebecca spoke again, "I would like it if you would come with me. I might need your help, and I'm not sure anyone there will believe this strange story."

Steven smiled. "Of course I'll go. I'll just make my annual trek early this year. And there is someone there who can help us. I called Frank this morning and spoke to him about this. He's already working on it at his end, and I'm sure he'd appreciate the help."

Rebecca had forgotten all about Frank. He would indeed be great help. But what would they find? What if her hunch was wrong? If it turned out to be nothing, at least she would be able to visit her mother for a few days.

But inside she didn't think it would be a wasted trip. Even if she was wrong about the nurse, there was something in Eastland waiting to be discovered, of this much she was certain.

They agreed between the two of them to meet in Eastland. Steven would go home first and gather his gear and his dog and make the two-day drive. Rebecca would stay here with Samantha for the next few days, waiting to see if she might have something to say to her before she met Steven in Eastland.

3

Timothy Watkins lay in his bed thinking about the monster. The old woman had something to do with the monster, he knew this. But she was not the monster. He had wanted so badly to knock on his mother's door and ask to spend the night, but he was trying so hard to be his Own Man, and he knew that smart people didn't knock on their mother's doors when they were scared, at least not the ones who were his age and their Own Man. But he was very afraid. He left a night-light plugged into the wall beside his bed. Usually it helped, but he didn't think it would help much this time. If the monster wanted to get him, it was going to get him.

It was a long time before he finally fell asleep. In the darkness of unconsciousness the colors of a dream began to come into his head.

He saw the old woman. She was standing at the entrance to a doorway, but he couldn't see what was on the other side.

"Come to me, Timothy," she said, but her mouth didn't move. "Come to me and I will help you through the door."

"But I don't want to go through the door," he objected. Even as he spoke he could feel himself being pulled across the distance. It was awful. He tried to run, but his dream legs were rubbery and heavy.

"Don't be afraid, Timothy. This doorway is inside you. It will lead you to a place where you will be smart. You will be smarter than all of those people who have made fun of you. You will be smarter than those doctors who ask you to make pictures out of splotches."

Timothy was still being pulled toward the doorway. "I know you want to trick me. Nothing can really make me smarter, nothing like that. My mom told me a long time ago, after I ate the dog poop, that things can't make me smart, only I can make me smart if I work real hard."

The old woman smiled and pointed a finger at him. Now she was very close. "Remember when I touched you today. That made you smart for just a few seconds. Your mother was wrong, Timothy. She didn't know about your inside doorway. This doorway will make you smart forever."

"It's not true." But it might be true. He did remember what had happened that day. Maybe she was telling him the truth. And it's true that his mom might not know about this, even though she knew about most important things.

Timothy turned until he faced the door. Now he could see through it. There was a dim light and swirling colors. They flowed to the edge of the door and to the base of it, but it didn't look like there was any floor. He was scared to go through.

"I'll show you how to go through," she said to him. "You have to trust me."

He looked back at her and she was smiling, but he was still afraid of her. What did he have to do? Would he have to do something bad? Maybe she wanted him to do something dirty, maybe a sex thing. He knew about that; he'd even seen pictures once in a stack of discarded magazines in an alley.

She laughed at him, then she gave him a shove.

He felt himself falling through the doorway and into the swirling colors. They wrapped around him and felt cold all over. He tried to push them away, but they were everywhere. He was falling slowly through the thick colors. He felt them get inside his head and tickle his brain. He could feel them trying to get inside, and he also felt something else, something like being smart.

Then the floor came. He hit it hard and felt dirt and rocks in his hands.

He was outside now, and it felt real. He got to his knees and looked around, and he knew he was not asleep anymore. He was behind the scary woman's house again. This time she was looking out her window at him. She wasn't waving, and she didn't seem angry, she just looked at him. Then she signaled for him to come inside.

He felt the warmth gather between his legs as he wet himself. Then he turned and ran to his mother's house.

4

Julie Curtis sat in her special room. She and Dean had built this house five years earlier when they had moved here shortly after marrying. This room had been specially designed by Julie. It was more like an arboretum than a room. Moonbeams streamed through a skylight in the ceiling, and plants and shrubs filled the room. Ivy grew along the walls and over some of the trees. It followed wires across the ceiling which was a sea of green, except where the moonlight came through. This was her private sanctuary. It would have been even more ideal to be outside, actually in nature instead of in a room. But the two of them had decided that it would be best if Julie's sanctuary be inside since they didn't want to risk someone stumbling upon her in the midst of one of her ceremonies. The people of Albany were generally very friendly people, but they didn't particularly take to any rituals being held outside the walls of one of the churches.

Julie possessed many skills which had been passed down through generations, from grandmother to granddaughter. Her own grandmother had passed these skills along to her, along with the ancient amulet which hung around her neck, thirty-five years ago. Julie had been a little girl then, and she had not completely understood what was happening.

Her grandmother had died, leaving her to explore her new skills on her own. Memories and experiences which were not hers had come with the years. She knew that once there had been many women like herself. She knew that some still lived, though she didn't know where or how to find them. She was a lost member of an ancient sisterhood.

In reality she did not want to find them. She had made a happy life for herself, and some day her daughter would have a daughter, and the legacy would continue.

Tonight she sat in her room with a special task. Dean had asked if she would help a friend of his, the sheriff from Eastland County. They had discussed before marrying Julie's understanding of what she was, and what she had decided she would and would not use her skills for. She did not feel guilt at not using these skills to help find lost dogs or lost people, she had saved more than her share of people in one big life-threatening effort back in New Orleans. But Dean had explained to her what was different about this situation. There were things which seemed to go beyond the realm of the natural, things which normal thinking would not comprehend. He needed her special perception to give his friend an idea of what was happening, and to even up the odds. She knew already that it had to do with the area they lived in. She had known on her first visit to Albany that they were close to something unnatural, that there was something wrong. She had finally explained to Dean that this was a place where the fabric between realities was thin. There were thousands upon thousands of doorways, doorways to different realms where things did not always have the same order as they did here. It did not surprise her when she learned what had happened in Cisco the year after they had moved out here. She had sensed at the time that one of those doorways had been opened. Only after it was over did she learn exactly what had gone on. She had believed Frank Sharp's account of what had happened, and she knew that the woman who had come down from Saint Louis had done more than save just one town from utter chaos. Now she was afraid that another doorway had been breached, though it did not affect her in the same way. This threshold had been crossed many years ago. Only now were the consequences of that crossing manifesting themselves. This evening she hoped to find out why.

She closed the skylight and sat down on a small cushion in the center of the room. Three small, white candles burnt gently as she closed her eyes and began singing her ancient song of discovery.

The room began to grow cold as she felt herself rising slowly through her own body.

Chapter Nine

1

It was almost noon before Steven got on the road. He'd caught the first flight back to Ontario and had been home only a couple of hours. Now he was back on the road again. Pat sat patiently in the back of the big Bronco. She had taken trips like this before. She knew from the bags and the gear it was going to be a long trip and she closed her eyes and sighed as the Bronco entered the freeway.

It was a sunny day, but not a particularly warm one. The Santa Ana's buffeted the utility vehicle as it passed through the Altamonte Pass on its way to Texas. Steven had made this trip about a dozen times over the past fifteen years. He turned on the radio and began listening to the talk stations. They would help to occupy his mind as the miles rolled by beneath him.

2

Julie sat in the Eastland County Sheriff's office. Frank had offered to pick her up at her home in Albany, but she didn't mind the forty-five-minute drive to Eastland, and she liked getting to a bigger town once in a while. She would pass through Cisco on the way home since the Thrift Mart there cut particularly large steaks to which Dean was quite partial.

Frank addressed Julie from across his big desk. "Were the kids good to you today?"

Julie smiled. She had been teaching the third grade at Albany Elementary for three years now, and she still loved the job. "Most of them were. One or two of them were not."

"I'll probably be seeing them in a few more years in one of my cells. Give me their names and I'll be sure to get back at them for you."

"Now sheriff, I don't think they're going to turn out to be criminals. They just need a little extra attention."

"What they probably need is some discipline at home."

Julie frowned. She knew this was partially true. "What they need at home is some attention. Some of these parents act like their children were just dropped on them, and it's not their responsibility to bring them up. School's just a place to get rid of them for most of the day."

Frank knew what she was talking about. But it wasn't the problem that was really on his mind today. "It is a shame."

Julie knew that the sheriff had to be anxious to get to the meat of the discussion, despite the small talk. She took a drink of the ice tea the sheriff had brought her. It was a warm day and the cool sweet tea was refreshing. "I'm pretty sure something unusual is going on around here."

"I was pretty sure of that myself." Frank shifted uncomfortably in his chair. "Is it bad?"

Julie knew what he was asking. "I really can't tell if it's anything like what happened in Cisco or not. I do know that another doorway has been breached, but there are many thresholds around here, and many of them have been crossed."

"But there's something special about this one," Frank prodded. "It has to do with seven people, all born about the same time, and all in a strange accident shortly after birth. It hasn't meant anything until now, but now it apparently does mean something to someone."

Julie was intrigued. Dean had mentioned nothing about an accident. "What do you mean, they were in an accident?"

Frank wasn't sure why Dean hadn't mentioned this to Julie, but he was sure Dean had his reasons. "There was some kind of strange electrical storm one night. They found the babies and the nurse all unconscious. The babies remained that way for three days before coming out of it. It took the nurse a little longer, but it left her crazy."

"What do you mean by 'strange storm'?"

It had been a long time since Frank had heard the story. "Now this is all second or third hand at best. There was some kind of electrical storm, but it was very localized. One or two of the mothers who were staying in the small hospital saw the lights and heard the sounds, but nobody actually witnessed anything, nobody who was left sane or who could remember it anyway."

Julie knew Dean had not told her these details so that her mind would be open to everything, not focused on any one thing. What was on the sheriff's mind might or might not be important to what she was looking for. But as he spoke to her she knew that it was important, very important.

"Is the room where this all happened still around?"

"The old doctor's office burned down about ten years ago. Nothing was built on the lot, it's next to an old auto shop and even has a couple of dead cars parked on it."

"I'd still like to have a look."

"Certainly."

The sheriff got to his feet and grabbed his keys from his desk. Julie stood and followed him to his patrol car.

3

The sun was bright and hot, but a bank of black clouds was gathering in the west. Julie stepped out of the patrol car and stepped onto the gravel which was more weeds than rock. To her right stood an old metal building. Sounds of metal on metal were emanating from inside of it, and she could see two men walking around an old pickup and shaking their heads. Sheriff Sharp walked around the front of the car and met Julie on her side. He adjusted his Straw Resistol hat and tilted his head just enough to block the sun from his eyes. He looked the grounds over intently, as if there might be something here he had missed. But there was nothing he could make out.

Julie walked across the weeds to the tall grass that covered most of the lot. She could see places where the foundation of the old building still protruded from the ground, corners of cracked concrete which would soon melt away completely. She heard a sizzling sound and jumped back. Then she saw the gray mottled skin slithering away toward a small pile of rocks.

"Did you find something?" the sheriff called to her. He was still standing near the road, allowing her to have her space.

"Just a snake." Just a snake. She wasn't particularly afraid of snakes, but these had rattles and fangs and venom, unlike the harmless version in her childhood home of Vermont, so these snakes certainly made her a little nervous. Where there was one there might be a hundred. She watched the ground closely as she continued.

As she approached the center of the lot she could feel something tugging at the corner of her mind. Colors began to appear at the periphery of her vision, but she continued to walk straight ahead. The sheriff was saying something, but it was far away and unimportant now. What had become important was the song which was coming from the air just above the ground, an ancient chant which called to something within her. It was not straight ahead; it was a little to the right. She veered in that direction and the chanting became more clear, her surroundings less distinct. The hot sun was beginning to fade and was being replaced by a cool winter evening and the images of dancing men.

The earth was speaking to her now. It told her of a doorway which had been opened long ago by a people who no longer existed. Through the doorway they had sent an invitation for the distant and ancient spirits which they believed would help them to defend the earth and conquer their foes. Their songs had been heard, but the people had died out long before the spirits had completed their long journey. Their dreams had given them the chants and dances which would open the doorway which rested in this place. The centuries had come and gone, and finally the spirits who had given them their dreams had come.

But the people who were to be their vessels, the ones who were to carry their existence into the new plane were not waiting for them. They had called but had not waited. Desperation as death approached. Existence for them had wavered, reality had flickered in and out.

Then they had found their vessels.

But there had been damage, and the vessels had not been those who had called for them. These vessels had not been prepared and did not understand their roles.

Then Julie understood what had happened. She didn't know all of the story, but what she knew now would no doubt be very valuable to the sheriff. The earth continued to speak to her, but the images were stagnant, shadowy remnants of a dead tale. She pulled away from the contact and the warmth of the afternoon sun returned.

4

"What happened in that place in 1956 was indeed a crossing of some kind."

The two of them had returned to the sheriff's office and sat across from each other at Frank's desk. Frank listened intently to Julie's explanation. He absorbed her words and laid any skepticism aside. He knew she was genuine. The story was amazing.

Julie continued, "There were two of them, partners of a sort. Perhaps mates. Either way, they were strongly bonded, yet separate entities."

"Why did they come?"

"They were invited by peoples who no longer exist here. The invitation was given hundreds or even thousands of years ago. They answered, unaware of the differences in our realities and theirs. They came quickly, yet it took hundreds or thousands of years for them to complete their journey. By the time they arrived those who had called them were gone. The people who had been waiting to carry their essence into this reality had long since died. Instead of finding waiting, eager vessels, they suddenly found themselves in a struggle for survival."

It was too strange, but he did not discount it. "So what happened to them?"

"I can't be sure, but based on the location, and based on what you've told me, I would guess that at least one of the entities broke up, split into different pieces and found itself in several different vessels, unable to pull itself together, and now unaware of what it is or where it is."

"You mean that the snow babies are possessed?"

Julie smiled. "Nothing quite that strong, and I'm only guessing. The only thing I'm sure of is that there was a struggle, and that both entities did make the crossing. Where they may be now, and what they may be now, is pure speculation. I only know that they made it across, and that the babies were present when it happened."

"So what are these things? Could they make someone turn into a killer?"

"These entities aren't inherently good or evil. There's no way to tell how they may have reacted to their new reality, or if their even conscious enough to understand it."

Frank thought immediately about the nurse. "The nurse that was caring for the babies went into a coma for a year. When she came out of it she was crazy, and she still is. She used to torment kids at school, and I only remember stories of her tormenting the snow babies. Do you think she might be possessed by one of these things?"

"Possession really isn't the right concept. If one of these entities has entered the nurse, then it has displaced her. It may have access to her memories, it may know who she was and everything she ever experienced, but she would no longer be in the body. As this entity tried to adjust to its new reality it would certainly appear insane by our standards."

The wheels began to turn inside the sheriff's head. There was something here, something which made perfect sense, yet which was too nonsensical to be a possibility. He tried to corner it but could not. "Can you think of any reason she might want to kill the snow babies?"

Julie thought about this. "Nothing comes to mind. I might venture to guess she is trying to eliminate any vessel which might hold her partner, but from what I picked up of their nature this doesn't seem consistent. Perhaps it's her partner whose doing the killing. Maybe he's finally gotten a grip on this reality and is looking for her. But there's no reason why he would kill the person who did not hold his partner.

I can't think of a good reason for the killings. I would say they weren't connected to all of this, but I'm afraid the coincidence is too much."

"Exactly. Why would anybody be after the snow babies? It's got to all come together somehow." Frank stared past Julie, his mind struggling with all of this.

"Maybe if I visited the nurse I could find something out. At least I could get a feel for if she's involved or not."

Frank wanted to be polite and tell her she'd done enough, but he had already been thinking of this himself. He would never have asked her on his own, but now she had brought it up. "Why don't you discuss it with Dean. I promised him I wouldn't put you on the payroll. I know you two are concerned about people finding out about what you can do, and I don't want you feeling obligated to help."

"But I already do," she explained. "And it was mostly my wish that I not spend my time solving crimes and finding dogs. But this is more than that. This is something that someone with my skills can make some progress on, much more quickly than someone whose mind is bound by conventional thought. Besides," Julie put on a mischievous grin, "I've become intrigued."

"You'll talk it over with Dean?"

Her smile softened. It brightened not only her face, but the entire room. "I'll even tell him it wasn't your idea. I'll make him think I talked you into it."

"If he goes for this, please thank him for me."

"I'm sure he won't have a problem with it."

"And I want to thank you too. You have no idea how this helps."

"Have we already accomplished that much?"

"Of course. At least now I know that this all ties together somehow. I know for certain who the targets are, and I can formulate some kind of plan of action. I need to know more, but the why of it all isn't so important as putting a stop to the killing. That's my job, putting a stop to the killing and incarcerating the criminal."

"Well, I wish you the best of luck, and I hope I will be of more help than I have been today." Julie glanced at her watch. It was a formality of politeness. "I really must get back to Albany. Dean's going to be waiting for those big rib-eyes I promised I'd pick up for him in Eastland."

Frank stood from his desk and thanked her again. Then he led her to the door. He returned to his desk thinking how much he had learned today, and how much he was still in the dark.

5

Julie stood staring blankly at the meats lined up in the store's refrigeration unit. Her mind was miles away, churning through the possibilities.

The more she thought about it, the more sense it made. *Reunification*. That's what this was all about. The nurse had probably been inhabited by one of the entities. The other had broken into pieces and found itself in many vessels, unaware yet somehow intact.

Reunification.

This second entity was not being systematically eliminated, it was being healed, brought back together as it became freed from each of its vessels and reunified in another.

This meant that one of these vessels had to be committing the murders.

Had this entity become conscious enough in one of the vessels to figure this all out and begin the killing, after almost forty years fighting for consciousness? Perhaps. If not, then what drove the killer, and who was it?

She would have to discuss this with Frank Sharp when she saw him again.

"You're a witch woman!"

The accusation came suddenly and loudly from behind her. Julie dropped the cut of meat she had been holding for too long as she turned to see a dirty woman pointing a finger at her face.

She knew in an instant this had to be Verna Calloway. She was dressed in soiled and tattered clothes, and she smelled badly. But there was something else here, something Julie had not expected.

She could indeed see Verna's physical body, but she could see more. There was an aura, a dirty brown glow which extended in all directions. It was not an extension of this woman, but more like the thing that was her essence was bursting at the seams, struggling to remain inside this body.

Verna whispered her accusation a second time. "You're unnatural. I'm warning you to stay away, stay away from those kids or you'll get hurt."

What did this mean? Was she trying to protect these people? It was more likely she was trying to protect what they held. The woman looked desperate. She truly looked crazy. But Julie knew that she was not, she merely operated on a different plane, still used to a different reality with a different set of rules.

She spoke to Verna. "I want to help."

"You stay away," Verna hissed, her finger still inches from Julie's face.

"Is he going to come back to you?" Julie asked. She had used the masculine term quite by accident, in response to the fact the Verna was a woman. But this seemed to strike a cord and Verna's hand dropped slowly to her side.

"Is he coming back?" Julie asked.

Verna's eyes lost their crazed look for a moment. "I will see him soon. We will leave this awful place together." She was looking down to the floor, speaking more to herself than to Julie.

Behind her the store clerk had already spotted the trouble and left to get help.

"Who is doing the killing?" Julie asked.

Verna's gaze came back up again and met her own. She looked confused. "Killing?"

"Who is killing the children?"

Her hand came up again, and the crazy look returned. "You're a witch woman," Verna spit out. "You stay away from the children."

Two stock boys, both members of the Cisco High football team, flanked Verna Calloway. One of them touched her shoulder, but she did not respond.

"You stay away!" she yelled. She wanted to threaten death, but knew this could lead to trouble, so she did not threaten but instead schemed on how to accomplish this goal.

Her voice was loud and when it was obvious she would not leave on her own the boys each grabbed an arm and turned her away from Julie. The head clerk appeared beside her and began his apology. Julie did not hear, instead she listed to the words of the crazed woman as she was hauled away, listening for any clue to what might be going on.

But there were no more clues, only veiled threats and incoherent babble.

She accepted Bill's apology and returned her attention to the steak selection.

Bill saw that two fresh cuts were made for Julie as she continued to try and piece it all together.

6

Verna Calloway sat on her rotting sofa as the sun set. The incident at the store was now hours behind her. It had not been planned. She had actually gone to pick up some groceries to help sustain this waning body. She had seen the witch woman, and she had known that this woman was different that any she had met, and that she had the power to destroy her plans. She had not meant to lose control, but she had. She had only come close to letting loose a real threat before realizing that would very possibly ruin everything. So she had let them haul her away and send her out of the store without her basket of food. That was okay. Now she would find a way to keep the witch woman out of the way. Already she had an idea.

She could feel the man coming closer, the one from the west. Two more were northeast and distant, but one of them would be coming soon. Samantha Chambers would live, and she would have to be brought in later. Two more were close by, not counting the filthy boy whom she had chosen to bring Him together. It pained her that he was so defiant. She wondered if it was time to summon the other vessel. The simple boy seemed to resist, but his mind would yield if she called. But the vessel she was working with, Derek, was already changing. He needed another soul, another piece of her companion to see Her as She truly was. She slapped him down now, and bridled his defiance, but inside it cut at her. Her companion was still in pieces. His soul still did not function on its own. What would he be like when he had been put back together? Would He remember any of this? Would He remember anything at all, or would it be like the beginning, so many millions of years ago.

Time again. She could not wait to be out of its incessant grasp.

Whatever survived would still be Him, of this much she was sure. It would take Him more time to adjust to this reality, just as it had taken her so many years to adjust, but she could wait, then they would leave this realm together. She had long ago abandoned the idea of staying and propagating. Those thoughts had come into her mind at the crossing as they left behind one of many realms they had populated with their offspring. Now she had no such desires, now she simply wished to leave this wretched place. It was not what they had imagined they would find when they had left the last place which also was not their home. They traveled on an endless journey, searching for and sometimes finding a pleasing reality. There they would remain, sometimes for eons, before moving on. Here they had seen the promise of senses and physicality they had never before seen or even imagined. But now she knew it was all a burden, that this accounting for time, these limitations of physicality were purgatory. This was not a good place, not a place to stay. She thought of home, and of a return a million years in the making. Now home seemed like a good goal. A place to heal up before beginning their journeys anew.

But she was beginning to fear that they would not be able to leave. She had feared this in other places, but He always knew how, and He always brought her along. She could not leave on her own. Even if it were possible, She would not leave without Him. She would rather cease to exist. He had cared for her and brought her on his journeys for endless eons. Now it was her time to repay his love for her.

Staying in this form was eternally confusing. It limited her, it affected her reasoning and clouded her essence. To stay here for a thousand years would be to lose oneself for certain, to stay for ten thousand would certainly mean death. Again, she found herself thinking in terms of time, and it made her furious. She thought about making a physical display of her anger, but she had learned to control that some time ago. Still she knew rage. She wanted to kill this body and try to join him in his various vessels, but she knew it would mean real death. They would both die in this terrible place.

So she would wait. And she would be careful.

And it was now this that concerned her. She was not convinced that Derek would not turn on her. She knew his strength. She was able to control him to some degree. But his own will was very strong, and his mind was dark and forceful. The more she thought about Derek, the more she thought that it might be time to make a change.

So she put her backup plan into action.

Z

It was getting dark, and the hunger was burning within Derek. How long would it be before Steven made it to Eastland? Would it be a day, or a week? He knew he couldn't make it for a week. He was beginning to doubt whether or not he could make it a day.

He knew all of the names of the ones he was supposed to kill. What did he need her for? He could take care of the preacher and the retard in the same night. Then he would be so powerful that nothing could stop him.

Still, he did not want to kill the old woman. She meant something that he did not understand. But when he had a killed a few more times, then he would know what part she played in all of this. On top of this, something inside told him that her threats were not vain ones. Each time he made up his mind to go visit one of the two who lived here a dark cloud descended into his mind and a coldness through his body. He could feel her watching him, and this changed his mind each time.

But as the night descended his hunger grew.

8

Samantha saw colors but did not know what they were. She did not know where she was. Her past was a blur, and her present was unclear. There had been darkness for a long time. Now there were colors, and a hint of consciousness. It was like a dream, but there were no concrete images. She had been here for a long time, and now questions were coming to her.

Rebecca was nearby. She could not see her, but she knew that she was near. She had been here for some time, but Samantha had just recently found her. She tried to reach out to Rebecca, but she did not know how. As time passed in this place she learned how to move within it. With still just a hint of consciousness, Samantha finally made contact. As she did the colors began to solidify and take on meaning. Her thoughts became more clear, though she was still trapped in this place of colors.

Rebecca's thoughts were confusing at first, but then they became synchronized with her own and Samantha was able to understand and communicate. Rebecca told her where she was and asked when she would return. Samantha did not know when she would be able to leave this place of colors, and she was unsure where she was supposed to go. She did not remember exactly where she was supposed to be as the secrets of her mind still lay locked behind the dark barrier. But she knew she would return.

Then she felt Rebecca slipping away. She tried to hold on, but she could not.

The colors faded some as exhaustion surrounded her.

Then she could not remember where she had just been.

2

Steven pulled into the La Quinta in Las Cruces and grabbed their last room. It was well past midnight and he found he had reached his limit. Even the caffeine was no longer enough to keep him from crossing the white line and running across the warning grooves once or twice in the past hour. It was time to stop. He could be in Eastland in another nine hours, a drive he would have to start on the other side of sleep.

He took Pat in through a door which was close to the room. They had told him that a small pet was okay, but Pat was only small when compared to a Mastiff or Great Dane. Pat followed closely and darted into the room as soon as the door was opened. She had been through the routine before and was in the middle of the bed before Steven had his bags on the floor.

Rebecca had left the number of the hotel she would be staying at in New York and had told him to feel free to call for an update on Samantha. But it was early morning in New York now, and Rebecca was probably in the midst of a sleep that had been elusive.

He did not unpack his bags but just unzipped his overnight bag and pulled out the clothes he would wear the next day, hanging them up to give them a few hours to work out some of the wrinkles. They looked pretty bad and he figured he would have to run an iron over them in the morning.

Steven reached into his bag and pulled out his 45. The gun caught the glint of the bedside light, and he checked the clip again to be sure it was full. He was glad he had kept up with his target practice, even if it was just because he enjoyed going to the range and running a box of shells through his gun. He had never shot anything with this gun besides paper targets and a few coke cans, though his dad had carried it at his side during the second world war. He hoped it would stay that way, but he was not going to be unprepared if the moment came when he needed to use it against a living target. He carried the gun to his bed and laid it on the night table, next to the phone. He would call Rebecca in the morning, then he would hit the road.

Pat let out a deep sigh and moved to the edge of the big bed as Steven climbed in and turned out the light.

10

Timothy dreamed.

Once again there was a doorway. He could not see the old woman, but he knew she was there. He had not seen her today. He had heard her door open as he pedaled past her house, but he hadn't looked, and he hadn't slowed down. But even then he had been touched somehow by her, and his brain had awakened for an instant. It had made him sad, and scared, and even angry. He wanted it badly. If he would go through the door it would be his. But he knew it would be wrong to go through the door, though he had no idea why.

"Go through the door, Timothy."

He could hear her voice, but her body was only a mist this time.

"You must go through the door. I can help you. I can make you well."

"I told you, I'm not sick."

"You are sick, Timothy. You've been sick all your life. They have all lied to you. They have all told you that you will always be this way. They say this so you won't be smart like them, so they won't have to worry about you getting smarter than them. But I can cure you, Timothy. Go through the door."

"I don't believe you," he replied. But the seed was planted. Maybe the doctors had lied? But his mother had not, she would never do such a thing to him.

"Your mother doesn't know."

He knew it wasn't right.

"All I'm asking is that you come to me. I will help you, then you can help me. I'll help you first. If you don't want to help me after that, then you can go. You can keep the gift even if you leave."

He was still scared. There was nothing she could say that would convince him. He knew inside that to go to her would be wrong.

Then the door slowly opened, and he felt himself being pulled through it.

"I don't want to go!" he cried out. "Don't put me in there!"

"I'll make you well," the voice whispered.

His own body seemed like a mist and the air carried him into the doorway. The other side was again full of a swirl of colors. He tried to resist, but his misty body crossed over nonetheless.

Then he felt himself falling into the swirling and churning colors. They surrounded him and teased him with hints of the gift she would give him.

Then he fell through the colors to the hard ground.

Again he awoke outside her home

Only this time the monster was there with him.

11

Rebecca stood outside the door of Samantha's apartment. She could see the line of glue where until this afternoon the yellow police tape had forbade entry. Now she had the permission of the police, the permission of Samantha's parents, and the keys to the apartment. She opened the door and walked in.

The apartment was much larger than she had expected. Samantha had never let on she was doing this well, but Rebecca could have guessed as much. Rebecca remembered how wonderful Samantha's art projects had always been. Most of them had actually been done outside the classroom and had covered the walls and shelves of the girl's bedroom. Rebecca still had one of these paintings from back then, when Samantha was just a child. People always commented on it, asking her who the artist was, which was quite a statement in San Francisco which had no shortage of good art. Samantha's apartment was not filled with her work as her childhood room had been. There were signs of Samantha's creativity everywhere, but her own personal artwork did not clutter the room. There were a few skillfully placed pieces of her own, mixed in with paintings and a few small sculptures from people she loved and admired in the art world. But it was all done quite well, it was not disconcerting or threatening, the apartment was still cozy and comfortable, a tribute to Samantha's skill as a true artist.

But there were things which did not look right, too. She could still see faded blood stains in places on the floor. Though the small table in the living room area had been set back on its legs, the items which rested on it were not arranged as Samantha would have arranged them. Rebecca stood at the edge of the living room, on the wood floor near the entrance to the kitchen. The kitchen was dark, but she knew that this was where it had started. The detective from the police department had told her this, but she sensed it as well. And this is why she was here, to see if she could solve this mystery. She had her ideas, but ideas only went so far. She needed proof, and she needed something she could focus on. Then her friend would be safe. Then they all would be safe.

Rebecca walked to the kitchen and turned on the light. Samantha's parents had paid a cleaning service to work the place over after the police had given the okay. The blood had been cleaned thoroughly from the kitchen floor, but she could still sense where it had run, not all of it Samantha's. As she stood near the sink with her eyes closed she knew that Samantha had fought, and that her attacker had, as the police had surmised, been seriously wounded. But there had been no leads at the hospital, no good descriptions, no real names to go on. Had this been a smaller city perhaps it would have been different. But there had been a dozen stabbing victims admitted that night, and perhaps a dozen the night before. The faces were anonymous to the hospital staff, the town was just too damn big.

Rebecca opened her eyes. There were images here, but nothing clear. If they had found the knife he had held, perhaps that would have given her what she needed. She knelt down and put her hands on the floor, but the images of maids and mops was stronger than the images of the conflict which had happened four nights ago.

She stood and walked again onto the wooden floor which separated the kitchen from the sunken living room. There was something here, but she could not focus on it. She closed her eyes again, and again she saw nothing but the waiting eyes.

Waiting eyes.

She kept her eyes closed and reached out with her arms. Nothing. She turned slowly in a circle, hoping something would reach out for her. As she turned past the living room, past the front door, something did. She kept her eyes closed and turned slowly as the misty image grew clearer in her mind. She turned until it was its strongest, though it still held no meaning for her. As she continued to turn toward the kitchen the image began to fade. She turned back until she found exactly where the images were the strongest. Then she stopped and opened her eyes.

She was facing the entry closet.

The waiting eyes.

She knew instantly that this was where he had waited for her, and she felt a chill run through her body. Nevertheless she walked over to the closet and opened it. As her hand touched the knob an icy chill ran up her arm. She let go for an instant, startled by the sensation, then she grabbed the knob and open the door all of the way.

A light inside the closet came on when she opened the door. Everything inside looked to be in order. She looked around the carpeted floor of the closet but found nothing unusual. She supposed the police had looked here for evidence, but they had not known as surely as she did that the killer had hidden here. And he was a killer. He had missed this time, but he had not missed in Atlanta. The police had found nothing which linked the two crimes, but Rebecca knew that they were linked, they were linked by the man who had stood in this closet, waiting for Samantha to return from the funeral of his last victim. As she ran her hands across the carpeted floor more images sank into her mind, but as yet they made no sense.

Rebecca stood and looked inside the closet. She knew what she had to do now, but it frightened her. Rebecca knew nothing would happen to her, but she feared what she might see. She proceeded nonetheless, hoping for an answer.

Rebecca walked to the front door and turned off the entry and living room lights. The apartment was dark except for the city lights which reflected off the kitchen floor. She walked back to the small closet and got inside of it. Then she pulled the door closed.

At first she felt only a chill. Then the room began to glow for her. It was a dim glow, as if someone had placed orange night lights in each corner of the apartment. The chill grew deeper, and she felt her body begin to change. Adrenaline rushed through her as her body prepared to escape, but there was no one here but her body and her mind. She stood and waited as the coldness deepened. She felt her arms changing, her chest heaved as it grew into the killer's. These things happened only in her mind, but for the moment they felt real.

This was the place. He had stood here and waited for a long time, waited for Samantha to come home, waited to drive the steel blade into her heart and watch as her life flowed out of her.

And into him.

What did that mean?

Jennifer was here too, somehow. It was not the Jennifer she had known, but it was much more than just a memory of Jennifer. Her hands and feet tingled; her head began to hurt as she awaited the greatest revelation.

Then it came.

She threw her head back and laughed, but it was not her own laugh, it was the killer's. She saw into his mind and it was a deep, black pit. She knew he would come for them all, but that it was for something she could never have imagined, and something she did not comprehend.

Then she saw him.

And she knew in an instant who it was.

She threw open the closet door, anxious to get away from the cold and the fear she had controlled. She hurried to the door and flipped on the lights as the room returned to normal for her.

Then she whispered his name.

"Derek."

Chapter Ten
1

Timothy's own body seemed like a mist and the air carried him into the doorway. The other side was again full of swirling colors. He tried to resist, but his misty body crossed over nonetheless.

Then he felt himself falling into the swirling and churning colors. They surrounded him and teased him with hints of the gift she would give him.

Then he fell through the colors to the hard ground.

Again he awoke outside her home

Only this time the monster was there with him.

2

The monster glared up at him with hungry eyes.

Timothy felt a shock run through his body. He knew this monster. It looked like a person, but he knew that it was not exactly a person. It was Derek, only the darkness which Timothy had always seen around Derek was much bigger now, and it seemed to have a life of its own.

"Kill him!" came the command from nearby.

Tim knew the voice. It was the crazy old nurse. She was here too. He heard her words, but it wasn't clear who she was speaking to. As she spoke Timothy felt something rise inside of him, something terrible yet something he needed now.

The monster rushed toward him.

Timothy was afraid, but he knew that if he did nothing, he would die here. There was also something helping him not to be afraid and something which helped him spring forward and meet the monster as it came toward him.

Timothy's response took Derek off guard. He wasn't ready, so Tim's powerful left fist took him by surprise and landed him on the wet ground. There was something else here, something was wrong. The power which had come to him with Jennifer's death had faded over the past five days until now he wasn't much stronger or faster than he had been before the kill. And there was something more, something like a terrible weight holding him down. It was almost like fighting underwater. He had heard Verna's words, and he, too, had been unsure who she was speaking to.

But Derek had always been a fighter and he turned over quickly before Tim could jump on top of him. He kicked out and caught Tim's right knee and the big man fell as his leg buckled.

Tim felt the pain shoot through his leg, but he knew he couldn't go down. He caught himself as he fell, both hands slipping into the mud, but before he could get up Derek leapt to his feet and kicked him in the side. It hurt bad. He kicked again. Timothy knew he couldn't get up fast enough, so he stayed on all fours, pretended like he was a very mean bull, and charged Derek.

Derek was used to fighting men who fought like himself. Timothy's mind did not work like theirs, and each move was a surprise. Before he could react, Tim had Derek on his back and was climbing up his body, landing punches in Derek's stomach and chest as he crawled.

"Kill him!" came the command again.

This time Derek knew the command was not for him. He tried to roll over to his stomach to push himself up, but Tim suddenly had a hold of his neck, and he could hear his own heartbeat in his ears.

Tim grabbed the monster's neck and squeezed. He knew this would make the monster sleep, long enough for him to escape. But something inside of him wanted more than this. He wanted to squeeze the monster's neck after it went to sleep, until its chest quit moving, until its tongue turned purple.

He was scared of the monster and wanted it dead. But there was something more. He knew that if he killed the monster that something wonderful would happen. But like the door in his dream, he knew that this wonderful thing was also very bad. He tried to resist the thought, but something was in his head with him, and it was very strong.

Derek's hand disappeared behind him for a moment, then it reappeared quickly with a knife in it. Tim saw the blade as it approached and reached out to keep it away. The blade was sharp, and it sliced through his left arm near the elbow. He saw the sliced flesh. The rain washed the blood down his soggy shirt and the hand holding the knife danced around, trying to put the blade in a place more lethal.

Tim grabbed the arm with both hands and held it down to the ground. Derek used his free hand to punch Tim hard in the side. Tim grunted, but he did not let go of the arm. Derek punch again, then Tim squeezed his wrist until he felt like it would shatter.

Then something did pop, and his hand opened, dropping the knife to the wet ground.

The rain poured down on them. A flash of light and clap of thunder added to the intensity.

"Kill him!" came the command again.

Timothy felt the electricity building inside of him. He knew exactly what to do and he snatched the knife up quickly as Derek punched at his side and his stomach. Then Tim was swinging the blade around, thrusting it down and around until he had cut both of Derek's hands and stabbed his shoulder once. Timothy could see the monster beneath him, fighting to get away. But he knew he would win now.

He put the knife in Derek, just below his last rib. Derek's eyes grew wide, and his fighting subsided. Tim quickly grabbed Derek's neck again with his left hand, with his right he drew the blade out of Derek's side. Derek's hands went immediately to the wound. It felt deep and Derek knew that this time death had finally come for him.

"Kill him!"

Timothy heard the voice and knew that it was time. Now the monster would be gone. Now he would be smart, and stronger than the monster ever was. He looked into Derek's eyes. They were not terrified eyes. They were not pleading eyes. They simply looked resigned to their fate.

Derek spoke even though the hand on his neck made it difficult. "So it was you." He managed to growl. "Who would have thought it was the retard?"

That's right, Tim thought to himself. It's me, and nobody's going to call me retard no more.

The power called to him.

Derek just glared at him and held his side. He wanted to see it coming. He was losing blood, and consciousness was slipping away. "Do it now!" he barked.

Tim knew where to put the knife this time. He looked at the monster's chest and found the place where his heart was pumping just inches below the flesh.

"Kill him now!" Verna cried behind him. "Do it now, and his gifts will be yours."

Derek's eyes were getting heavy. The rain made soothing noises on the old woman's roof. The sound reminded Timothy of the house he had grown up in.

Then the old woman screamed out again. "No! No! You get out of here! No!"

Verna felt a presence, and she knew what was happening. She had not felt it before, she had not known that the woman could be this strong. Now it was too late. She had hidden herself until the most crucial moment, then she had spoiled everything.

Whatever had held Tim was slipping away. Something else was coming out now, something which released him from her spell and reminded him of who he was.

Derek's eyes closed.

Timothy stood from the wounded body and looked at it. He threw the knife away, as far as he could throw it. Then he ran.

"No!" the old woman screamed at him as the one who was to have been her new champion stood. "You must kill him!"

Then she watched as Tim turned and disappeared into the night.

She looked back to Derek. His chest rose and fell slowly. The body was wounded, but she did not know how badly. Luckily the real Verna Calloway had been a nurse, so she knew what needed to be done to help him. She couldn't take him to a hospital, not now. She had to keep him close. He was still her best hope. She could make him forget.

She walked over to his body and placed her arms under him. It was a tremendous strain on her body, but she lifted him from the wet ground. Blood ran down his side and across her arm. He had to live. If the body passed away now, He would never be whole.

She carried Derek's limp body across her small yard and took him inside her house. There she would care for him until he was ready. Then she would make him even stronger.

3

Julie opened her eyes and let the hemlock leaves fall from between her hands.

She had seen the battle coming and knew it would be critical. Timothy was a strong man, his mind was strong, his sense of right and wrong was strong. If this had not been so, he might have defeated the beast which would then have consumed him completely.

But she had been there for him, and with her quiet help he had been able to resist. Now he was gone into the night, and even she could not see where he had gone. She had caught a glimpse of his thoughts which had wandered first to his mother, then away from her to a place where he would not put her in danger. She had let go then, exhausted from her efforts, drained to the limit, but satisfied for the time being.

She was still recovering from the experience when the window at the back of the atrium popped, letting a small piece of lead come through. The bullet deflected from its intended angle, but still caught her in the shoulder.

It took her a moment to realize what was happening.

She fell to the floor and called out to her husband and two more shots entered her body.

4

Sheriff Frank Sharp knocked twice on Verna's front door. The call had come in around 11 p.m. Mrs. Carlin reported seeing a fight in her neighbor's back yard. Her neighbor was Verna Calloway. Mrs. Carlin hadn't seen any faces or even any distinct forms since the yard was lit only by Verna's small porch light.

Frank had received a couple of calls late in the afternoon which had been what he would consider major breaks. The first had been from Julie Curtis. She had described a strange encounter at the grocery store with this woman, one which he knew implicated her somehow in what was going on. Less than an hour later he had received another call, this one from Rebecca Robinson. He hadn't heard from her since their ten-year reunion in '84, and it had taken him a moment to remember who she was. Steven had spoken to him and had talked about her. That had helped him to remember faster. She told him what she thought, including the fact the Derek Lowrance was the person killing the snow babies. He had already been to Derek's place, but he had been gone, or had refused to answer, and the sheriff didn't have a warrant, or sufficient cause to get one. Now he stood in front of Verna's door, answering a call on a domestic dispute. There was a connection, there had to be.

He knocked again and Verna's face appeared in the small window beside the front door. She didn't look surprised, and she opened the door a moment later.

"Did you come because of the fight?" she asked him.

"Yes, Verna, I did. Did you see anything?" His eyes wandered about the inside of her house as he spoke. She sensed this and appeared to grow uneasy.

"I heard some strange noises, but by the time I got out of bed and got to the window, there was nothing there."

"May I have a look around?" he asked, being vague on purpose, hoping it would give him legal grounds to get inside.

"You may look in my yard, if you like."

She pointed around the house. She clearly did not want him inside. Perhaps she was conspiring somehow in these murders and there was evidence to be seen. Perhaps even Derek was staying here now. He would have to test that theory out later. For now he was limited to the task at hand.

He smiled pleasantly at Verna and thanked her before turning on his big flashlight and walking around the side of the house. The ground was wet and soggy, and his boots made a sucking sound as the ground tried to pull them from his feet. He scanned the yard quickly, looking for anything obviously wrong. The rain still drizzled out of the sky, and the clouds covered what little light the slice of the moon had to offer. She had said something about her yard, hadn't she? If she hadn't seen anything, how could she have known it had been in her own back yard and not her neighbor's? He walked over the small yard until his light picked up the location of the scuffle. The mud was washed in odd patterns, and there were hints of blood, which meant there had to have been a lot or the rain would have washed it away by now. He tried to pick up a trail, but the only other place he found was a few feet toward Verna's house. The fight had been concentrated in a relatively small area, and somebody had been hurt badly. There was nothing more here, though. Not now. He would have to return in daylight to search the whole area. Maybe he could bring Julie with him.

He returned to the back of the house and knocked, hoping to get a view of this side of her dwelling. Her face appeared at the window and she shook the door.

"I don't have the key," she called out. "Go to the front."

He looked down and noticed the muddy footprints on the porch before obliging. Something was definitely wrong here. Did he have probable cause? Perhaps. What if Derek was in there? Could he arrest him? If so, what for? He had no hard evidence; he had no victim. What if Derek wasn't in there? Certainly Verna would complain about the search. Tomorrow he would make some calls and try to build a case. Until then he would have to play it safe.

The sheriff walked around to the front of the house where Verna stood with the door propped open.

"May I use your phone?" He asked her. "I need to make a call."

"I'm sorry, sheriff, I don't have a phone."

He grinned at her. Of course she did. The game was over, for now.

"Very well," he said. "I'll be heading back to the station then."

"Did you find anything?" she asked with mock interest.

"Not a thing," he replied. He made note of the relief which flashed across her features. "Must have been some kids playing around." He was definitely coming back tomorrow, but he wasn't warning her about it.

"Darned kids," she commented. Then she grinned oddly at him. He felt a chill run down his back.

Verna thanked him for his help, and closed the door behind him as he left. It was not a cold night, but a chill lingered with him nonetheless.

5

The room was dark when she awoke. Everything was unfamiliar, and her mouth was painfully dry. She tried to lift her arm, but it would only twitch.

'What's happened to me?' was all Samantha could think. Now that she was awake she could not remember her unconscious struggle to get here. Now that she was here she could not remember why.

She looked around, but the room was black and she could only make out the outlines of strange objects which surrounded her. Her body felt numb, almost as if it wasn't there. She looked down slowly, even her eyes did not follow directions very well. Her body was there. This eased her fear that she had died, a fear which had intensified with the strange dreams.

She tried again to move her arm. It tingled, and it was as heavy as lead. She tried to move her fingers but could not see if they were responding. Samantha looked around the room one last time as exhaustion came over her. She had been motionless for two days and nights, but she had been fighting a battle inside which had left her drained and weary. She did not want to sleep. She feared that this sleep might be as long as the last one.

In defiance of this, her mind slipped into restfulness once again.

6

Verna turned the light on in the large closet in the corner of her room. The string which led to the light socket dangled and danced above her as she knelt closer to him. He lay on the wood floor in the midst of clothing which she had arranged for him. It was not a bed, but she could not risk having him out where he might be seen.

There was blood on one of her shirts. It still seeped from his chest and soaked the torn dress she had wrapped around his waist to cover the wound. The worst damage was inside of him. Had he been alone, without the other power which lingered inside of him, he would have been dead now. If the injuries were severe enough he would die anyway.

But already he was healing, of this much she was sure. If he was not dead now, there was very little chance he was going to leave her.

Things had not gone as they should have. The simple boy should have killed this vessel. He would have been more cooperative, and his body was bigger and stronger as well. The three elements which would have been inside of him would have made him understand more, and would have made him obey her, even if he didn't really understand. The more of her lover that was joined inside, the less of the person remained.

But the witch woman had interfered and now she was left with Derek. She had been very specific, the witch woman was to have been dead before this confrontation took place. She did not know if Derek had given the wrong instructions, or if his boys had simply screwed up. She would find out.

Verna would stay with him not only to heal him, but to muddy his mind as well. She could not do this to any human, just those with whom she had this secret contact. When he healed he would not remember that she had betrayed him. He would have to believe that it had been no more than a failed plan. Then he would have to kill and kill quickly. One more element of her lover was all he needed inside of him to take the edge off his resistance and stubbornness. He would belong to her then, and he would be powerful enough to gather the elements that remained quickly. Time, time had never before ruled so much of what she was. She would be glad to finally be rid of it.

Derek would have to kill as soon as he was able.

She began to work on a plan.

Z

Pat moaned and stretched as Steven threw his sack of dirty clothes into his travel bag and zipped it shut.

"Time to move again, girl." he explained.

Pat just looked at him and raised one of her eyebrows. She had not gotten the sleep she was used to. They had driven until it was so late, now the sun had barely risen and Steven was heading for the door. But they would be getting into the small moving house, and she could sleep in there.

Pat followed Steven out of the room and to the Bronco. He left her inside while he checked out, and she found her sleeping spot and nested in it by the time he returned.

"You've had it too easy, girl," he chided her. Then he laughed out loud as she raised her eyebrow again, then closed her eyes.

Steven filled the vehicle with gas before pulling onto the highway. In half an hour he would be in Texas. Seven and a half hours after that he would be at the airport in Abilene where he had agreed to pick Rebecca up. Between here and there he would stop only for gas and food, at the same time. He would like to have included Carlsbad caverns on this trip. It had been three years since his last visit. True, the caverns had become quite commercialized, but the monumental calcite formations as well as the layout of the cave still awed him. There were formations in there which were a hundred feet tall, formations which would grow only an inch or so in his entire lifetime. There were still portions of the cave which had not yet been explored. He hoped to go sometime with the approval of the U.S.G.S. and do some off-trail exploring of his own. Perhaps next year.

It was a cool morning with clouds only far to the east. He suspected he would not see rain today, not, at least, until he got past Big Spring. That would help his driving time.

Steven checked his home messages, and there was one from Rebecca. She said that Samantha had been awake for a few moments, but she had not been there when it happened. She also told him about Derek. When she said his name it all came together for him. It didn't make sense, but he knew she was right. Somehow he had always known that Derek was one of them, but not one of them. He had always known Derek was a 'snow baby', but had never considered him a part of the special group. He remembered the Derek that gave him icy stares, the one that pulled a knife on Frank Sharp in the seventh grade, and who had a high incidence of unfortunate deaths surrounding him. Rebecca had called from the hospital where she was going to stay with Samantha until noon before catching her flight to Abilene.

Rebecca's mother had grown fearful of driving alone around Abilene, so Steven was going to pick Rebecca up at the airport, then drive her home on the way to his own parents' house. Rebecca had said she would call Frank and tell him what she knew. Steven would wait until he got to Eastland to speak with Frank.

But tonight he would be home, in a house he had spent many good years in. And he would see Rebecca again. The thought stirred something inside him as it always did. Now their special ties meant something more. They were in this fight together, a fight which threatened there very lives.

He reached forward and turned on the radio, scanning for some interesting talk. In the back, Pat moaned again as they passed a truck load of cast iron pipe on its way to El Paso.

8

"I saw it again," Richard explained to the Sheriff. "I saw through the beast's eyes."

Frank Sharp sat in his office. The sun had risen only hours ago, but Frank had gotten little sleep last night. After the incident at Verna's house he had gone home and lain awake trying to figure out how to get inside. Rebecca had called. She told him what he had come to suspect. It was Derek. Now Richard had called to tell him of his latest vision.

"What exactly did you see?" he asked Richard.

"It was very different. It was dark, and wet, and there were other people there."

"Did you recognize them?" Frank asked.

"There was a woman in the shadows. I never saw her, he never looked directly at her. But I did see who he was attacking, it was Tim Watkins."

The sheriff struggled with whether or not to tell Richard that he knew who the monster was now. Frank knew that it was Derek's eyes he was seeing through, that it was Derek's hand he had seen holding the blade which had claimed Jennifer and attacked Samantha. If he were Richard he would want to know. But there were reasons not to tell, most of them dealing with technicalities and courtroom procedures.

"What happened? Is Tim dead?"

"I don't know," Richard answered. "Some very strange things happened. One instant I was attacking Tim, then I was floating between the two men, then I saw Tim again. It was like I was really there, and I was slipping in and out of the killers body."

"Did you get a good look at the killer?" Frank asked, knowing who it was and hoping for confirmation.

"It was dark, and my vision was very blurry when I wasn't actually seeing through his eyes."

"You don't know what happened to Tim?"

"The images faded. I know he was injured, but I don't think he was killed right there. There was something about the time that Jennifer died, something that wasn't there when Samantha was attacked. It wasn't there this time either, and I think he got away."

"Thank you, Richard. I suggest you protect yourself and your family. Keep your doors locked at night and put a gun by your bed."

Richard did not own a gun, and he was not going to get one. His trust was in his God, not in this world's tools of violence.

Richard said good-bye, and Frank hung up his phone.

Frank knew he had to get to Derek.

Dean's feed store opened early for the farmers and Frank had already called and found out what had happened to Julie. Dean assured Frank that she would be fine, that he did not hold Frank responsible, and that Julie was not going to walk away now. Frank hoped she would be able to tell him if Derek really was inside the woman's house. In another hour he would call Judge Years to see what it would take to get that warrant. Arresting Derek just to let him go later would be the worst thing. He would get out and kill the rest of them. There had to be a way to get to him, and Frank was going to figure it out.

As he waited for Julie to arrive he phoned the airlines to check passenger manifests on flights Derek might have taken to Atlanta or New York before the attacks on Jennifer and Samantha. None of them would release that information over the phone. But he knew people in Abilene who could help him out, and Derek would certainly have flown in and out of there. That meant it had to be Delta for the Atlanta flight, and American or Delta for the New York flight. He would go to Abilene after he went to Verna's house and check on the flights. If what he needed was there, then he would get his warrant and make his arrest.

Hopefully Derek would do nothing in the meantime.

2

Frank drove into Timothy's Watkin's small driveway. Julie was in the car with him, her right arm in a sling, and got out when he stopped.

It was a cool morning, and the clouds were wisps in the sky. Last night it had rained almost an inch over most of Eastland. This morning the pavement was still damp. By noon the pavement would be dried completely by the warm spring sun.

Timothy's mother saw them pull up to the house and she came across the yard to meet them at the front door. Frank had spoken to her from his office after talking to the judge. Mrs. Watkins had called him because the newspaper had called her. None of Tim's papers had been delivered and they were concerned.

The Sheriff greeted Myrna Watkins and introduced Julie as an observer. Myrna was trying to keep her composure, but Frank could see that she was shaken. She had a key to the small house and she let Frank and Julie in.

Frank walked through the one-bedroom house and looked around. There were pictures on the walls of flowers and waterfalls, things arranged to make the place more comfortable.

"It's a nice little house," Frank commented.

"He decorated it himself," Myrna replied.

Julie looked around the house and smiled. Something about this reminded her of her own boy, Aaron. Aaron was deaf, but he had a knack for doing his own decorating, and he did it in things that made him comfortable. Tim's choices were childlike, but they were also refreshing. She held the ancient amulet which hung around her neck and sensed no darkness here.

After a quick look through the house Frank and Julie left. Nothing had been out of the ordinary except that Tim's bed had not been made. Frank wouldn't have thought this to be so usual, since it was a rare thing for his own bed to be made. But Myrna commented that Timothy always made his bed, and he must have gone somewhere in a hurry in the night.

Frank told Julie what he knew about the fight, and about how he believed Tim was involved as they drove to Verna's house.

Julie was intrigued. There was more here that Frank wasn't telling her, but she knew he had his reasons. "So is Timothy one of the 'snow babies'."

"Yes."

"Do you think that Derek is the person trying to kill them all."

"I'm sure of it."

"Why?"

Frank turned onto Verna's street. "I don't feel comfortable telling you everything, but I feel you have a right to know."

"That's okay," she agreed. "Only tell me what you want to tell me. I won't be offended."

Frank relaxed some. He looked over to Julie. "It's absolutely nothing personal," he explained, "but I spoke to the Judge this morning and I've got to be very careful how I proceed from here on out. If Derek is hiding in Verna's house, I've got to find a way to get in there and arrest him. I've got to watch my steps or Judge Years will throw it all out. He hates having his decisions overturned, so he's very tough on procedure. I didn't even tell him I was bringing you over here."

"I understand. Just let me know what you can, and I'll help as much as I'm able."

"You've helped plenty already." Frank smiled at her. She had told him about the gunfire that had torn into her sanctuary the previous night, and they had agreed that this woman they were going to see had something to do with it.

The two of them walked to Verna's front door and Frank knocked. He had not mentioned to Verna that he would be back, and he hoped the surprise would give him some advantage. Her face appeared at the small window next to the door and she quickly looked them both over. She indeed did look surprised, though Frank could not tell if it was because he had returned, or because Julie was alive and standing next to him.

Verna opened her door and stood before them. She spoke first.

"Did you find out who was fighting back there last night?" she asked.

"No," Frank answered. "But we have some ideas. I wanted to ask you a few more questions, if that's okay with you?"

She gave her best false smile. "Of course."

"May we come in?" Frank asked.

Her face dropped for an instant, then she turned and looked behind her. "Oh, I'm afraid it's just too messy in here," she explained. Then she stepped outside and pulled her door shut. "I'll be glad to join you outside though," she explained through her fake grin.

Julie held her amulet and concentrated. Whatever was here was beyond her. She could sense very little. She could sense absolutely no thoughts, which was a first. The woman looked at her for an instant and Julie smiled back.

Frank asked a few general questions as Julie tried to pry through the woman's will. Nothing seemed to work, and finally he grew frustrated with the whole process.

Julie held the amulet tightly and tried her best powers of persuasion. "Do you know where Derek is?" she asked.

The Sheriff winced. He had not mentioned Derek's name on purpose, but he saw Verna's fake smile waver when Julie did.

Verna looked directly into Julie's eyes and said she did not. Julie could not tell if her persuasive powers were working or not, she could not tell if Verna was telling the truth or not. This was too big a puzzle for her.

Finally, Verna asked if there was anything more, to which the Sheriff answered that there was not.

Julie held to her amulet and tried one last time. "May I use your restroom before we go?"

Verna's eyes shifted. She had done well to deflect these two so far, but now she wondered just how much they knew. She did not want to give them reason to be more suspicious than they might be already. She could see the anticipation in Sheriff Sharp's eyes as he waited for her response. Unaware of Julie's influence over the decision, Verna agreed and led Julie inside, asking the Sheriff to please wait outside, considering the condition of the house.

Julie followed the woman through the living room and to her bedroom. The inside really was a mess, and it smelled of rotten food and urine. Her eyes roamed about, taking in everything possible as she followed Verna to the small bathroom in the back of her little bedroom. Verna opened the door and let Julie in. Moments later Julie emerged, and Verna was waiting just outside the door.

"Thank you," Julie offered.

The woman did not respond, but instead made a deep, guttural growling sound. Julie could sense her frustration and knew that someone was going to be made to pay for the fact that she was still alive.

Verna followed Julie back to the front of the house where she let her out the door. The Sheriff was waiting with anxious eyes.

"I hope you find those people," Verna said to him. "We don't need that kind of stuff in this town."

"Thank you, Verna," he replied. "Thanks for answering my questions."

"You're both welcome," she replied. Then she closed her door firmly. They heard the lock click into place as they turned to walk down the steps.

Once inside the car Julie told him about the blood she had seen in Verna's room, at the bottom of her closet door.

Chapter Eleven
1

She saw his death coming while she was on the plane.

Rebecca had been traveling all day, thinking about where she was going and concentrating on her friends when it came to her.

Why it hadn't come with Jennifer and Samantha she could not be sure. Sometimes her vision worked with her, sometimes it did not. Perhaps it was because she was so close now. She looked out the window of the small commuter plane and saw the highway to the north. The southernmost portion of Eastland ran along that highway. That's where the killer was. But that was not her premonition.

Richard was going to be killed.

She didn't know when or how. It had simply come to her as the hum of the commuter's twin props lulled her into a trance-like state. On the jet from New York to Dallas there had been phones on every row of seats. Here there were none. She could not call a warning down to Richard or to the Sheriff. Here she was helpless. All she could do was hope that it didn't happen before she landed, which was only minutes from now.

Rebecca assumed that her premonition meant the Sheriff had not picked Derek up yet. Perhaps he would. But not unless she interfered somehow, of this much she was sure. Her premonitions were deadly accurate, and this was a strong one

She signaled the cabin attendant and asked her again how long it would be before they landed.

2

Frank Sharp sat across from the judge who sat at his desk. The judge was frowning, which was what he always did when reviewing a warrant. He was thinking carefully about this.

"You know I can't let you hold him for long on these charges?"

"I understand that."

Frank had worked up enough evidence to arrest Derek on charges of assault on Timothy Watkins and had presented just enough evidence to convince the judge that he was hiding in Verna's house. He had also gotten confirmation through visual identification that Derek had boarded commuter planes for Dallas on the dates surrounding the murders. While this was not enough to convict Derek of anything, it was enough to get the judge's interest.

"I'm only signing this because of the blood that the woman saw inside Verna's house. That's not probable cause for much, but it should give you the excuse you need to look in that closet. But I'm warning you, don't search the entire house unless you've got clear evidence that he was in that closet."

"Of course, sir."

Frank waited anxiously as the judge's pen hovered over the piece of paper.

The judge looked at Frank again. "I wouldn't do this if I didn't think Derek wasn't involved in the murders you've described to me. I've seen that man in my courtroom before, and I'm well aware of the rumors about the death of his sister and that Matson boy. There are other things as well which convince me that you may have something." He paused and looked at the warrant. "But if you aren't able to put together sufficient evidence for these charges by the time he shows up in front of my bench, I'm going to have to set bail fairly low. If you can't find Tim Watkins I may even have to dismiss charges and have him released. In either case, you're only going to have about twenty-four hours to keep him in a cell. Do you think you can put together what you need, or are you wasting my time?"

"I'll put it together, sir. I can't have him loose, waiting to kill again. Let me lock him up, and I'll stay awake for twenty-four hours putting together whatever I need to keep him there."

The judge frowned again. "You shouldn't have taken that woman with you."

Then he signed the warrant.

3

Steven waited in the terminal as Rebecca's plane taxied in. The afternoon had turned out to be comfortably warm. It was May. The hot afternoons were not far away.

He watched as the passengers got off the plane and walked to the terminal. He saw Rebecca and his heart leapt, which actually surprised him. She looked bothered, but he supposed that had to do with the circumstances, at least until she got inside the doors and spotted him.

Rebecca hurried to him and threw her arms around him. She was warm. He felt himself glowing. That wasn't exactly what was happening, but that's what it felt like. Then she was looking at him.

"I need a phone. Fast."

Steven led her to the pay phones across the terminal and she rummaged through her purse for her phone book. He watched as she dialed a number, waited, then dialed another. He listened to her end of the conversation with much interest, sure she would fill him in when the urgency passed.

When she finished with her calls she returned her attention to him. She realized how much she needed him now. His strength was physical and spiritual, and their bond went beyond what anyone else could understand. He gave her a strength of her own. These past few days had been frantic, and she had been alone. Samantha's parents had arrived, but Rebecca had still been alone. With Steven she was not alone. He understood.

"Richard's in trouble?" he asked.

They walked together to get her suitcase. "Yes. I think Derek will kill him next."

"Did you try to call him?"

"That was the first call."

"No answer?" Steven asked.

"Busy."

Steven carried her suitcase as they walked outside to his Bronco. Pat waited for them with her nose pressed against the back window. Her tail wagged gently as they approached.

"Nice dog," Rebecca commented.

"She's usually a little hesitant with strangers, but she won't bite."

Steven opened the hatch and threw her bags inside. Pat reached her head out and nudged him. Then she did the same to Rebecca. She petted Pat's head and asked her name.

"Her name's Pat, and she doesn't usually nudge strangers like that. I think you two will get along fine."

Pat wagged her tail as the woman petted her head. This woman was like her master, she had the same light, the good light.

They got into the Bronco and resumed their discussion as Steven headed back toward the interstate. Pat licked his ear once, then Rebecca's, then she laid back in her spot.

"Did you get a hold of Frank last night?" Steven asked her.

"Yes. He said he had just gotten back from a disturbance of some kind behind Verna Calloway's house. He didn't say too much about it, but he agreed that Derek was probably involved somehow. He also seemed open to the idea that Derek was the killer. He says he's had some help from a woman who has a gift like mine, and that she told him someone was trying to bring something together by killing the snow babies."

"Her name's Julie, she's the wife of a friend of mine from Albany."

"Is she legitimate?" Rebecca had seen many women and men in her line of work over the years, the bulk of them frauds.

"According to my friend Dean, and he can be trusted."

"Maybe she can be of some help," Rebecca suggested.

"It sounds like she already has."

Steven pulled onto Interstate Twenty and headed eastward. It was nice to have Rebecca in the vehicle. She was strong, and it helped him to be even stronger. Now they shared something more than their birthdays. Now death was on their heels, and it somehow made their relationship even more special. They would have to beat this thing together.

"Do you think Richard is in immediate danger?" Steven asked.

"I don't know. I know I picked it up as I flew near Eastland. That could have been only because I was close, or because it was imminent, or both. I just wish I could have gotten through to him."

"Do you want me to pull over?" he asked.

"No. The station said they'd get the message through to Frank. We'll do better to get to Eastland."

"You want to go by Richard's house?" he asked.

She had really been looking forward to spending some time with her mother this evening. Once again this thing had intruded on her life. She hadn't seen Richard since the summer after graduation. He had not come to the reunion. Going to see him now seemed like a strange idea. She always knew that they, too, were linked. But they had never been close, not like she and Steven and Samantha and Jennifer. Richard's parents had kept in separated, in his own world.

"I guess that might be a good idea. Maybe we should stop and see Tim too."

Steven hadn't even thought about Tim Watkins. "Of course. Do you want to go by your mother's house first?"

"I think we should see Richard first. Then I can go to the house. We'll visit Timothy tomorrow. I don't have any reason to believe that he's in any more danger than we are."

"I wonder how much danger that is?" Steven mused.

Rebecca looked at him. His face was strong, but worried. She reached over and squeezed his hand.

It helped.

4

Richard was holding the hand of an old widow when the vision came. She was dying slowly of a bad kidney. Richard was there to comfort her. Only now something terrible was happening, something which again took his mind from his task.

This was the most terrible vision he had ever had.

The images were dark and misty, not clear at all in his mind. But even through the mist he knew what he was seeing.

It was the inside of his own home.

He opened his eyes and the images still overlay reality. He could see well enough, however, to run out of the nursing home and get to his car.

5

Sheriff Sharp approached Verna's house carefully. He brought Deputy Max Perry with him in case there was any trouble. They walked up the steps to her home together. Frank knocked loudly on her door.

He waited for her face to appear at the small window, but it didn't show. He knocked again, longer and harder this time. The glass rattled in the door. "Mrs. Calloway. We need to talk with you."

There was no response.

"We have a search warrant for your premises. I'd like you to open the door for me, or I'll have to open it by force."

They waited, but there was no response.

"Want me to break it in?" the big deputy asked.

Frank reached forward and turned the knob. It wasn't locked. "No," he answered his deputy. Max looked chagrined. Frank walked in cautiously.

The house was a mess and smelled awful. Roaches ran across the floor, hiding under the couch and in the walls. Torn clothing lay strewn about the room. The television sat crooked and shattered on a rotting old stand. The lights didn't work. The shades had rotted, but she had hung sheets in their place. All the windows were covered and the oppressiveness of it all blocked out the afternoon sun.

The deputy followed Sheriff Sharp carefully. He had been warned about the specific nature of the warrant. They were here to get Derek Lowrance, that was all. The old woman was out right now, and that would make their job easier.

Frank walked into her room. There were no sheets on the bed, and the mattress was sagging and covered in shades of yellow. He walked to the closet, which was about three feet from the foot of the bed. It was a small door, and Julie had been right, there was blood on the floor, near the door. It looked to be fairly fresh, and it was streaked in the direction of the door. He had decided that if Derek was in here he was probably armed and waiting. With this in mind he knocked.

"Derek. I know you're in there. We're going to open this door. There are three of us, and our weapons are drawn. If you have a weapon I suggest you put it down now so we don't have an accident."

He listened, but there was no sound. He waited a few moments longer, then decided that if Derek had been in here, he certainly wasn't now.

He signaled the deputy to step to one side of the closet and he stepped to the other. He turned the knob on the closet door and opened it quickly, staying out of the line of sight of anyone who might be inside. A light came on by itself inside the closet as it opened, and this startled Frank. He put his head cautiously around the doorway to take a look inside.

There was no one there.

But there was more blood.

Frank led the way into the long closet. He could see that Verna had made a bed out of old clothes; clothes now covered with Derek's blood. Timothy had apparently wounded Derek pretty severely in that fight, and Derek was not healing quickly. But why had she moved him, and where had they gone?

"Want me to take a look around the room?" the deputy asked.

Frank thought only briefly about the Judge's admonition. "Yes. But don't touch anything."

The deputy left the closet as Frank sifted through the clothing for clues. He found a piece of paper which was wet with water and blood and had apparently fallen out of Derek's pocket. On it were directions to Samantha's apartment in New York. This was good. It was enough to get Derek locked up for more than twenty-four hours. If they could find him. There was also some change, and a card with some local phone numbers. He slipped the card in his pocket and sifted through the clothes some more. There was nothing else here.

Sheriff Sharp stood and looked around the inside of the closet. There was a shelf which ran along one wall, near the ceiling. It was bare, for the most part, except for one very interesting box. The warrant was specific. It gave him access only to the closet. This box was in the closet, and was, therefore, subject to search. But Frank was smarter than this. He knew that the box was not material to his search for Derek. It was probably not even Derek's property. It was evidence which would be thrown out on a technicality. But he could still look. If there was evidence in there, he could find a means to get a proper warrant for the box. For now he simply had to look inside.

"Everything okay in there?" the deputy asked.

"I'm fine." He reached up and took the box down. It was the size of a large shoebox with a removable lid.

"What'ca got there?" Max asked as he returned to the closet entrance.

"Nothing."

Max understood. He watched nonetheless.

Frank opened the lid to the box. Inside was a jumble of photos and newspaper articles. It didn't take long to discern their significance.

He took one newspaper clipping out and looked at it. It was about Steven. It was an article about the big game in 1974 when he gained over 200 yards rushing and made three touchdowns. There was more. There were several articles paper-clipped together which showed pictures of Jennifer as she grew, each article outlining one pageant or another which she had won. There were pictures which had been clipped from school yearbooks and class pictures, all of them of the snow babies. There were even some Polaroids which someone had taken from various hiding places, Verna had probably taken these herself.

He had to have the box, but he could not take it with him. If he did it would not be admitted as evidence. But if he left it she might return for it.

Frank put the box back on the shelf and left the closet.

His deputy looked at him. "Were those pictures important?"

"Absolutely."

"Why did you leave them? Don't we have a warrant?"

"Not for them."

"But they're important?"

"Definitely."

Frank walked out of the bedroom and back into the kitchen. His deputy followed close behind.

"Then why did you leave them?"

"The warrant doesn't cover them. If I take them, or if you mention that we even saw them, they can't be used in court."

"That stinks." The disgust was evident in Max's voice.

"That's the law." He stopped and faced his deputy, ready to give him a quick lesson. "And it's the law for a good reason. We just have to figure out a way to use the law to get that box. That box in any court will put them both behind bars for good, no bail."

Frank walked to the stove and looked it over carefully. He lifted the top of it and saw that the pilot lights were lit. He blew them both out. Max just watched in silence. He knew his boss had a reason for what he was doing. Frank put the lid down and walked back through the living room to the front door.

"I want you to stay here at the house, around the side. Stay out of sight. If she comes back with Derek, arrest them both. We can say I just wanted her for questioning about the fighting. If she comes alone just keep her out of the house. Tell her there's a gas leak inside and you can't let her in until the gas company shows up. If she gets belligerent, throw her in the car.

"Got it."

Frank knew he was pushing it, but he could not, under any circumstances, let her back in the house until he had that box. In the meantime he would call the judge and ask for the safest way to search the contents of the closet. If there was no way, then he would take the box for his own evidence.

He radioed to the office and told them to send the gas company to Verna Calloway's house if Max called in. Jill took his instructions, then gave Frank the message from Rebecca. It didn't sound urgent, but Frank knew that it was. It simply said 'please check on Richard.' He asked Jill to call Richard's house as he headed that way.

Jill came back on the radio moments later and said the line to Richard Hall's house was busy. Frank told her to try the church and he drove a little faster.

6

Frank pulled up to the front of Richard Hall's house. It was a peaceful place with nicely placed bushes and a thick green carpet of St. Augustine grass. But it was too peaceful right now. It was silent, and it seemed ominous to Frank. He knew he was overreacting to Rebecca's message, but he also knew that things seemed to be getting out of hand.

Richard worked at home when he was not at the church or visiting the sick at the hospital. Richard also spent a lot of time at the nursing homes around the towns between Eastland and Abilene. Frank hoped Richard was out now. It was almost five o'clock, so he might be on his way home. Frank wasn't exactly sure what preacher's hours were.

Frank knocked on the door and waited. Nobody answered. He rang the bell, but still no one came. The children would not be at school, but perhaps they were at a friend's house. He walked back to the car and had Jill call the house again. Again, Jill reported that the line was busy. It could be nothing, a cat that had knocked the phone off the hook, a broken answering machine, anything. But Rebecca's message stuck in his head, and he knew this was very bad.

Frank walked to the picture window in front of the house and looked through a gap in the curtains. The kitchen light was on. The living room looked well kept. He watched for a few moments, but there was no motion. He decided to take a look around the house.

First he tried the front door. It was locked. He walked around the house, being careful not to step on the landscaped areas on the way. The curtains were all drawn, which seemed odd to Frank, though not unheard of. The back yard was fenced in, so he jumped the short chain link fence and walked to the first window. These curtains, too, were drawn closed. He walked along the back of the house, looking for an opened curtain or window, maybe an unlocked door. There was a small window over the kitchen sink, and the curtains here were opened. He stood on his toes and looked inside, but all he could see was the kitchen. He could see the phone, and it was still on the hook. The kitchen was clean, except for a few things which rested on the white countertop by the stove.

And there was a pot on the stove.

Steam was coming out of it.

Something was wrong. He looked at the items on the counter. There was a bag of carrots, and a pack of hamburger which looked wet. Someone was making dinner. Actually, someone had started to make dinner, but something had taken her from the job.

And the phone was still busy.

He wanted to break in. But if Mrs. Hall was sitting in her bedroom on the phone he would be more than a little embarrassed.

As he sat pondering his dilemma he heard a car come around the corner so fast its tires were squealing. As the vehicle raced to the front of Richard's house the Sheriff saw that it was Richard's car. Frank raced to the front of the house, leaping back over the fence as he ran. If something was wrong here, he needed to be the one to go inside first, not Richard.

But by the time Frank got to the front of the house Richard was already at the front door.

"Richard! Stop!" he shouted.

"They got my wife!" he shouted back without looking. He threw the front door open and ran inside. The sheriff was only a few seconds behind him, his service revolver drawn and ready.

He stepped inside the house but had no idea where Richard had disappeared to.

"Richard!" he shouted out. "Where are you?"

There was no answer, but he heard the sobbing coming from the back of the house. He walked slowly and carefully watching his surroundings as he tried to hurry to that room. When he got to the room he raised his gun instinctively.

There was blood on the carpet, lots of blood. Richard's wife Bonnie lay in the middle of most of it. Richard was on his knees, holding her in his arms.

But they were not alone. Derek was there. So was Verna Calloway. Derek stood over Richard, a gleaming blade in his right hand. They were fifteen feet from the sheriff. Verna was behind Derek. She, too, had a weapon. It was a small gun, and it was pointed behind the bed. The sheriff couldn't see what she was pointing her gun at, but she was looking directly at him. Then she spoke.

"Drop your gun and come this way or I'll kill the children."

The children were lying on the floor behind the bed. He could not see them, and there were no sounds. Was she bluffing? Were the children already dead?

"Do it now!" she shouted as her gun wavered.

He couldn't lower his gun. He had to get help. He took a step back.

She fired her gun once.

He could hear the sound of muffled screaming and his finger tensed on the trigger of his own gun.

"Don't you dare!" she shouted. She stared at him hard. "That time I shot a leg. Next time I shoot a head. If you don't lower your gun, I'll kill them both. If you run away, I'll kill them both. If you shoot me I'll probably still get one of them, Derek will kill the preacher. You must comply. That's all there is to it."

If Richard would run, if he would bolt for the door Frank knew he could take them both out. He could get a bullet in Verna before she could fire another shot, and he was close enough to be sure it would be lethal.

But Richard would not move. None of this mattered to him. All that was real to him right now was his dead wife in his own arms.

Frank had always thought that there was no such thing as a no-win scenario. This was certainly as close as it got.

Then Verna turned suddenly and fired.

Z

His mind was still racing, and he was not prepared for this. The bullet took him in the right shoulder. His instinct was to return fire, but the situation made him hesitate. He couldn't release his gun, but he couldn't fire it either.

These thoughts raced through his mind as his arm flew back in slow motion. Before he could bring his gun back around, she fired again. This time he felt a burning in his side. He fired a shot of his own, but his shoulder was on fire and is aim was too far to the right. She didn't move. Instead she just shot and shot and shot until her bullets were gone. After the first two shots only two more hit the sheriff, the remaining four penetrated the wall and door behind him. One bullet tore through his left leg, nicking the femur but missing the main artery. The other grazed his neck, and he felt the warm blood soaking into his collar as he fell to the floor.

It was over now. There was too much pain and burning here, and he couldn't move his legs. His gun was lost somewhere, hopefully where she wouldn't find it. His brought his left hand slowly to his neck where the bleeding was the worst. Maybe someone heard the shots. Maybe someone would be coming now. If he held on until then...

From where he lay the bed blocked his view of the nurse. He heard her talking to Derek who just looked at him, then nodded his head. His mouth moved and Frank understood the word 'hurry.'

Then he witnessed something which amazed and horrified him.

Derek drove his knife into Richard's back. Richard had never turned to face him. Even now, with the blade buried in his back, he simply curled tighter to his wife and cried out something to his God.

But Derek would not allow this. The crazed man withdrew the knife and buried it in Richard's back again, then he grabbed Richard by the hair and pulled back his head. He stared into the preacher's eyes as he twisted the knife in his back.

Richard's legs kicked out oddly as blood seeped from his mouth.

Frank tried to move, but his legs would not cooperate. Then came the terror.

Richard slowly began to relax. Then, a moment after his arms finally released his wife, something leapt from his eyes. It looked to Frank like a bright yellow mist. It leapt from the preacher and forced its way into Derek through his own eyes. It lasted only a second, but Frank knew he had seen it.

When it finished, Derek released the preacher's head and let him fall back to the ground.

Derek suddenly looked strong again. The weakness had left the man completely. He literally leapt up and yelled out something which Frank could not understand, this time because it was not in English.

Then Derek was upon him. It happened just like that. One moment Derek was crying out his victory, the next he simply appeared looking down upon him. Death was in his eyes, and Frank could see into that deep pit.

Now it was as if the room had disappeared. There was nothing here but him and this madman. But Frank could see more than that now. He could see into this dark creature and he knew that something different than just Derek, something more than Derek was here. It was something he could never possibly comprehend.

But consciousness was slipping away.

He thought for a moment that he heard the sound of sirens.

Then he heard the voice which must have come from Derek, but which was deeper and much darker than any he had ever heard.

"I will have your soul," it said.

Then the blackness overtook him.

Chapter Twelve
1

Steven visited his parents in Eastland every year. He had remained familiar with the town, and he knew where Richard Hall lived. They arrived in Eastland before dark, so Steven drove straight to Richard's home.

About thirty minutes earlier the conversation in the Bronco had come to an abrupt halt and Rebecca had arched her back oddly. Steven had felt something too, and they had come to expect the worst.

When they turned the last corner they saw the flashing lights and police cars. Rebecca's hand went to her mouth. She knew instantly what had happened. She had seen this all before. Richard was dead.

Steven parked two houses away. The two of them walked together toward the house but were stopped short by Deputy Bill Carroll.

"Can I help you two?" he asked.

"Is Richard all right?" Steven asked. He already knew the answer.

"Are you friends of Richard's?" the deputy asked.

"We went to school with him. We know about the killings that the sheriff is working on. That's why we're here."

Steven looked around but couldn't see Frank. "Can I speak to Sheriff Sharp for a minute."

"I'm afraid not," the deputy responded.

Steven gave the man a cold look. "Why not."

Rebecca grabbed Steven's arm. "Because he's dead too."

The deputy looked at Rebecca for a moment, then back to Steven. "He's not available right now."

Steven looked to Rebecca. She'd just said that Frank was dead. "Are you sure?"

She looked toward the house. "I can't be sure, not from here."

"I can tell you they're not going to let you get any closer than this for now." He returned his eyes to the concerned deputy. "Look, we're friends of the sheriff, Frank and I went to school together. We're two of the people he's been trying to protect. Did he tell you about the 'snow babies?'" The deputy looked puzzled. "Did he tell you anything about what he was working on?"

"I'm afraid this mess has got us all real busy right now. Why don't you come by the station tomorrow."

Steven stood to his full intimidating height and the deputy visibly shrank. "This can't wait until tomorrow, damn it. Get me someone who knows what's going on."

The deputy didn't like to feel threatened. But if the sheriff had been looking for these people, maybe they could help sort out this mess.

"Wait here, I'll go get deputy Perry."

Steven and Rebecca stood on the sidewalk about fifty yards from Richard's home, which was cordoned off with yellow police tape.

"Derek's already been here," Steven observed.

Rebecca just stared at the house, trying to pick something up, something that would help her understand what she should do now. She thought of Timothy and wondered if he was being protected.

Behind them, in the Bronco, Pat stood suddenly and looked to the west. She felt a coldness pass through her brain, and she could smell the evil, even through the glass of the Bronco. Her hackles raised and she began barking viciously as she felt the darkness pass close by, then head away. It hadn't seen her, but knew it had come close. And she knew it held malice for her master. She would protect him from this thing, and she knew it would be back.

Steven heard the barking and looked back to the Bronco. Pat was barking away from all of the commotion. He looked to see what she was barking at, but could see nothing. But he, too, felt the chill she had felt, though he did not sense the malice.

A moment later Deputy Perry approached them. He spoke to Steven. "The sheriff told me a little about what he was working on. He mentioned that there were people who were in danger, and I remember your name. He said you'd be coming, and he had left a message with your parents for you to come to the station as soon as you got in. He wanted to talk to you about Verna Calloway."

"Is he dead?" Steven asked.

"No."

Rebecca raised an eyebrow. She was glad she had been wrong.

Steven asked the deputy, "Can I talk to him now?"

"He's on his way to the hospital, may be there by now. He took quite a few bullets and lost a lot of blood. He was slipping in and out of consciousness when I saw him, he wasn't saying anything I could make any sense out of." The deputy looked back to the house. "I was with him at Verna's house earlier today, and I have a pretty good idea who did this. But we still have no real proof. If the sheriff pulls through, he'll be all we need. Without him we still have a mystery, and a suspect who can't be found."

Rebecca interrupted. "Derek has disappeared?"

The deputy seemed surprised that she knew the name, but he continued. "The last we knew he was hiding out in Verna's place. He'd been injured in a fight behind her house. I'm not sure how he was able to pull this off, obviously with her help. I'm sure they won't be going back to her house now. I have no idea where they may be hiding."

Rebecca looked at the house again. "If I could go in there now, while everything is still fresh, I may be able to help."

"I appreciate the offer Ma'am, but we've got our best people sifting through it all right now. And we've still got a couple of bodies in there."

"A couple?" Steven asked.

The deputy looked uncomfortable. "They got his wife and one of his kids. The other kid wasn't wounded, but she's not in good shape."

Steven pressed out a frown and felt his blood begin to boil. He would find Derek himself and tear him into pieces.

Rebecca felt the anger too. "I don't mean to sound too odd, but I work with the police in San Francisco from time to time. I can see things that most people can't, things which might help us find Verna and Derek."

Deputy Perry was skeptical. "I appreciate that, Ma'am. But I'd rather wait until we've gone over things ourselves, and gotten it cleaned up a little."

"But if you clean it all up, I won't be able to see anything."

Max wasn't persuaded, and he was beginning to grow impatient. "You'll have to come back later. This is my scene, and I won't allow it."

Steven grabbed her hand as her eyes focused firmly on the window which led to the bedroom where it had all happened. "Rebecca, let's go home now." She looked at him. "I'll take you to your mother's, and I'll go to my parent's house. We'll get together in the morning and go see the Sheriff. They're not going to let us in tonight anyway, and I don't think it'll make a lot of difference."

Rebecca returned her gaze to the deputy.

"I think that would be best ma'am," the man said to her. "I'll do what I can to let you in here tomorrow."

She was irritated, but she did not let it affect her manners. She knew he was doing his job. He had every right to be skeptical. After all, this was 'his scene.'

Suddenly she remembered the other special person. "What about Timothy Watkins?" she asked. "Has anybody gotten hold of him?"

"He's disappeared," the deputy explained. "We don't know if he's alive, wounded, or if he just ran away. His mother has been instructed to call if he returns, but she hasn't called us. If we can't find him, maybe he's safe already."

"Maybe so." Rebecca didn't know. Timothy was a mystery to her.

She smiled, thanked the deputy, then followed Steven to the Bronco. Pat seemed agitated and greeted them both vigorously as they got in.

2

Steven took Rebecca to her mother's house as the sun began to set. Emily invited him in, and he accepted.

"But only for a couple of minutes," he commented. "My parents have to be getting pretty worried by now."

"Why don't you give them a call?" Emily suggested.

Steven agreed that this was a good idea. Another one occurred to him as he made the call and he asked his parents if they would mind some additional company for the night. Then he came back into the den and made the offer.

Rebecca looked relived. "I hate to impose like this," she commented, "but I think it's a very good idea."

Emily wasn't fond of sleeping somewhere besides her own bed and said she would stay at her own home. Then Steven explained the situation for her in terms which would concern her, but not terrify her.

"Even if you stay here alone, there's a chance that Derek won't know Rebecca isn't here and he may come in anyway. Besides, you and my mother probably haven't had a good visit in years."

Emily was definitely concerned. "I feel awkward imposing like that. But you say he may try to harm me and Rebecca, then maybe it's not such a bad idea."

"I think it's a great idea, mom." Rebecca prodded.

Emily smiled at her daughter. She was still her only and special child. She only wished Andy could have seen her now, he would have been so proud of who she had become. "Give me a few minutes to put my things together," she commented. Then she went to the back of the house.

When she was gone Rebecca spoke. "You'll have to thank your parents. I don't think we're safe here at all. I didn't even think to ask to stay with your folks, I just figured I was going to have to sleep with my mom and try my best to make it through the night. I can see now that it wasn't a very good plan. My mind just isn't working at its best. There's too much going on."

"I know," Steven agreed. "But we need to make plans to stick together as much as possible now, and to stay around other people at night if we can. He's going to be coming after us, that much is a fact. We just need to be ready."

The shock of Richard's death hit her again. "What is Derek doing? Why now?"

Steven stepped forward and took Rebecca into his arms. She had not appeared weak, her voice had been strong, but Steven had felt her need. His arms were strong and comforting, and she felt calmness run through her body. With him she would be safe.

"Let's get over to my mom and dad's. We'll talk about it there, then we'll get some sleep. Tomorrow we'll go see Frank. If he's well enough to talk, we'll take what he has to say and go from there. That's all we can do."

Rebecca smiled faintly. "Okay."

Moments later her mother appeared. Then they loaded back into Steven's Bronco and headed for his parents' house.

3

Verna sat down with her back against the rocks. It was cool, but she had brought a blanket and it kept her warm. Derek was sitting beside her, staring at the floor of the cave in front of him. It seemed both familiar and foreign. Richard's death had brought a new vision to him. With it had come a new understanding, but not a complete understanding. He was changing. He had known this when Jennifer had helped him to make the first change. Now he realized that it was not the change he had originally suspected. This change meant more than better sight or faster reflexes. Those were just some of the physical manifestations of a greater change, a change that would take him beyond mere humanity.

He also understood that the woman sitting behind him had made this change already. She was waiting for him. He still felt both attracted and repulsed, but he understood that where he had to go he could not go alone. And he could not go until he had killed them all.

"It's very hot here now," she said, breaking the silence.

He continued to stare at the floor. Her words echoed inside his head. "What do you mean."

"I mean that we have to do it all now. We have to kill them fast. The police may already know what's going on. If they do, they'll be looking for us. You may be strong now, but you're not fully healed, and you're not impervious to bullets. If they shoot you, you will die. If they capture you, we may never accomplish what we have set out to do."

"What are you saying?"

"I'm saying that these rocks can't hide us forever. I'm saying that we must move again tonight when they are sleeping. We will kill the woman first; she will be easier to kill, and her power will make killing the man easier too."

He was ready for this. He was not tired, and he was hungry for another soul. He felt more complete than he had ever felt, yet he understood that much was missing. "Then we will find the stupid man?"

"We will search together, or we will wait. He is not our match. He longs for his mother; he will return to her soon. Then we will finish him. He will be the last. Then we will leave these worthless shells and move on."

What did she mean by 'worthless shells?' He knew she was referring to this body, but how did she intend to leave these bodies behind, and where would they go?

Derek was confused, but his defiance had subsided now that Richard's essence was a part of him. There was understanding here now, understanding he had lacked before. It tempered his anger and brought him closer to his destiny.

Whatever that might be.

4

Steven and Rebecca sat at the kitchen table drinking the flavored coffee's which Steven's mother had bought for his visit. It was late, everyone had finished visiting and gone to bed except for the two of them. Rebecca's mother was lying awake in the back bedroom, unable to sleep in a strange bed. Steven had gotten an old mattress out of the attic and placed it in the floor of that bedroom for Rebecca. Rebecca said she wanted to sleep in the same room with her mother, more for her mother's sake than for her own.

Rebecca spoke. "He's got to come after us, you know."

"I know," Steven replied, "but I don't understand."

"Frank said some things to me on the phone last night when I called to tell him that Derek was the killer."

Steven shifted in his chair. "What did he say."

"He said that the woman he had gotten some help from, he said her name was Julie, told him that the snow babies all hold a piece of an ancient entity which split into pieces as it crossed some kind of barrier."

"Did Julie say why Derek or Verna felt compelled to kill us?"

"She didn't know that they were involved. As far as she knew, it was someone outside trying to kill us all. Now we know that it's one of the snow babies who's doing all of the killing."

"Maybe I can give her a call in the morning, see if this bit of information gives her any ideas."

"We should go see the sheriff first," Rebecca suggested. "See if he's talking, and if there's anything he can tell us."

"I agree." He sipped the hot coffee. "But we've got to be careful. There's no telling when or where Derek may strike again. We need to stay close to each other, and we should both be armed."

Steven patted his waist as he said this. Underneath was the heavy handle of his dad's old .45 service pistol. The gun he had brought with him. He had also gotten his dad's .380 Beretta out of the entry closet and made sure it was loaded. It now lay on the kitchen counter. He had shown it to Rebecca, but he had not shown her how to use it yet. She was unsure about carrying a gun but knew that it was best. She was not going to let Derek take her, not without taking her best shot at him first.

Rebecca looked out the window behind Steven. "I wonder where they are now?"

"Somewhere around town, I'm sure. There are dozens of old buildings. They could be in any one of them. A person could hide out in this town for a long time, if he was trying to stay out of sight."

She looked at him hard. Steven was not the boy she had known twenty-three years ago, yet he was similar. He was strong willed, he seemed to know what he wanted, and what needed to be done. He still liked to take charge but did so in a way which offended no one.

But he was different. He had matured. His movements were patient and deliberate, not fast and reckless as they had once been. He seemed to think carefully about each word before he said it, and his mind always seemed to be at work behind those otherwise restful eyes. He grew stronger and more attractive with age. She could see that he was going to be irresistible as he matured into a gray headed patriarch of sorts. Already he was much more attractive than she had ever remembered. He had always been good looking, but now he was more attractive. His calmness and strength were almost sexy. No, it absolutely was sexy.

Steven had no idea what was running through Rebecca's mind. He just sat in the silence and let her think. She was a very special woman. He felt drawn to her in ways he had never felt before. Both Jennifer and Samantha had been special, but this was different. Perhaps it would have been different with Jennifer is they hadn't been children when they had fallen in love, not knowing exactly what that meant. But Jennifer had grown into something that had seemed too hard to reach, too fragile to touch. Samantha was strong, but her world was her own. Rebecca was the closest to him. She wanted the things he wanted, she asked the same questions and thought the same way. He would never have imagined that she would be drawn to him. She never had been before, not as any more than a special friend. She would always be his special friend. He was beginning to fear that he would want more than this, and that it might destroy the friendship that they had. So he would keep this to himself. He would bury it with all of his strength.

She reached across the table and took his hand. Warmth ran through his body, but his face did not show what was in his heart.

"Steven, what can we do?"

"We can find them," he replied. "Or wait for them to find us. We can hunt them down, or we can set a trap for them. Either way, we have to kill them. I'm sorry if the word is too strong, but it's the truth."

The word did shock her. It was the truth, she had known it was the truth, but until now it had been an unspoken truth. Kill them. She had helped people live and find and hope for most of her adult life. Now she had to kill. For what? Just for self-defense?

Steven sensed her hesitation. "It's them or us, Rebecca. If you value your life, and the lives of those you touch and help, then it has to be them that dies."

He made it sound so cut and dried. "It can't be that simple."

"Think how your mother would feel with you gone. Think about all of the people you could help who would never have your help. I wouldn't be too happy about it either."

"But why death? Can't we hide out until they're captured by the police? Then they'll be locked up for murder, and we'll never have to worry about them again."

"That would mean finding a place they would never find us in. Maybe we can hide, maybe not. What about Samantha? How can she hide? Even if they are captured and put away, do you want to live the rest of your life wondering if they'll ever escape, or if maybe one of them will get out for good behavior. Surely they'd put Verna back in the mental hospital, maybe Derek too. What if they played sane for enough years? I can't live like that, and I can justify hunting them down. I can live with that. I would like to have your help, but even without it I've got to try."

"Of course I'll try," she commented, sounding slightly offended. "But I just don't know if it will be as easy for me to live with."

"It will be easier than the alternative."

"Perhaps." She took a drink of her coffee. It was all very confusing, but again Steven had made it so simple. She knew he was right, she just had to adjust to the thought of trying to kill someone. It helped that they had already lost one close friend to these two, and that another had been brought close to death. But revenge was not a good enough reason, not by itself. When coupled with self-preservation, and all of the people Steven had mentioned who would be lost without her, then it was easier to grasp. Easier, but not easy.

He took a moment to show her where the safety was, and how to point and shoot the gun. He would take her out back in the morning to let her try actually firing it.

Then Steven stood from the table and walked over to her. He got down on one knee and put his strong hand on her shoulder. "I know it's a struggle for you, but I'll be here with you. We'll be in this together to the end, I promise."

She looked at his eyes. They were strong, yet soft. "I know," she said.

Then he kissed her. It happened all of the sudden, but it seemed quite natural, as if they had been lovers for a long time.

He led her to the couch in the living room where he put his arm around here and they talked some more about what had been and what must be. Finally silence fell upon the dark room and she fell asleep, worn out from the travel and the day. He held onto her and listened to her soft breathing as he closed his eyes and waited for sleep.

5

"They're not here."

Derek lifted the bed from the floor and threw it against the wall. The lamp fell from its stand and the bulb shattered as it hit the ground. Now he could not think, he could only act. His power of reasoning had become clouded by this new reality, and he had to rely on the woman for judgment. He had never been this helpless, and it infuriated him even further.

"They must be together," Verna said to him in the darkness. "At his parents' place."

"Then we'll go there. We'll get them both and be done with it."

"No!" she shouted at him. If they're together then they probably expect us. We need to wait until they are not so prepared, wait until their guard is down."

"Perhaps it is down now," he suggested. "If he is sleeping alone in his room, or if she is sleeping alone, we can get one of them for sure."

"The house may have five people in it. We can't move that fast."

"I can," he protested.

She thought it over. He could move in and out of the room before anyone could react. He could descend on her bed and drive the blade into her chest, then escape before anyone came to her aid.

But Steven was dangerous. She could not see him so clearly, and he was the one most likely to resist, and provide the greatest amount of resistance.

"We will go and look. Then we will decide."

Derek grinned. An instant later he was outside, waiting for her to join him.

6

Rebecca saw the cloudy mist. It was flowing toward her, and she knew it was coming for her. It terrified her, but all she could do was watch it come. She knew that something was wrong, that she needed to get out of this world and into another. But reality was elusive, and she could not awaken.

Steven drew the hand crocheted afghan closer around them as he, too, felt the chill.

7

Pat found herself in a doggy nightmare, running from a giant black cat that only moments before had been the fleeing subject of a good doggy dream. Now it chased her and cornered her and slashed out at her with claws which grew larger as they came toward her.

She came awake in the darkness of the back yard and was on her feet in an instant.

Before her first bark escaped something struck out at her from the darkness, breaking her muzzle and sending her to the ground.

Then she felt something pressing down on her chest and head and found she could not move or breathe.

Then darkness.

8

They stood together outside the house, the big dog lying motionless at Derek's feet. Steven's car was out front, the one with the California license tags. Verna had been right, he was here, and she probably was too. It was time to take a closer look. Verna could not allow Derek to do it on his own. He lacked the judgment he needed, something Steven's force would give him. She led Derek to the first window and told him to look inside.

The curtains were drawn, but still he could see. It was not the same as seeing with his physical eyes, but he knew what was in the room. "There are two bodies, a man and a woman. They are too old."

"His parents," she whispered.

Derek followed her to the next window, then looked again into the dark room. "It's an older woman. She is alone."

They had already checked the rooms in the front of the house, but they had been empty. Where was Steven? Where was Rebecca? Had they left the house and gone into hiding? She doubted that, not with what she knew of that man.

Something moved behind them.

Verna turned and looked but saw nothing. Derek's eyes were fixed on the house. He knew his prey was in there, and his heart was beating loudly in his ears. He left Verna and began walking along the side of the house to the glass door which led to the living room. He was halfway there before Verna's attention returned to him. She knew they were being watched, but by whom she could not fathom. Right now she had to get the reigns on Derek.

She met him on the back porch, and he confirmed his find. The curtains were slightly drawn and even she could see the two bodies at rest on the couch.

"They are both together," he said in a loud whisper.

"Yes," she agreed. But the house was full of people, and someone was watching.

He felt his pulse begin to race. His body shook with the excitement, and he put his hands on the glass. Steven stirred, but only for a moment.

"This is no good," Verna said.

Derek turned around quickly and stared hard into her eyes. "They are here. They are together. I can have them both before they even awake."

"But they must awake first, or their forces will escape. You can only wait for one, the other will have time."

His eyes returned to their outlines. "I will break both their necks. I will take one while the other waits, then I will kill the other."

"We have time. There will be a better time for this."

Derek stared at the bodies. They were so close. In moments they could be his. Everything around him seemed to glow. His body shook and felt electrified. He could not turn away. "You said time is short."

She could see she had made a mistake bringing him here. She put her hand on his arm to pull him away from the glass before he made a worse one.

But it was too late. He turned quickly and pushed her away. She fell down to the porch with the force of his shove. He tried the door, but it was locked. He could not wait; something was building inside of him and he had to have them now.

"Derek, don't," Verna said aloud.

He looked at her for only a moment, then he leapt across the porch and grabbed the barbecue grill. He rushed back to the glass door and held it in front of him as he flew toward the glass.

2

Rebecca screamed out a second before the glass shattered. Steven awoke instantly at the sound of her scream. In an instant his hand went to his waist and removed the gun from its hiding place.

But before he could stand he felt a powerful arm around his head, turning it sharply to his left. Steven felt a terrible pain, but he did not release the gun. Instead he aimed it as best he could and fired twice. The pressure on his neck lessened and he knew he had hit something.

Then he felt a sharp pain in his hand and the gun was out of his grip. Then he was flying from the couch, across the coffee table and into the living room floor. His neck hurt badly, but he raised his head to see his assailant.

It was dark, but he knew this man in an instant. Derek stood looking at him. Derek quickly drew his knife and leapt over the couch and the coffee table in one fluid movement. Steven knew that it was a futile fight, but he rolled away as quickly as he could and got to his feet before Derek could make a lethal slice.

But Derek was lightning fast and in a moment was standing in front of Steven, just a few feet away. Steven did not hesitate. As Derek drew back his blade Steven ran straight at him and grabbed him around the waist. He drove as hard as he could and he felt the blade enter his back once before smashing Derek into the wall. He drove his fist hard into Derek's stomach twice, then leapt away again, afraid Derek might find a lethal place to drive his blade.

Derek was slow getting up. Steven was a powerful man. Derek's head ached where it had gone through the wall, and his right arm was dangling oddly at his side. It would repair, he knew this. But right now it was a disadvantage.

And his knife was gone.

Steven could see that Derek did not have his knife. He could also see that he was not advancing, that he was momentarily dazed. Steven took the opportunity to step forward and land a powerful punch to Derek's face. Derek stepped back, but he did not go down.

A cry came from outside, "Derek, later! It must be later!"

Derek hesitated. Steven punched again. This time it dazed him slightly and he pulled back his fist to land a punch of his own.

The impact of the blow sent Steven to the floor. He landed on his hands and knees. When he turned back around he could see that Derek had found his knife and now held it in his right hand.

There was an explosion, and Derek heard the wall pop beside him. There was another, and the wall popped again.

He looked to the source of the explosions and saw Rebecca, standing in the kitchen, firing a small gun she had figured out how to operate.

Another pop.

Steven was on his feet.

The hall light came on.

The fire inside Derek was dwindling.

The final shot would have taken him in the head had he continued to stand still. Instead he leapt again, crossing the room in an instant and disappearing out the shattered back door.

Steven looked out the door and held his back where the blade had cut him. It wasn't deep, but there was plenty of blood.

His father appeared with his own gun and looked at his son. He made a quick survey of the room. Whatever had happened was over now.

Steven looked at Rebecca. "He'll be back."

She knew he was right. This wouldn't be over until someone was dead. She looked down at the gun and decided that she could live with it now. She could do what had to be done.

"Is everyone all right?" Steven's dad asked.

"I'm cut," Steven answered. "But it's not bad." "You?" he asked Rebecca.

"I'm fine," she answered, but her voice was shaky.

Steven walked across the floor and took the gun from her hand. Then he put his arms around her and held her tight.

In the morning they buried his good friend, Pat. She didn't deserve this, and he would miss her forever.

Chapter Thirteen
1

Steven and Rebecca stood at the side of Frank Sharp's bed. Frank had intravenous tubes running into his arm, and his face was little pale. Other than that he looked good, much better than their recent images of Samantha. His eyes were open and there had been no coma, only unconsciousness which he had overcome during the night. Feeling had returned to areas he feared it would never return, and with it had come some pain as well, but he welcomed the pain in the face of the alternative.

"You two are here early," he commented.

Steven walked over and grabbed the good shoulder of his old friend. "Good to see you too, Frank. You sure screwed up this time."

Frank winced slightly, but his friend's grip felt good. "Hey Rebecca, I haven't seen you since you were just a girl."

"And I haven't seen you since you were a boy," she threw back.

They had known each other in school, Frank had even dated her a couple of times, but nothing serious had developed. The story of Frank's life.

Steven looked at his wounded pal. "Hey, what's going on here, Frank?"

"You know about as much as I do," he responded. Then he looked to Rebecca. "Maybe even more."

Rebecca knew what he was referring to. "I can't get much on all of this, Frank," she commented. "I don't know where they are, and I can't get near anything that might help me. We were hoping you might be able to help."

"What do you mean?" he asked.

Steven answered, "They wouldn't let us in Richard's house last night, and that probably would have helped some."

"Damn it," Frank exclaimed. "I hate not being up and running. Well, I can get you in there now, if it'll do any good."

Rebecca commented, "It's probably too late. If they've cleaned it all up and handled the evidence, then there's probably very little I can get from it all."

Steven looked to her. "Still, it wouldn't hurt?"

"Of course not. Just don't expect anything."

The sheriff sat up slowly. "Max was just doing his job. He's a good deputy, but he follows the rules too carefully." An idea came to him. "I'll tell Max to take you over to Verna's house before the crew gets there. You can go through that box of things in her closet, and whatever else might be of help."

"Box?" Rebecca asked.

"There's a box in her closet full of pictures and clippings of you guys, all of you. She was keeping Derek in that closet until he was well enough to kill Richard, that much I'm sure of."

A box of pictures which she had handled over the years. "That would be great." Rebecca replied. There was no telling what all she would be able to pick up in there.

Steven looked at his wounded friend. "Why is it still there? Why don't you have it?"

"There wasn't enough cause to even look in that box. It would have been useless as evidence."

"And now?" Steven asked.

"I've already taken care of all that. If I'd died everything would still be at a standstill, maybe even worse off. But I saw what happened at Richard's house, I have all the cause I need now to search every inch of that house. Those pictures will provide the link I need to the other murders, and that will get me some federal help, which I'm sure I'll need at this point."

"Why feds?" Steven asked.

Frank smiled. "We've got a good force here, Steven. But I'm not too proud to ask for help when we need it. The two of them are gone by now, no telling where they may be hiding. You know as well as I do that we couldn't search ten percent of the hiding places in this county if everyone in the county was looking. We need the feds to help us find them and bring them in before they do any more damage. I'm not too proud to admit that, and I'm not going to risk more lives just so I can get my picture in the paper and credit for the arrests. Besides, this one crosses both county *and* state lines. Even if I wanted it all to myself, I'd be asking for trouble by not inviting my federal counterparts. I'd rather have them show up with an invitation than some nasty paperwork that'll keep me tied up for days behind my desk. They did that once to Pritchard when he was sheriff here, a kind of retribution for not bringing them in early enough."

Rebecca tilted her head inquisitively. "But we know where they'll be going."

Frank looked at Rebecca with interest. "What?"

"They'll be coming after us. They already did last night."

Frank looked to Steven. "You didn't tell me about that."

"I just haven't gotten to that part yet."

Steven recounted the encounter for Frank. It made the sheriff furious that he had been on the operating table then, unable to warn or help them. But that had passed. Now he would do all he could to protect them.

Frank advised his friend. "I would like to suggest you sit in a little room surrounded by police officers, or maybe even feds when I get them in on this. But I know you too well Steven. You won't go for that."

"You're right. And you know damn well why."

"I know," Frank responded. "Because if you do those two will haunt you for the rest of your lives. Someday, maybe thirty years from now, you may be sitting outside your tent in the woods when Derek comes screaming out of the trees and tries to stick his knife in you. It probably wouldn't happen that way, but you'll probably dream that one, and probably some other ways too."

"But it's more than that."

Frank listened.

"This has got to come to an end. Not just for me, but for all of us. And for Richard and Jennifer too."

Frank could see Steven was trying to make a point. "What's on your mind, Steven?"

"Frank, don't bring in the feds. Not yet."

"You don't want them found." It was a statement, not a question.

"Right."

"You want to find them yourselves and take care of it all."

"Right."

Frank took in a deep breath and let it out. "How do you propose to find them by yourselves when you know they could be anywhere?"

"Rebecca can find them, especially if we get to that box. Besides, even if we can't find them, we know they're coming for us."

Frank closed his eyes for a minute. "You're right, of course. But what about Samantha?"

Rebecca didn't understand. "What do you mean?"

"She's lying unprotected in a hospital bed in New York. How can you protect her?"

"Can't you just call the police up there; tell them you suspect she's in danger?"

"I can try, but they're stretched so thin in that place that they probably wouldn't help. I'd have to bring in the feds for that. They can ask, and then it'll get done."

"But you'll call anyway?" Rebecca asked, deeply concerned for her friend.

"Of course I will, I'll do it when we're finished here."

Steven spoke. "And you won't bring in the feds?"

"I'll put it off. I can't bring them in without the evidence in the box anyway, and theoretically I don't even know about that box. We'll search her place late this afternoon. I'll tell Max to keep the box safe, and to look through it last. But I'm going to have to bring them in sometime soon, especially once we've made the connection between what's happening here and what happened in Atlanta. Remember, it wasn't just Jennifer he killed out there. I could get in real trouble if I drag this out too long. I think they call it obstruction of justice."

Steven patted his friend's shoulder. "Thanks."

"Don't mention it."

Rebecca finally asked the question that had been on her mind all morning. "So what exactly did happen at Richard's house?"

The Sheriff took another deep breath and lay back down. Then he told them everything he had seen. Finally he shared with them everything he knew about the case, including what Julie had shared with him. Rebecca's eyes were fixed on him as her mind whirred, trying to put it all together. Perhaps the visit to Verna's house would help her put the final pieces in place.

2

Steven entered the house first. Deputy Max Perry stood just outside the front door as Steven and Rebecca went in. He was not to go in, not yet anyway. He didn't like bending the rules like this, but he knew that Frank had his reasons. The deputy hoped that perhaps later he would get an explanation.

The house was a mess. It smelled rank, and there was a lingering odor of natural gas. The gas company had come to fix the 'problem' yesterday, but Max had already left the house to go to the scene at Richard Hall's house. Since no one had been in the house, the gas company had simply shut the gas off, as they always did when a leak was reported and they were unable to gain entry to the home.

Rebecca instantly picked up images which were bizarre yet familiar. Verna had lived here for five years, and there was a lot to be sensed. But the things which came into her mind were not understandable.

Steven led the way to the closet in Verna's room. He could see the dried blood still at the base of the door. He opened it and a light came on, then they entered together.

Rebecca spotted the box first and pointed it out to Steven. He pulled it down from its perch and opened it up. The first thing he saw was a picture of himself in football garb. It took him aback. He instantly remembered the game, that they had won, and he had contributed in a big way.

"Let's take it out of the closet," Rebecca suggested.

They walked to Verna's bed together and sat down on the stained mattress. It was filthy, but better than sitting on the floor. Together they began going through the old pictures and articles. There were memories here too, memories they had lost or buried and which brought it all back to them with such force that it saddened them both.

Jennifer in a beauty pageant at age twelve. She was a beautiful little girl. But now she was dead. Samantha in junior high standing next to a sculpture which won her a state art award. Now she was lying unconscious in a hospital in New York. There were some programs from the Abilene Philharmonic with Timothy's name circled. There was no telling where Tim had gone to. There were pictures of Richard from the high school yearbooks, and an article about the seminars he had given on the family and raising children in modern times. Richard was with his God now. Perhaps it was better than all of this.

Rebecca handled the photos with care. They carried the warmth of good memories, but they also carried the remnants of something else, something that Verna had felt when she collected these things and looked them over. There was a sense of loss, of mourning. There was need, and a quest. Verna needed them all, but she needed them together.

"Are you okay?" Steven asked.

She put down the picture of Jennifer in the high school lunchroom. "Yea, I'm okay." She looked into the box. "It's just very confusing."

Steven looked at an article about the junior varsity football team and their fight in the playoffs. His numbers were good. It was no wonder his father had preferred him playing football to climbing rocks. "These are things I might expect to find in my mother's closet, not here."

"I know. That's just it. In a way Verna cares for us all deeply."

"But in another way she wants to kill us?"

Rebecca put her hand on Steven's leg. "She wants to bring us together."

Steven sat up straight. "Through Derek."

"Yes."

"Okay, well, let's assume then that Verna is trying to put us back together, that she's trying to repair this entity. The way she's doing this is through Derek. He's killing us off and setting these pieces of the entity free."

"That's what Frank believes, and it seems to make sense, if anything here does."

Steven grabbed her hand. "You said she wants to bring us together. I think that Derek is a vessel, just like we are. When he kills one of us, our 'piece' is drawn to him. He absorbs that part of us and becomes more complete."

Together.

Suddenly she began sifting through the box again, trying to see if this idea made sense with the feelings she was picking up. It did.

She looked at Steven. "Then she has to kill us all. There is no alternative."

"Exactly."

"And she'll do whatever it takes."

"She's been waiting forty years. It's all her life has meant in that time. Nothing else matters, not even her own life."

"But what will happen? What happens when Derek puts it all together?"

Steven shook his head. "I have no idea. Maybe he'll become like her and they'll run off together. Maybe they'll go back to where they came from and leave the bodies behind. Who knows." He squeezed her hand. "And I hope we don't find out."

Rebecca smiled. Then she winced as if a shock ran through her. Her other hand, the one near the box, was cold.

"What's wrong?" Steven asked.

"I'm not sure." She began looking through the items again. There was something important here. She rifled through the articles and pictures until something shocked her hand. She looked at it closely. It was a picture of Samantha.

"We've got to get out of here Steven," she warned.

He reached for his gun. "Are they coming for us?"

"No. No that's not it. They're gone. They're not even here now."

"Gone, where?"

As soon as the words has left his lips, he knew the answer.

"New York."

Steven put the items back in the box and returned it to the closet. They would have to tell Frank, tell him what was about to happen. Maybe the police in New York could deter Derek. Maybe they could stop him. Maybe they could just delay him a while.

Rebecca looked at him. "We have to go."

Steven knew this already. He knew that they might be of little help, but he knew she was right. They had to go and protect their friend.

They left Verna's house in a hurry. The deputy locked up the house and watched as they left together in Steven's truck.

3

It was nightfall by the time they got to New York. They could only hope that Derek and Verna would wait, that the two killers would not act before they got there. Sheriff Sharp had called the New York city police for help, and they had said they would do what they could. When Rebecca and Steven arrived at the hospital they found out that this meant one officer reading a magazine in the waiting room on Samantha's floor. There were several other people there too, people who had relatives who were sick or dying. Steven approached the officer and he looked up from his magazine, seemingly indifferent.

"Excuse me, are you here on the Samantha Chambers case?"

"My chief asked me to come watch the floor for suspicious characters. Who are you?"

"We're friends of Samantha's. Is anyone else coming to help you."

"I'll be relived in a couple of hours if that's what you mean. If you want to know why we can't post two officers here, it's because this is a favor, and because we don't have any evidence of danger here. We've got a lot of things going on in this city which are immediate and urgent. We need every cop on the street we can get out there."

Steven hadn't meant to provoke the man, not realizing that this was simply this cop's demeanor. "Can we go visit with her?"

"Be my guest," he slid out sarcastically, then he returned to his magazine.

Rebecca followed Steven out of the waiting room and down the hall. "That's it?"

Steven just shook his head. "It could have been us. We're even carrying guns, and we're going to walk right in that room where she's sleeping. This is ridiculous. I'm going to give Frank a call."

They entered Samantha's room together. A woman was in the room at the foot of Samantha's bed. She jumped as the door opened, then grew relieved as she recognized them. It took Steven a moment to recognize Samantha's mother, but then again, it had been decades since he had seen the woman, and she had aged much more than his own parents had.

She recognized both of them right away. "Steven, Rebecca, it's so good to see you two."

Steven responded. "It's good to see you, Mrs. Chambers."

"Please, call me Nancy. You're not in high school anymore."

They walked to Samantha's bed and looked at her. She was pale, but she looked better than she had when they had left.

Rebecca also thought that Nancy had not aged well. Of course, she couldn't be expected to look her best today considering what she had been through. "Is she doing better?"

"Oh yes. She actually came out of the coma yesterday. She never stays awake long, and she's only been lucid for a few moments, but the doctor says her brain is just trying to retrain itself."

Steven looked puzzled. "Retrain itself?"

"She lost a lot of blood, and part of her brain was damaged. But brains are resilient, at least that's what the doctor told us. Right now it's trying to reassign old tasks to new places. He's spoken to her in one of her lucid moments, and he says that it looks good. It may take some time, but she'll have most of her faculties back, along with her memories."

Relief flashed across Rebecca's face. "Thank God for that."

"Yes, indeed," Nancy agreed.

Steven looked to Rebecca. "I'm going to go make that call. Can you stay here?"

Rebecca looked at Nancy, "If it's all right with you, I'd like to stay here for a while."

Nancy smiled. "Of course."

Rebecca tried not to let her concern show. She didn't want to alarm Samantha's mom. Still, it was good to know that the gun that had helped to save Steven was tucked securely in her coat pocket, ready to defend again.

Steven assured them he would be right back, then left to call Sheriff Sharp.

When he returned it was just Rebecca. She explained that Samantha's mother had gone to the cafeteria for something to eat.

"Good. Let me tell you what Frank said. He can't get us more help without involving the feds. I wanted more time to find them myself, but I think her life may depend on it now, so I told him to go ahead. He said he'll get it going as fast as he can, and she should have more protection by tomorrow at the latest."

"We may not have that long."

"I know. That's why I want you to stay here with Samantha. Stay awake and keep your hand in your pocket. Sit on the other side of the bed so you'll be behind it and so you can clearly see anyone coming in the door."

"What are you going to do?"

Steven looked into her warm eyes. "I'm going to see if I can't find them first."

"New York is a big town," she reminded him.

"I have some ideas. If they haven't been to this hospital yet, then I may be able to track them down. I've got to give it a try."

Rebecca looked at her silent sleeping friend again. "I think you should. I can handle this here. I know he's fast, but I'll be awake and waiting, and I won't leave the room."

"I'll be back as soon as I can."

She stood and gave him a kiss. "Be careful."

He smiled. "I will."

Then he left the room and headed into the city.

4

Steven started by phoning the airport for flight schedules. If Derek and Verna had arrived in New York before he and Rebecca had, and Rebecca seemed to be pretty sure of this, there was only one flight they could have made on an airline which connected out of Abilene. He called that airline and said his name was Derek Lowrance and he needed to confirm his return flight. But the airline had no record of Derek flying in on that earlier flight. Steven knew he couldn't get that information from them, but he was sure they had taken that flight, probably paying cash and flying under different names.

The next best place to start looking would be the hotels nearest the hospital. He hired a cab to take him to all of the hotels nearby, both the nice ones and the seedy places that charged by the hour. He took a picture of Derek with him, one that Rebecca had taken from the box, and showed it around. Finally, after about three hours of this, he got lucky.

"Yea. I seen 'im. He came in here earlier tonight. You lookin' for 'im?"

"Yes. I need to give him a message."

The man behind the counter smiled. "I know what kind of message you want to give him. What's the matter, he with your wife?"

Steven resisted the urge to punch the man. "Can you please tell me which room they're in?"

"You'll have to ask nicer than that."

Steven was growing hot. "What words did you have in mind?"

The man leaned forward. His breath reeked of hard liquor. "Green words. The kind that will get me the things I need to keep this old body of mine going."

It took Steven a second, but he understood. He took a ten out of his wallet and held it out. The man reached for it, but Steven did not let go.

"Which room?"

"Not enough."

Steven took out another ten. "Which room?"

"More."

Steven knew the man would rather have twenty than nothing and he pulled the bills from the man's hand and turned to leave. His gamble worked and the man called out the number to him before he reached the door. Steven gave the man his twenty dollars, then headed up the stairs.

Hack loved it when it worked out this way. He knew how to play them, really knew how. He had just gotten twenty dollars from someone looking for the man and woman who had come in earlier that night. They had paid him fifty to warn them if someone was looking for them, and had threatened to kill him if he did not. He knew they were more dangerous. They were much more of a threat. He picked up his phone and called their room. The woman answered. He told them that a man was coming up the stairs, and he wasn't a cop. The woman didn't say anything, she just hung up the phone.

Hack put the phone down and looked at his gun which lay on the shelf just below the counter. If they didn't win, that guy was going to be pissed. He grabbed the gun and held it nervously as he waited for the outcome.

5

Steven walked carefully to the third floor. The stairs were loud, but the noise from the street and the rooms covered him. He made his way quickly, eyes following him from time to time as he passed them.

He reached the third floor and drew his gun. He would be careful, but not too careful. This was his chance to get it over with. He could get them both here and now. There would be no questions. If there were, Frank would help him out. Even if he did go to jail for a while, it would be better than letting them live.

Steven came to their door and stayed out of the line of sight of the peep hole. He listened and could hear the television blaring some old program through a worn-out speaker. He couldn't make out the show, but that didn't really matter. He was going to have to be fast, because Derek was faster.

He counted to three, then kicked at the door hard. Splinters of wood flew from the door frame and the door swung into the room, crashing against the wall and bouncing half way back. The room was dark except for the television. He could see no one.

It looked like a trap.

He approached the room carefully. They were not going to shoot him from a distance, they needed to be close, Derek needed to be close. Steven understood now why he had stared into Richard's eyes at Richard's death. Steven knew Derek would need to stare into his eyes too. He felt for the light switch and found it, but no light came on when he flipped it. He made a quick visual sweep of the room. There was nobody in sight. They could be behind the bed, or in the closet, or in the bathroom. It would be safest to leave, but that was not an option. Instead he walked carefully toward the bed, pointing his gun over it as he approached. They were not there. He checked under the bed. Nothing. The room was chilly, and he noticed a breeze coming through an open window. He would have to check this out last because it would put him too far away from the closet and in an unprotected position. He made his way to the closet and threw the door open. An old plastic jacket fluttered out, sending more adrenaline into his blood, but doing nothing more. The bathroom was the same, empty. Finally, when he was sure the room was empty, he went back to the window and looked out.

There was a fire escape here. Outside the window there were fresh footprints on the dirty steel. They had left. The man at the front had blown it for him. Steven would get his money back on the way out.

Before Steven left he looked around the room for anything which might help the police. It was clean except for some used tissues in the bathroom and a dirty sock on the floor by the bed. It probably wasn't either of theirs.

He had gotten so close.

Steven left the room and headed down the stairs to the front desk. The man there acted like he had never seen Steven before, so Steven surprised him with a quick and unexpected left hook which sent the man to the floor. Steven leapt the counter and took his money back, then kicked the man one more time for screwing things up for him. He saw the gun under the counter and grabbed it on his way out. He wasn't going to take the chance of being shot in the back.

Outside it had grown cold, and it was beginning to rain.

Steven paid the cab driver and told him he would walk on his own back to the hospital. The cab driver told Steven it wasn't safe, but Steven insisted, so the cab left him there.

Steven stood at the side of the hotel for a moment, staring into the alley behind it. There was nothing there. He tried to sense them, but it was no use, he was not Rebecca.

He had been so close.

He walked back toward the hospital, knowing now that he would not find them at all now that they knew he had come. Now they would wait.

And he would wait for them.

Chapter Fourteen
1

Steven was still gritting his teeth when he boarded the elevator to the third floor of the hospital, the floor where an indifferent cop was sitting in a waiting room, waiting for the arrival of Derek and Verna so they could kill Samantha and he could get back to his beat.

The doors slid open and Steven stepped out, heading for Samantha's room. He was still a good fifteen yards away when he was met by a man in street clothes.

"Excuse me," the man said. "Who are you here to see."

"Samantha Chambers. Why, is something wrong?"

"Are you family?"

"No, I'm a friend."

Steven heard Rebecca's voice behind him. "Steven, I've been waiting for you."

The man in front of him looked nervous, but he turned around and faced Rebecca.

"What's going on?" Steven asked her.

"Come with me to the waiting room for a minute, we need to talk."

Steven looked at the man again. The man was obviously alarmed at Steven's height and build. He seemed to be measuring Steven up, trying to guess if he would be able to take him on or not. Steven knew that look. With his size he had gotten used to seeing it.

He backed away from the man and walked to Rebecca who stood a few feet away, waiting. She did not want to approach Steven or the man, and she would explain why this was to Steven later.

Steven looked at Rebecca. "Has there been some kind of trouble?" he asked.

Rebecca led the way toward the waiting room. "He's a cop, Steven. FBI."

"And he's patrolling the hallway outside the room? Don't they know there are windows in that room?"

"There's a man inside the room, and there's one more that keeps wandering around, checking the waiting areas and restrooms."

The tension left his face. "So Frank did some convincing."

"Apparently so," Rebecca answered. "They even checked me out." Her eyes darted back to the man she had met once tonight. "He found my gun and went kind of crazy, like I was an enemy agent or something. They even handcuffed me for a few minutes."

"Jesus, are you serious?"

"It was only a few minutes. They checked my story out with the Sheriff's office in Eastland. They let me out of the cuffs, but they're not giving me back my gun. I mean, your gun. Sorry."

Steven remembered the motel keeper's gun which was now in his waistband, along with his own. "That's okay. I got you another one."

"What?"

The second agent came into the waiting room and looked around. He eyed Steven suspiciously, then looked at Rebecca for a minute. Then he left.

"Let's get out of here," Steven suggested. "We'll get some decent food and a place to sleep, and I'll tell you what happened."

"What about Samantha?"

"There's nothing we can do here now. Even if something did happen, all we could do is watch. Besides, I don't feel too comfortable in here with two guns on me."

Rebecca thought it over. Steven was right. They weren't doing any good here, and she needed sleep badly. She grabbed her purse and bag and followed Steven to the elevators. The man near Samantha's room didn't take his eyes off of them until the door closed.

Even though she despised the scrutiny, she was glad that he was there.

2

They ate Chinese food together and talked. Steven had never cared much for Chinese food, but Rebecca had acquired quite a taste for it working in the San Francisco Bay area. She knew what Steven liked in food, and she recommended a dish to him that he found quite good. Not as good as a thick rib-eye, but good nonetheless.

It was almost four o'clock Saturday morning by the time they checked into the hotel. Steven had decided that something nice was in order, so they got a room at the Marriott. It was over twice as much as he had spent most recently on a hotel room, but this was New York, and he had some savings for times such as these.

They agreed to share a room, but Steven insisted on paying for it. It didn't seem odd. Neither of them was married, and they had been friends since high school. Still, deep inside, each of them harbored a secret hope that something special might happen, despite the hour and circumstances.

They each took quick showers. Both were exhausted. Steven always slept in just his underwear, and now realized that he had nothing more decent to wear. He stuck his head out of the bathroom door and warned Rebecca.

"I'm afraid I don't have pajamas, so you may avert your eyes, if your southern upbringing so demands."

She laughed and watched as he emerged from the bathroom and walked quickly to his full-size bed.

She realized then that she had never seen him like this before. She might have seen him with his shirt off once or twice, but she didn't remember this being the case. Now it was difficult not to be a little aroused as his chest muscles rippled and his thigh muscles tightened and relaxed on his short walk to the bed. She glanced down his frame quickly, then looked away so she would not be caught.

Steven crawled into the soft bed. He loved the feel of soft, clean hotel sheets. They were cool and relaxing, and he felt his big muscles relax as he rolled over to face Rebecca who lay in the same size bed a few feet away. She was in a night gown of some kind, her head in the pillow and her eyes full of something he hadn't seen there before. Was it anticipation? Perhaps just relaxation? He couldn't tell, but it made her look beautiful.

The light beside her bed was off. The shadows accented her sharp cheekbones.

The silence was almost awkward.

"Good night," Steven said.

Rebecca smiled. "Good night."

Steven reached over and turned out the light.

There was silence again for several minutes as a thousand scenarios ran through both of their heads. It was Rebecca who spoke first.

"Would it put a strain on our friendship if you were to hold me tonight?"

Steven said nothing but climbed out of his bed and into hers. He put his arms around her slowly. She needed this. There was so much going on, it was so disorienting. She needed his strength. His strength was a part of her, more so than she had ever thought. It was good to have this part of herself so near.

She was also aroused by this strength.

She knew this was not the right time or place, but she kissed his chest nonetheless, knowing what it might lead to, but neither expecting nor caring.

He felt her kiss and a warmness ran through him, down his chest and between and into his powerful legs.

He wanted more. They had not spent much time together, and they had not even discussed feelings towards each other. With any other woman he would not have felt it appropriate. But he had known Rebecca for a lifetime, and he had special ties to her, something inside himself that came from the same place and something which she held inside her. He ran his hand inside her gown, up and down her side. The skin was warm and soft, and she let out a soft sigh.

He knew it was going to be all right. They didn't need to talk about it.

She let his hands explore, and she buried her face in his neck. The movements of his chest as he breathed were soothing and exciting. It had been a very long time since she had been with a man, and she didn't remember ever being this excited about it. She wanted more than just tonight, but was willing to accept less as part of the price, if it came to that. But she wanted more, and she prayed it would be there.

She helped him ease off her clothes, then she ran her fingers down his chest. Goosebumps rose on his belly, and she could feel his firmness against her stomach. She continued downward and reached gently into his underwear. It was waiting just below the band of elastic, firm and a little wet on the tip. She ran her hand down its length, and it seemed to go on forever. He was a big man in every sense of the word.

She stroked him gently as they kissed, then she removed his underwear completely. She lingered near his legs and kissed his thighs gently.

Steven felt as if he would explode, but he continued to be gentle. He held her by her shoulders and pulled her slowly up until her lips met his. He rolled slowly over, careful not to make her uncomfortable with his weight.

Then, as he kissed her gently on the neck, he slid slowly inside her.

She let out a gasp, and he moved slowly so he would not hurt her.

It was wonderful. They moved together, every nerve in their bodies tingling with excitement and anticipation. But there was more, there was something inside of each of them which reached out and joined with its missing part. They each felt a oneness they had never before experienced with anyone.

The excitement went beyond all bounds as their bodies reached together toward that peak.

And when the moment came, their souls touched.

3

Derek walked quietly down the stairs which lead to the basement of the big hospital. Down there, next to the boilers and laundry equipment, were the janitors' lockers.

There were a lot of people in a hospital. He should have been able to simply make his way to her room and take care of her before anyone knew what was happening. But they were on to him now. There was a chance she was being protected. He had to get close, fast. This was the best way to do it.

He grabbed the lock on the first locker of the second row and twisted slowly. It had been only hours since he had taken that part of Richard that was truly his own, and his strength was again near its peak. But this was only temporary. Until he had killed Steven, he would have no lasting strength. But his temporary state helped him as the lock gave way and snapped as if it were made only of heavy plastic. He checked the contents of the locker, but the uniform was too large for him. The next locker was empty, this janitor was on duty, but the next one held what he was looking for.

The door to the room opened and someone entered. Before the man had even stepped into the room, Derek removed the contents of the open locker and rushed back into the shadows. He watched and waited as a man walked to the second row of lockers and began heading in his direction. Derek tensed as the man came, and he prepared himself for what he might have to do. But the man stopped about half way down the aisle and turned the combination on his own lock. Derek watched patiently as the man withdrew his own clothes from the small locker and put them on. The man hummed softly as Derek waited and watched. A moment later another man entered. It had to be the beginning of a shift. This was bad luck.

This man was much more observant than the first. As he walked down the second row of lockers he stopped for a moment and looked at the locks which Derek had broken. He looked to the man getting dressed.

"Hey, Les, you see this?"

The short, fat man, apparently named Les, looked up. "See what?"

"These broken locks. Somebody broke-in here."

Les continued to dress. "So they did." He seemed unimpressed.

"Nobody uses this first locker, but these belong to Dave and Peter."

"Well, I'm glad they didn't get into mine, because I'm running a little late as it is. And so are you."

"But don't you think this is weird?"

Les was getting agitated. "Sure it's weird, but what are you going to do about it? Get dressed and forget it. You can tell the supervisor when he comes in tomorrow."

The first man still looked concerned, but he seemed to be willing to listen to Les's suggestion. He walked away from the lockers and toward Les. But his eyes wandered. He seemed spooked, and he was walking slowly. His eyes ran across Derek once, but the shadows hid Derek from him.

He walked past Les as Les put on his hat and closed his own locker. "You better get a move on. It's almost fifteen after."

The nameless man kept walking past Les, two lockers, then three. He was very close now, less than fifteen feet away. The man was about to turn around and face his own locker when he saw the strange shadow.

"Hey Les?"

Les was heading out when the tall man called to him. He shouted over his shoulder. "What is it?"

The tall man stepped closer to the strange shadow. The pipes didn't look like they were supposed to. Then he saw the eyes.

The tall man lost his composure and screamed. Derek flashed out of the shadows and drove his knife into his chest, twisting it when it was buried in the man's heart.

Les stood only for a moment, unsure of what he was seeing. Then he turned and ran.

Derek let the tall man drop to the floor in his own blood and ran down the aisle of lockers in a flash. As Les turned the knob on the door he felt the knife drive into his back. How could this be? There was no way the man could have caught up with him so quickly.

But Derek had, and Derek turned the knife quickly, bursting Les's left kidney.

Derek picked Les up and carried him back into the shadows. Then retrieved the tall one. They were expected for a shift, apparently they were late. There might even be more men coming, he couldn't know.

Derek changed into the clothes he had stolen before this had all gotten out of control. He took Les's name tag and identification and then carried the two men into the boiler room and shoved them firmly behind one of the boiler units where they would be safe and oh so quiet for as long as he needed.

And he did not need very long.

4

They had only been asleep for two hours when Rebecca woke up, her heart racing, images of death still fresh in her mind.

"Steven," she cried out. "We've got to get over there!"

Steven awoke to Rebecca's cry and knew in an instant what she meant. He did not reply, but merely jumped out of the bed and got dressed as quickly as he could.

Rebecca sat in a daze for only a couple of seconds. The vision had been gruesome, and she was not sure if it was a glance of things to come or if it had already come to pass. A moment later she, too, was up and getting dressed.

"I'd better go alone," Steven explained as he pulled on his boots.

"I can take care of myself," Rebecca objected.

"I know you can, but I can't wait on you."

"I'll be ready in thirty seconds."

Steven was dressed and heading for the door. "That's not what I mean. If time is critical I've got to go now, and I've got to go fast."

Rebecca protested, "I can keep up!"

Steven opened the door and looked back. Rebecca was trying frantically to pull her pants on and get them zipped before he was gone. He wished she understood.

He couldn't go.

"You need my help, dammit!" she cried out as she slipped her white shoes on and got to her feet, not bothering to tie them.

He knew these seconds were crucial, along with those that would follow. But this was her crisis too, and she had a right to be involved. It might cost them the advantage, but it was the right thing to do.

Rebecca felt otherwise. She knew that Steven would do better with her help than without, otherwise she would have let him go on his own. He would need her help. And if he failed, she would need to be right there behind him, firing the fatal shot. It would be harder for Derek to face them both down.

If he had not taken Samantha already.

Rebecca grabbed her gun from the dresser and ran to Steven's side. He said nothing but pulled the door shut and hurried down the hall, his own gun hidden in his belt. She hid her own gun under her arm as she ran with him to the stairs, but there was no one to see them as they were all in their hotel beds, hours away from rising to a new morning.

Hours which would decide the fate of their friend.

And their own fate as well.

5

Derek left the basement by the stairs which led to a hallway and followed the gray concrete floor to its end, at the doorway to the service elevator. He had armed himself with a mop and a pail from the storeroom near the lockers, and he grinned slightly as the elevator doors opened.

He knew which floor Samantha was on, but not which room she was in. But that wouldn't matter. He could feel them now, just like he had felt Steven approaching their hotel room. He would have to be close to her, but even if there were no names on the doors he would know which room she was in.

The elevator stopped on the third floor and the doors slid open. He was met there by a man dressed like himself, obviously one of the janitorial staff whose shift was coming to an end. The man waited for Derek to step out, but Derek stood in the back of the elevator with his eyes down, so the man got in. As the doors closed the man looked at Derek's name tag, then up to Derek. Although Derek's face was hidden, the man knew this man was not the right build to be the man whose name was on the tag.

"Hey, you're not Les."

Derek looked up. "No shit." Then he brought out his blade and made quick work of silencing the scream that was trying to emerge from the man's neck. Derek stayed in the elevator holding the limp body off the floor. He rode the elevator down and carried the man back to the dressing room. This was getting out of control. It was getting complicated quickly. Verna had said that if it did he was to abort and try again later. But he was not about to try again later. He was so close, and he needed Samantha so badly.

He tried again, riding the elevator to the third floor. This time no one met him as he got off, which was a good thing considering the blood which had gotten on his clothes, and which was smeared along the floor of the elevator. Derek stepped out, pushing his pail ahead of him, heading for the double doors which lead to the rooms where Samantha was hiding.

He passed through the double doors and walked slowly past the rooms, pushing the bucket in front of him. He walked the length of the hall, knowing he was getting closer, but knowing he was not yet close. As he came to the end of the first hallway and turned the corner he saw a man. He knew in an instant this was trouble. The man's eyes came to him quickly and began scanning him carefully. As Derek approached the man, the man turned and faced him. This was not just a man in the hallway, this was protection of some kind. And there might be more.

The man walked to the center of the hall. "I'll need to see your identification," he said. Jeff Walker had been through this exercise three times tonight already. The last man had just left, he'd said it was the end of his shift. He was supposed to be replaced by Les. Jeff had reviewed photos of all of the janitors, but he could not tell yet if this was Les. If he'd remembered the height and weight statistics, he would have known it was not. If he had seen the blood on this man's uniform in time he could have prevented what happened next.

Seeing the blood, the man took a step back and reached inside his jacket. Derek reacted like lightning and instantly the man's hand was crushed by Derek's grip. The man looked surprised for a second, then brought his other hand up quickly. But Derek was much faster as he drew his blade and drove it home with lightning speed. The man let out a cry, but Derek covered his mouth. Derek left the knife in the man's chest as he quickly grabbed the gun which the man had been reaching for. He held firmly to the man's face as he went down so no sound would escape. Then the man's eyes glazed over and Derek let him go and swiftly removed the blade from his chest.

It was still a lot of noise, and Derek watched the hallway as he concealed the knife and the gun. If they had posted this man to walk the halls there was most likely one in the room. There might even be two.

Derek continued down the hallway, his senses heightened and his heart racing.

Then a scream came from behind him.

He did not look. Instead he walked to the wall and watched both ends of the hallway. In a moment a man appeared around the corner which stood between Derek and his goal.

6

It took too long to get the cab, and Steven promised the man twenty dollars if he could get them there in less than ten minutes. It was going to be close, but even that ten minutes seemed too long.

"Is he there?" he asked Rebecca.

"I don't know. I know that he was on his way, but I don't know if he is there now, or if he's still heading that way." She was silent for a moment. The cold steel of her gun pressed against her belly. "It may even be all over by now."

"I hope to God not."

The cab came to rest in front of the hospital. The cabby had missed his time by a minute and a half, but Steven threw him a twenty anyway. He couldn't wait for the change.

As they approached the hospital Steven noted that the police were not swarming the entrances. That was good. Either Derek was not here yet, or he had not completed his task. Steven hoped it was the first of these two.

Then Steven heard the sirens, and his heart sank.

Rebecca followed Steven into the hospital and up the stairs. The elevator would be too slow. Steven hoped that they would see a cop that Rebecca knew already. They were, after all, running to the room of a woman whose life had been threatened, running, no less, with guns in their possession.

But it was happening too quickly. The strategy he had made up on the cab ride over would have to be the one they used now. Rebecca would just follow him; he had asked her for this and she trusted him.

As they emerged onto the third floor they heard the gunshots and knew the time had come.

Z

Derek stood in the hall and fired three shots rapidly. The first and third hit his target. The man fired back once, but then dropped to the floor as one of the bullets took him in the side. He tried to raise up to shoot again, but the wound in his side burned badly. Before he could raise up, and much too quickly to be possible, Derek was upon him with his blade, slicing through his neck and twisting his head at the same time. Then Derek was away from the body, throwing the severed head against the wall behind him and waiting for another man to appear.

The scream behind him continued, but no one else came. There had to be another, but he was apparently staying put. The third man was in Samantha's room, he was sure of this. He had probably already radioed for help. Derek could hear the sirens now. He would reach his goal, of this much he was certain. But escape was now becoming more difficult. He could turn back now and increase his odds dramatically. He could even hear Verna calling to him to abandon his task. But he could not. The call from Samantha's soul was closer and stronger. He would have that soul, then he would worry about escape.

Derek hurried down the third hallway, gun in hand. This was the right hallway, he could feel the excitement growing as he approached her room. He was there in an instant, a moment later he had thrown her door inward and ducked the bullet which came for him. The man inside was going to try to keep Derek out until help came.

But the only help that could arrive in time was Samantha's two friends, a hundred yards away and closing fast.

8

Samantha was in the back corner of the room. She was stirring as if she knew she was in danger but could not wake from a bad dream. She probably did know. She could probably sense that he had come back for her. The cop was behind a second, empty bed on the right. The cop was well covered, and he had a good clear shot at the door.

But he could not suspect Derek's speed and strength.

Derek rushed into the room, pulled the door closed, and turned the light off in one fluid motion. The man fired and hit Derek once in the arm, but Derek moved too quickly, and then the man could not see him at all. Once the lights were out the cop's eyes did not have time to adjust before Derek's blade was deep into his neck.

There were sirens.

Samantha screamed.

9

Steven and Rebecca rushed past the second dead agent. It was the one who had challenged Steven. Now he was lying in a bloody pile, his head ten feet away. They heard Samantha scream and Steven picked up speed running down the hall, toward Samantha's door. Behind him Rebecca slipped on the man's blood and watched Steven pulling away, heading for the door.

Then Rebecca cried out and doubled over. Steven couldn't look back, not now, now he had to concentrate on one goal and nothing else. Behind him Rebecca felt steel entering her body as if she were the one under attack. The pain sent her to the floor, her gun sliding away from her hand as she grabbed her chest with both hands.

She knew they were too late to save Samantha and prayed Steven would get there in time to put an end to Derek.

10

Derek pulled the blade from the man's neck and rushed to Samantha's side. He could see her terrified eyes, even in the darkness. "You can't get away from me this time," he spit at her.

Samantha tried to raise herself out of her bed, but her muscles would not respond. She tried to cry out, but her help was all dead now. She knew he was right. The struggle was over.

She closed her eyes tight, knowing that he needed them to be open.

But it did not matter. She felt the steel as it slid slowly into her body. She tried to resist, but something inside of her wanted out, and it wanted out through her eyes.

He stared and he waited, his hand wrapped firmly around the handle of the knife. His arm burned where the bullet had torn him, but already the healing had begun. He waited. He knew she could not resist.

She felt the burning pain where the blade had entered. She felt her blood leaving her body and she began to cry. It wasn't fair. She remembered her childhood and her parents. Then she remembered her special friends. In that moment she understood why they had always been so special, and she understood the tie they all shared. She knew they were close by and she tried to warn them.

She also knew she could no longer resist.

As her life left her, her eyes slowly opened. The electricity started deep inside her brain and worked its way forward.

Then she felt a sharp pain in her eyes, followed by a bright light that consumed her entire being.

Then it was warm.

And dark.

And she could feel that something had left her. Something which had been a part of her for her entire life pulled away from her and left her alone in the darkness which had come for her.

Then there was another, different kind of light which descended upon her from above.

11

Derek watched the fire as it leapt from her eyes and into his own. It rushed into his brain and set off the fireworks, more powerful than ever. He felt bigger than his body, as if he could leave it now if he wished. But the body felt more powerful now, more complete.

He understood that this was not his home, though he did not know what that meant. He felt the grace and beauty of what had been lodged in Samantha, and it brought understanding and a hint of remorse. But this had to be done. And there was more to do.

The sirens grew louder.

He stood and looked at the lifeless body on the bed before him. It was now an empty shell. Inside of him he now held what it had contained.

Then the door exploded inward and Steven entered, gun drawn, eyes probing the darkness for Derek. Derek considered only for a moment if he should take Steven on here and now, at the peak of his strength. But he knew Steven was not alone, and the risk was too great. There would be a better time.

As the police rushed up the stairwell and bullets from Steven's drawn gun peppered the wall behind him Derek flew along the wall to the window. It was sealed shut, and there was a heavy screen on the outside to keep the more depressed patients from putting an end to their hospital stay. It was nothing. As Steven continued to fire his gun, Derek put his shoulder into the glass, and it shattered outward. The screen bent and snapped as he forced his way through it, the safety glass hanging together in odd patterns, unable to cut him deeply. He swung out through the twisted metal and wiry glass and found himself on the outside of the building.

It was an older building and there were ledges to hold onto. They were not close together, but his fingers held like steel, and he could fly from one to the other almost effortlessly. He felt the exhilaration as he scaled down the side of the building to the ground level. The cops were all on the other side, covering the entrances and exits.

Steven ran to the window, not knowing if he had hit Derek or not, unsure of his aim in the dark room. Rebecca was still in the hall, getting slowly to her feet, knowing Samantha was gone now. As she made it to Samantha's dark room Steven stuck the gun and his head out of the window, but only in time to see Derek's shadowy figure disappear into the night.

Chapter Fifteen
1

Derek stood on a street corner with his woman, waiting for a cab to come take them to the airport.

It was becoming clearer in his mind now. Since he had brought both Richard and Samantha in it had all begun to make sense. He didn't know exactly where home was now, and he didn't know how he would get there, but soon even these things would become known.

Steven and Rebecca were here, in New York. They knew now, and they were staying together. They were prepared for him and had stood in his way twice already. With the two new souls had also come more wisdom. He knew he could not simply come charging after them here. As strong as he was, a bullet to the head or heart would still end it all suddenly. He had to form a strategy.

He and his woman would go back to Texas now and wait. It would be better that way. This would not be expected, and it would give him and the woman a great advantage. He would call out to them and let them come to him, but he would deceive them as well. He had not developed any new psychic powers, not yet anyway. It was simply his tie to them, that part of himself that rested in their minds, which allowed him to reach out to them. They knew that Samantha was dead. They would also know he was returning to Eastland. But they would not know why. They would think he was running, hiding from them to attack at a later time, a time when they were apart from each other.

A cab came into sight, but its light was off and a passenger was inside.

His mind was working almost as quickly as his body now. He knew that they had not come here only to save their friend, but also to come after him. They would try again, of this much he was sure. So he would let them come. But not in this place. He would need another advantage.

Finally a taxi pulled to the curb. Derek opened the door and threw in their two bags, then let his woman climb in first. He knew now why he needed her too. He no longer felt repulsed by her, and he could sense her joy. He climbed into the cab and closed the door. She was silent now.

"To the airport."

The cab pulled back into the early morning traffic as they sat in silence. She knew she no longer had to chastise him. Now she would answer his questions, and he would know how and what to ask.

But this was not the time or the place. He would ask when they were alone in west Texas.

The road hummed beneath them as they began their journey back.

2

The drone of the big plane's engines filled Steven's mind. Rebecca sat at his side as they passed over the rolling white puffs of moisture which were dropping a warm spring rain on northern Louisiana. In a few more hours they would be home. But Samantha would never go home. Or she was there now. It was a matter of perspective.

The horror of the past week ran through Rebecca's mind. Where had this nightmare come from? Had it always been with them? Rebecca looked back on her own life with a new perspective. This time, the present, has always been with them. What was happening now was what they were all destined for from their birth, or from shortly thereafter. She knew that it was the storm which had changed them, and that for just an instant they had been just seven more new babies, wonders to the world, yet common in their humanity. Moments later, in the flash of light, that had all changed. Their lives, even who they were, their very fiber of existence, had all changed. She wondered who she would have been if there had been no storm. Where would she be now if not for her gifts? Surely she would not be the same person. The woman she would have been had disappeared back then.

Suddenly she did not feel real. She felt as if something so much larger than herself had controlled who she was and who she had become.

Steven looked over at her and she smiled at him. She felt the warmth inside of herself and was reminded that she was, in fact, very real. There were things in everyone's lives which changed who they were and who they would be. For some people it was the family they were born into, for some the town they grew up in. Everybody was adrift in the ocean of life, at the mercy of the rolling waves which shaped their destinies.

She was no different.

She squeezed Steven's hand and closed her eyes, glad that he was drifting so closely to her in that ocean.

3

The Sheriff lay in his hospital bed wishing he was almost anywhere else. This was not his style. He flipped through the pages of a magazine he had never even heard of before this stay, and hoped never to hear of again. He was beyond reading the articles on civil wars and inner peace. Now the ads were the last bastion of interest, and not so much the ads as the way they were shaped and worded.

It was all an exercise to keep from going crazy.

He dropped the magazine on his lap in frustration and looked up to the television. It was the middle of the day on a Friday. Nothing was on. It was a little different nothing than what had been on this morning, but it was nothing, nonetheless. In an hour or two one of his deputies would come by to check on him and ask some odd procedural question. It was a routine he had gotten used to and now had begun looking forward to. They had let him use a phone for a while yesterday, but had taken it away when they realized he was working from his hospital bed when what he needed was rest, not the tension of being the sheriff of Eastland County. Deputy Cox was running things for him for now. The man was not an innovator, or particularly brilliant, but he knew what the rules were, and he followed them to the 'T'. Cox was reliable if not predicable.

The sun beamed through the slit in the curtains. It was a welcomed greeting from the outside, a gloriously sunny day which he would not be able to participate in. The evaporative coolers would be humming in the old part of town, and the hills north of Cisco would be green and teaming with squirrels and wild turkey.

The hills of Cisco.

The image had presented itself more than once since the incident at Richard's house. Only now was it becoming clear to him that it had done so.

Before his murder, Richard had said something about those hills. At the time it had seemed enlightened, but then it had become buried in the sheriff's subconscious. Until now.

Richard had said that there would be death in the hills. He had said something about a beast, something about life and eternity.

Frank closed his eyes, but he could not remember more. He knew that it was important. Maybe it would mean something to Rebecca.

He had not heard from Steven or Rebecca since they has left his room the day before. He felt out of touch and he hated it.

He buzzed his call button and asked the nurse for the phone when she appeared. She frowned for a moment, then reminded him that he needed his rest.

4

It was dark but not cold in the hills just north of Cisco. From their cave in the rocks they could see a valley below them with trees and a small stream.

Eastland County was vast and empty, thousands of square miles inhabited by twenty thousand people, most of whom were located in the two small towns of Cisco and Eastland. There were certainly counties in Texas with fewer people in them, but there were also city blocks in Dallas and Houston which had more people in them at one time than had ever lived in the entire county of Eastland. Derek hadn't thought much about that either until recently. He been to Dallas twice, never to Houston, and never out of the state until his trip to Atlanta. Now he realized that he should have left long ago. Atlanta and New York had been full and alive, yet dead at the same time. He could have lived in any of a dozen big cities and killed every week, maybe even every night, if he'd been careful. In Cisco his opportunities had been limited, as had been his cover. In a city like Houston there were a million rocks to climb under.

But if he had left town he would not be here now, on the verge of this greatness. In fact, if Verna had contacted one of the other 'snow babies', he might even be a victim by now.

Derek and Verna had made their home in a large cave in the rocky hills outside of Cisco. They would need a portal to leave this place, but when he had gathered the energies of the remaining souls they would be able to open their own doorway. That was how they had come to this place. This place was full of doorways, and they were near to its center. It was a place which was ancient, doorways which had existed since before man had set foot on the land, before creatures of any kind had wandered through. It was a place which was held tight by the gravity of the rotating ball it was on, as were many such doorways throughout the universe. It had been formed at the dawn of this ball's creation when the magnetic forces and gravitational energies had given birth also to a moon and the planet's surface had flowed as hot liquid.

The doorways would be here until the day this planet melted as its growing red sun burned the last of its fuel.

Perhaps they would return then, to see what new wonders this place might offer. For now it was hostile and uninhabitable. They would flee to another place, one which was not so material as this. The concepts of the fabric of this place were too difficult to work with, the limitations were enormous, it was the closest thing to hell he had ever seen.

And he had seen many places. Some were silent and as immaterial as dreams, some were brilliant and expansive, but none were and material and constraining as this one.

The time they had spent here had been but a millisecond compared to their entire existence, but time had become such a reality here that it had seemed an eternity. Never before had he understood time, now he loathed that this knowledge would stay with him, and hoped that he would forget what it meant to be made of flesh and blood and be held accountable to the passing of time.

He remembered being in pieces, though only in the pieces which had been reunited. Memories as well as talents which resided in those who were alive were still lost. He remembered lying in the darkness of night, watching pieces of a foreign and hostile world go by for endless day after endless day. It had truly been a terrible eternity.

And now it was finally coming to an end.

He turned to the south and felt the swirling warm winds as he faced the souls which would soon be his.

5

"They're here." Rebecca sat in the living room of Steven's parent's house holding a cup of decaffeinated coffee. This was the same living-room where Derek had made his first attempt to "reclaim" them and had taken Pat from them. He would probably come here again, he and Verna both, only this time he would be stronger, and they would come in a different way. Steven's dad sat in the chair across from Rebecca and regarded her with concern and respect. He wondered if she was using her special gifts now, or if what she felt was just the intuition of the hunted.

Steven sat next to Rebecca and he squeezed her hand. It was as much for his own comfort as it was for hers. They were not going to return to New York for Samantha's funeral. It would bring them out in the open, and he would hunt them down. They could not win, not traveling as they would have to, unguarded and ill prepared. He could come from anywhere, and now Derek, or whatever he had become, didn't care if he was seen or not. They couldn't risk it.

Steven's mother came back into the room with a cup of coffee for herself and for Rebecca's mother. "What are you going to do now?" she asked. They had just finished listening to the horrible story of what had taken place in New York. It was late, but now none of them could sleep.

Outside the house two deputies sat in a car, a loaded shotgun and two pistols accompanied them. It made their parents feel better, but Steven and Rebecca knew it wasn't enough. They had seen Derek in action twice, and his display at the hospital had made it clear that he was too fast to counter. Perhaps the sounds of gunshots would give Steven and Rebecca a head start, if either of the men could get a shot off before Derek got to them.

Rebecca answered the question which had hung in the air a little too long. "We're going to stick close to each other and stay as hidden as possible. There will be protection outside the house twenty-four hours a day, we'll have our inside protection near at all times." She patted the gun at her side as she said these last few words. Of all of the futures she had imagined, the one of being back in a small west Texas town and hiding a gun in her pants had never crossed her mind.

"Did Frank say something about the feds hiding you?"

Steven answered his dad, "he did, but we discussed it and decided we'd be safer here, like this. He might be able to swing some more protection for us here though, but not for a day or two."

"What about the search?"

"Frank said that they were traveling under aliases, and there was no evidence that they came back to Cisco. No matter how much we think they did, this is only one place they could be. The feds have sent one man to work with Frank's men to put up some posters and to do a general search, but they're not going to put on a manhunt or anything like that, not without some proof that this is where he is."

Rebecca's mother sat forward. "But you know he is."

Rebecca answered, "that doesn't count for much with the feds, I'm afraid. Frank knows we're right, and he's done everything he can. The man the feds sent wants to concentrate on the grocery store and the hardware store, stakeouts and posters. Frank remembered something Richard said about the hills, and I feel like he's right, so he'll have a couple of men looking in the hills outside of town tomorrow, but the rest of them are assigned to the feds, guard duty here, and he had to leave a couple available for calls. Frank has them all working overtime."

Steven's dad spoke, "I guess our county taxes will be going up again this year."

It was light humor, and it was the first of it all evening. It lifted the weight of the heavy air slightly, and Rebecca let a slight smile come to her lips.

"So, how is Frank doing?" Steven's mother asked.

Steven turned to his mom. "He's recovering pretty well, but it's going to be a couple of days before they let him out. They want to keep an eye on a couple of his wounds, make sure they continue to heal." Steven took a breath. "They're probably just afraid that if they let him out he'll jump right back into work and tear something up again."

"And he probably would," Steven's mom replied, remembering Frank's determined nature for as long as she had known him, remembering the time Frank had played a full quarter with a broken rib before collapsing on the field from the pain. That was Frank, loyal and determined, but not always real bright.

Amanda could see in her son's eyes that he, too, was remembering earlier days with fondness, days which now seemed so uncomplicated but at that time had seemed so full of import and meaning. It was funny how time did that to your perspective. She was sure, however, that no passage of time would decrease the significance of what had happened to them all this past week.

<u>6</u>

It was dark, but Frank couldn't sleep. There was pain, but it wasn't the pain which kept him awake. His friends were at home, trying to protect themselves against Derek Lowrance and Verna Calloway, or whatever it was the two of them had become. People had died. People had been shot at, knifed, pummeled, and worse. He felt helpless laying in his bed, knowing he was of no use to anyone here, knowing he was needed now more than ever.

His mind kept returning to the hills. What hills? There were many patches of rolling terrain in the county that could be considered hills, many of them would be good hiding places. Tomorrow some of his men would begin searching those hills, and he would feel much better when they had found an abandoned campfire or other sign of activity. They could be on either private or public land, and they would have no problem searching both.

But there had to be one place that was better than most for hiding.

But where could that be?

He thought long and hard about the terrain of the land surrounding the towns of Cisco and Eastland. They would not wander too far from town because they would need food and water, unless they were in someone's house. The latter was unlikely, it would be too visible and have too many hazards. They would want to avoid the roads now, so they would likely be traveling on foot. And they would have to know they were being searched for now, so they would be wearing disguises, or they would already have food and water stashed, in which case they could be even farther from town.

Then he remembered the summer of 1973. It had been a hot day, and a very warm night had followed. He and Steven had sat in Steven's truck drinking a few beers and talking, waiting for the traffic to lighten up, waiting for darkness to hide their activities.

He remembered tying a rope to the rail at the top of the dam and watching Steven climb down it with a can of spray paint to put up the biggest, most dominating two numbers as had ever been put on the Cisco dam. Even now the faded remnants were more discernible than many of the numbers that had been painted since.

Rattlesnake Canyon. That had to be the place. More caves and dens per square mile than anywhere else in the county. And there was one cave in particular that was better than most, one where each of them had taken girls from time to time to both scare and romance them. Since those days the trail had been damaged, a second kid had been killed trying to get out there, the first had been a big kid they all knew in grade school. The man who never stepped on the land but actually owned it had put up a stink with the authorities to keep the kids out. So it was, once again, a secret place where no one went.

It was perfect, and Derek would have known about this place. So would Richard.

It made the most sense.

If he told Rebecca, she would know for sure if he was right.

He rang his alarm and had to raise his voice at the nurse, but he finally talked her into getting him a telephone.

Chapter Sixteen

1

They went as far as they could in Steven's Bronco, then got out. Frank had given his word he wouldn't tell anyone else for a couple of hours. Steven hoped that was all they would need. Inside he knew it was because within that time someone would be dead. He felt the handle of his .45 and hoped it would be Derek and Verna.

They were still a mile away from Rattlesnake Canyon. They would go on foot from here because it would be too rough on the Bronco, and because they needed to be stealthy. If they could surprise Derek and Verna, then they would have one more advantage. But inside Steven doubted that he and Rebecca would be able to surprise the two who had been killing their friends. Even now they probably already knew that Steven and Rebecca were on their way. Would they hide from them and wait for a better time, or would they try to set a trap? Either was possible. They had to be more than careful.

"I never knew about this place," Rebecca said. It was hot. The sun had risen on a clear morning, and the rocks beneath their feet still held the heat from the previous day's sun.

"Remember when we in were in grade school, and we heard about this big kid, it was Mrs. Gilbert's boy, who died 'in the hills outside of Cisco?'"

Rebecca shifted nervously as she looked around at the forbidding rock formations which climbed and jutted, narrow paths evident between crushing boulders. "This is the place?"

"About a hundred yards ahead. There's a part of this path that is really narrow, and you have to hold on to some rocks beside the path to make it past this cavern. He didn't make it. We were always leery of that place, because there were stories that they never recovered the body, and his bones were waiting down there for companionship."

"Steven, stop. I'm already terrified."

He grabbed her hand. "I'm sorry. I was just remembering it for myself. Of course his body was recovered, and it's not that dangerous as long as you keep your eyes on the rocks and not the cavern. Actually, I used to love this place. I guess it's really where I got started with my interest in climbing and hiking and camping. It's challenging and dangerous, yet beautiful."

Rebecca looked down the path they would take. "One mile?"

"About that."

"How long will it take us?"

Steven thought back, trying to remember the layout of the trail. "Probably forty-five minutes." He looked at Rebecca. "Not much longer."

She took a deep breath and felt the gun she was carrying. They had to know. But the time for hiding and waiting was over. At Steven's house would not be better. A year from now in San Francisco would not be better. It had to be now.

"They can wait for a very long time," Rebecca said, looking down the trail.

"They already have," Steven answered. "If we don't do this now, we do it later. And I'd rather fight them now when I'm ready, than ten years from now when I'm older, sitting on my couch some evening falling asleep after watching reruns of Seinfeld."

Normally Rebecca would have laughed. But nothing was normal about this moment.

Then Steven stepped over to her and kissed her.

A tear came to her eye. "I'm sorry," she said suddenly.

"For what?"

She looked into his eyes. "I don't know. I just am." She buried her face in his warm and dusty shirt. It felt nice. She wished this was all behind them, and that death was not going to meet one or both of them at the end of this trail.

Steven held her shoulders. "There's nothing to be sorry for. We're in this together." He looked into the hills and took a deep breath. "Now let's go before we lose our nerve."

2

It was tougher than he remembered. Of course, his memory had been fogged by more than two decades, and he had been a little more limber and lithe back then.

The trail quickly degraded and became extremely narrow. In many places it disappeared altogether, buried under rocks which had fallen from the hills above them. This trail had not been kept over the years as had the trails he traveled in southern California working for the USGS.

Rebecca noticed that Steven had stopped and was staring at the trail ahead. "What's wrong?"

"No tracks," he replied, still surveying the path.

"Do you think they got in a different way?" she asked.

"I don't mean just human tracks; I mean no tracks at all."

"Is that bad?"

"Yes." He looked ahead but did not see anything blocking the way. "There used to be a stream a little further down the trail. If the animals aren't using the trail any longer it probably means that it has become impassable."

"Couldn't it just mean that the stream has dried up?"

Steven thought. "It's possible, but even if it had, there would probably still be some kind of tracks. Animals don't just stop using an old trail completely."

"Could the rain have cleared all of the tracks."

The trail was dry and dusty. There were no droppings, no signs of droppings or other disturbances not wholly attributable to rocks and wind. "This trail is dead."

She didn't like the sound of it. "What do we do?"

"For now we go on. When we find out what killed it, then we decide."

Rebecca agreed. "Let's go then."

Steven led the way through the rock-strewn trail. As they rounded a corner they came to a large boulder which had broken free from the ledge above and now blocked the path in front of them.

"Is that the problem?" Rebecca asked.

"No. There's space under it for small animals, and a deer could scale it much easier than we're about to have to."

As he said this he grabbed hold of the boulder at the greatest protrusion and pulled himself up. The rock was about ten feet from bottom to top, but it was jagged and broken, and had many good placed to grab and hold. In just a minute he was on the relatively flat top. When he got there he saw the real problem.

Rebecca had started up the boulder, so he did not have time to take a good look down the trail. Instead he crouched down and offered his hand to her. He helped her get her chest and shoulders to the top, then began climbing down the opposite side since there was clearly not room for two people on top of the great rock. Rebecca slid across the top, not looking down the trail. Steven helped her down, then stood as both of them rubbed their sore spots and caught their breaths.

Rebecca grabbed her water bottle. "Damn, it's hot."

"Climbing over that well heated rock didn't help any," Steven offered.

Rebecca could see that he was distracted, looking down the trail instead of at her.

"Did you hear something?" she asked in a hushed voice.

"No." He looked back at her. "It's what I saw, from the top of that rock."

Rebecca looked down the trail and saw that from here forward it changed its character completely. They had been gradually climbing upward, but with rock walls on either side of them. Ahead the trail was a steep climb, and the wall on the right fell away quickly into a canyon. At first the canyon was a narrow but deep crack in the rocks, but further ahead it opened up into a small valley with trees and a pond, about a hundred yards below them.

But the worst part was that the trail disappeared, right where the canyon began.

"Is that what killed the trail?" Rebecca asked.

Steven walked down the trail, toward where the small valley began.. "I would guess so."

As they walked down the trail Rebecca noticed what Steven already knew. The deep crack in the rock was a separate feature, like a crevasse in the ice. It was not connected to the valley but was its own deep black pit. It was probably as deep as the valley, only you could not see the bottom, so it looked even deeper.

"That must be where that kid died," Rebecca observed.

Steven looked at the place where the trail disappeared. "That's the place."

The rocks which had once supported his feet across the edge of the crevasse were now gone, presumably down in the canyon covering the bones of whatever animals had fallen in over the years. The rocks they had held onto to keep them on the then narrow trail were still intact, only the side of the hill beneath them had given in to gravity.

"You crossed that thing?" she asked.

"It wasn't like that." He looked to the ground where the trail disappeared into the now widened crevasse. "There was some trail left, pretty good footing, but not very wide. You could make it without grabbing rocks if you were good, but there are some real good grips there, so it was really pretty safe."

"Except for those two kids."

"I'll bet this spot was traversed hundreds of times, if not thousands. I probably did it twenty or thirty times myself."

"You were crazy."

He had looked it over carefully. "You're going to think I still am."

She knew what he was going to say. "No way in hell." She couldn't help it.

He turned and looked at her. "I do this kind of thing all of the time. There's no trail, but there are still some great grips. I can make it around to the other side where the trail picks up again by climbing."

"I won't go."

"I wasn't planning on it."

Rebecca just then realized what he was thinking. "You can't go alone. You need my help."

"You can't do this," he explained. "You'll end up down there." He was pointing into the dark crevasse.

"We need to get the right equipment and come back."

"They don't carry climbing ropes and pitons in Cisco," he explained.

"We can go to Abilene."

"It's an hour each way, they probably don't have the supplies, and I can be across in less than a minute."

Rebecca looked down the crevasse. It looked as if it were a gaping mouth, waiting for its next meal. She knew she could not talk Steven out of this, and that they were wasting time. "Okay. But I'm going with you."

"I don't think so. It's too dangerous."

"But not for you."

"Of course it's dangerous for me, but I do this all of the time. I'm used to the stress."

"But you'll need my help on the other side."

She was right. But it was still too much of a risk.

Rebecca looked up the steep wall to their right. "Is there another way around?"

Steven thought about it. "There might be, but I don't know where it is, and the cave is just minutes away from us now."

"Not if we're dead."

"I can make it," Steven protested. "I'll go by myself, and if I fail on the other side, at least one of us will still be around to stop them."

"But with the two of us we both stand a better chance."

Steven looked at the rocks ahead of them. He knew he could make it. She could probably make it, but he didn't want to risk her life.

"Look, Steven, we're already taking a huge risk here. What difference does a little valley make now?"

She was trying to lighten the atmosphere, but the effort failed. It was too serious now; it was all too serious now.

"Watch me carefully. Watch my hands and do the same."

A moment later Steven was on his way, his feet dangling over the open mouth below while his hands groped and grabbed at the handles which had been used a thousand times before. As long as it had been it still felt familiar. It was a short trip but seemed to take a lifetime as that was clearly what was at risk.

When he reached the other side he turned to help Rebecca across, but she had already started the trip.

The rocks were not familiar in any way to her hands. They felt slick, and she felt heavy. Her arms were not used to this kind of work, and her heart raced.

"Feel for the big rocks, don't grab anything you can't get your hand around."

She didn't answer but concentrated on the task. She could sense the ground was gradually recovering beneath her, but there still was not enough there to keep her from feeding the hungry rock beast below.

She felt above her head and grabbed a rock that was too small. It came free and spun past her head, bouncing off her shoulder on its way down. She cried out, but held firmly with her left hand, dangling precariously in the air while Steven told her to reach further than she had, that there was a deep groove in the rock she should use. She found the groove and held firmly to it. For a moment she did not move. Then she gathered her strength and her nerve and continued.

She covered the final five feet quickly but carefully. She felt the earth beneath her feet just as the rocks above her receded into the hillside, the grips becoming smooth, then nonexistent. As she released her last grip the ground beneath her moved. At first she thought she had stepped on a loose stone, but then realized that everything beneath her was giving way, moving back into the cavern. She looked up to Steven, afraid to move, yet knowing she must.

Steven saw the look of terror in Rebecca's eyes and knew what he had to do. The trail between them was sliding away, already loosened by whatever had sent the rest of it below. The gap which had covered twenty feet would soon cover thirty, the last ten feet taking them both with it if he did not hurry, and perhaps even if he did. He jumped to the ground, his chest over the cavern, his arm held out. Rebecca was already reaching for him and their hands met as her knees hit the moving trail, her feet on their way into the gaping maw. She slid with the earth into the pit, swinging oddly by the arm which Steven held tightly in his grip.

"Climb up me!" he shouted as she swung from his right to his left. He could not reach out for her with his left hand and keep his grip, so he stabilized himself as she came up, grabbing at his left shoulder.

Rebecca got a handful of shirt and began to climb, not thinking about what was happening. She pulled herself out of the pit, climbing over Steven's head and back, trying not to hurt him, yet pushing quickly, anxious to get away from the edge. She rolled off of him as soon as she could, and he pushed himself away from the edge which was already soft, pieces still slipping down into the crevasse.

Rebecca was out of breath. "That was too close."

Steven turned, a look of exhaustion and disapproval on his face. "We just about lost you down there."

"Well, we're over here now. And so are they." She got up and brushed the dirt from his shirt and pants, new holes at the knees. She looked back at what they had just traversed. "How did they do it?"

Steven stood, checking to be sure all of his equipment was still strapped to his belt. "Maybe they floated across. Maybe Derek carried the old woman on his back and climbed across. There's no telling."

Rebecca was thinking differently. "Maybe they came in another way."

Steven was looking down the trail, past Rebecca. "Maybe so." He walked over to her and grabbed her shoulders, looking again into her eyes. "Are you sure you're ready for this?"

"I have to be. If I don't face them now, with you, I'll have to face them later, probably alone."

"Perhaps not. If I fail alone, Frank will call in the artillery, bring everyone in here to get them."

Rebecca shook her head. "They don't know what they're up against. They won't catch them both, certainly not Derek."

Steven ran his hands down her arms and held to her hands. "You're right, of course."

"So we have to do this now, because our chances only get worse from here on out."

Steven looked over her shoulder again at the trail which wound gently to the left, then disappeared behind the stone wall. Around that bend was the cave. And perhaps more. Certainly death was there, but death for whom? He was as prepared as he could be, and Rebecca was right. The two of them would have a better chance.

"Just like we planned," Rebecca reminded him.

Somehow the plan now seemed inadequate. But it was all they had.

She kissed him, then looked into his eyes. "We're going to win either way."

Steven knew she was right. Whether they lived or died, Derek would be denied one of them. They had made a horrible, yet necessary plan. If one was killed, then the other would die then too, down the hillside, away from Derek and his invasive being. It was suicide. But they would win. He just didn't like the idea of winning by default, especially if it meant shooting himself in the head while jumping off a two-hundred-foot cliff.

But it was too late for this kind of retrospection now. Now it was time to go down that trail and face whatever future awaited them both.

3

It was eerily silent. Steven could hear where the water from the small stream slipped down the hillside into the valley below to fill the small pond there. This was private land, but nobody was sure who really owned it now, and no one had disturbed most of the 800 acres in half a century.

A hundred yards ahead of them was the cave. It was afternoon and the sun hung near the top of the cave, lighting the valley but leaving the inside of the cave in contrasting darkness. Sunrise would have been much better, the sun shining into the cave. A small but important error, but one realized too late.

The cave had been carved into the hillside ten thousand years earlier and used as a home by the ancient peoples of the area seven thousand years ago. In front of the cave was a large, flat area which extended about fifteen feet in front of the cave before dropping about twenty-five feet to a small, flat area with rocks and shrubs. This platform extended another fifty feet or so and was relatively flat to its edge, which then fell on an almost vertical line for over two hundred feet to the rocky valley floor.

Steven regarded the valley floor and guessed where he might land if he were the one to jump. Rebecca was thinking the same thing, and it was clear neither of them would survive either with or without a gunshot to the head.

"I can't see anything," Steven said looking ahead into the darkness.

"They're here somewhere." Rebecca replied.

Steven took the first tenuous steps toward the cave, heading up the steep trail which led to its southern edge. It was the safest approach. Rebecca followed behind him, grabbing at the shrubs to help her balance on the way up. Moments later they were at the top, looking around the southern edge of the cave into its interior. Steven took the flashlight and the gun from his belt and scanned the cave. There were signs of activity, but no people.

"They're staying here for sure, but there not here now."

That was the best of the possibilities. Now they would have a chance to get settled into advantageous positions before Derek and Verna returned. This would give them their greatest chance of success.

Rebecca still felt unsettled. Something wasn't right. "Are you sure?"

"Come look," he said, stepping forward in front of the cave entrance.

Rebecca watched as Steven swept the flashlight beam from left to right. There was an old campfire, a pile of trash, some candy wrappers dancing around the cave floor, but no people. She could see all of the way back into the cave, about one hundred feet. There were only a couple of good hiding places, and only one of them would still be able to conceal an adult human.

"What about there?" she asked.

"They can't both be there, but Derek could be, and that's all that matters. I don't think he would wait for us there, but I'm going to walk around the mouth of the cave until I can see the other side. When I'm sure it's clear, we'll go in."

Rebecca had her hand on Steven's hip and hated to feel it slip away as he left her, walking slowly across the front of the cave, his light and gun pointing at the one large rock that could be Derek's hiding place. If he was not there, then Steven would go there and wait while she waited outside the cave, in the brush near the entrance. This way they would trap them, shoot at them from two angles. More importantly they would be apart from each other if one of them should be caught and killed, leaving time for the other to do what needed to be done.

When Steven reached the opposite end of the cave he gave Rebecca the okay signal and walked in. Rebecca stepped into the open and watched as Steven quickly inspected the inside of the cave more closely before coming back out. Together they found her hiding place, outside the cave and near the edge of the first small drop. There was an outcropping of rock and a couple of shrubs which would conceal her from anyone coming up the only path to the caves entrance. They would walk past her, coming no closer than thirty feet, and then into the cave. Once inside the cave she would wait for Steven to start shooting. That would be her signal that they were in a position where they could be shot at from both sides without the danger of Rebecca and Steven shooting each other. It seemed to be a good plan, but she knew that there were too many unknowns to get a guarantee. Her biggest concern was simply that Derek would 'sense' her presence and snap her neck before she knew what was happening, or that they had been waiting for this and would spring a trap of their own.

But none of these fears mattered now, and she had to put them out of her mind as she squatted down into her hiding place.

Then she thought she heard odd noises coming from inside the cave, and as the gunshots began she realized too late that their targets were already there.

4

Steven had not yet gotten to his hiding place when he saw something out of the corner of his eye. He turned quickly, pointing his flashlight and gun upward. As he did he saw a shadow descend from the ceiling of the cave, something dark and evil which almost floated to the ground.

Steven began firing even before Derek hit the ground, but it was impossible to hit the dark moving target and in seconds Derek was before him, swatting both the flashlight and gun away in one fluid movement. At the same time Steven dropped to his knees and pulled a hunting knife from his boot. He felt Derek's powerful hands encircling his neck as he drove the knife upward, thrusting with all of his strength into the dark mass above him.

The air was split with a blood curdling scream as Steven drove the blade home. Rebecca stood outside the cave, unable to see the struggle, unable to decide if Steven was in need of her assistance or if she should simply begin firing.

Then she heard the scream inside the cave, followed by another behind her. A searing pain shot through her side and suddenly someone was on her, pummeling her head with some metal object which tore at her flesh and dented her skull. She had dropped her gun and now lay on her side taking the blows and trying to understand what was happening. Then she felt the weight magically pull away from her. She heard screaming and shouting but was losing consciousness. Then she heard a final scream, followed by a soft thud, then nothing. As she slipped into darkness she felt big hands pulling her away from the cave.

Steven felt the pressure around his neck loosen and he lunged forward, pulling the knife upward with all of his strength and pushing Derek away with his free hand. He hoped to gut the man, then flee to the light outside where the battle would be more even. He did not search for his gun but withdrew his knife as Derek fell back and sprinted for the opening of the cave. As he reached daylight Derek landed on him from behind, pushing forward to the edge of the first small ledge. Derek's hands were on his neck again, this time from behind. Steven got to his knees. Derek was still strong, but he was not heavy, and Steven, using moves he had learned years before in high-school wrestling and modified for a life and death struggle, planted his right foot, stayed on his left knee, reached over his own head, grabbing Derek by the hair on the back of his head, tucked his left shoulder and pulled down hard. Derek went flying over his shoulder, over the ledge dropping the twenty-five feet to the ground below.

Steven looked over the ledge in time to see Derek land about fifteen feet from the unconscious Verna. He landed on his feet, but spinning and off balance. The force of the fall pushed him forward to the ground, landing on his face and one arm. Even from twenty-five feet away Steven could hear the arm snap.

But Derek was starting to get up.

Knowing he must take every possible advantage, Steven leapt.

He landed hard on his feet and fell forward. He felt a sharp pain and knew he had sprained his ankle, and his knees took a beating as he hit the solid ground. But he was up in an instant, his bloodied fingers still wrapped around the hunting knife, lunging forward toward Derek who was miraculously up and facing him.

Blood covered Derek's front and gushed from the wound near his belly. His face was covered with blood from his last fall, his nose crushed and his skull above his right eye exposed. But he looked alert. And furious.

In a flash Derek was on him again, this time in the light. Steven was ready, and he was prepared for Derek's speed. He held the knife tightly, the blade in line with his knuckles, and punched. The shot took Derek square in the face, but only dazed him for a moment. Steven took that moment to step forward and punch again, this time chest high, with the sharp point of the knife forward. Derek stepped into the blade, causing Steven to miss his mark. The blade sunk in nevertheless, piercing Derek's shoulder, sticking in the bone.

Steven heard no gunshots and knew Rebecca was in trouble. But that thought flashed quickly through his mind as Derek came forward with his own blow, knocking Steven back against the stone wall he had just jumped from. Steven hit his head and was dazed for a moment, then he was looking at Derek, the blade protruding from his shoulder, the blood covering him from head to toe. Any normal man would be on the ground breathing his last. But Derek was no normal man, and he kept coming, not even aware of the knife, intent on his quarry before him.

Steven lunged forward, tackling Derek around the waist and driving him back. He drove forward an upward, trying to keep Derek on his feet until he reached his goal. They would both go over the edge together, then it would be done with.

But Derek lifted his feet off the ground and went down too early. The men tumbled, and Steven felt his feet slide over the edge of the cliff. Derek was on the ground too, now aware of some pain and weakened, but still focused on his goal. Before Steven could get to his feet Derek was there, kicking him once in the head. It was a powerful kick and Steven slid sideways, more of his body slipping over the edge. Then he was too far, he felt stone tearing at his chest as he slid away. Death awaited him on the rocks two hundred feet below, and he felt it pulling him toward it.

That would be fine. Derek could not reach him in time. From what he had seen the beast had to be close when it happened, and Steven knew he would be dead long before Derek could be near enough to capture his essence.

Then he felt a strong hand on his arm, holding him in place over the edge of the cliff. He looked up to see Derek's bloodied face looking down at him.

"It's not going to work," the face hissed at him.

Steven got a hold on the ledge with his free hand, and his feet found protruding rock.

Derek looked now at the knife protruding from his shoulder. He grasped it firmly and pulled, flesh and blood covering the blade as he did. "I'm going to help you up here and slit your throat as I do. Then you will be mine. Then I will go to Rebecca, who is unconscious on the rocks above. Then she will be mine."

Steven grabbed firmly onto Derek's arm. With all of his strength he planted his feet and pulled.

But Derek did not budge. Instead he laughed and began to pull Steven upwards, toward him and the bloodied blade. "I admire your valor. Soon it will be mine."

Then, suddenly, Derek began to float. His body rose slowly from the ground and began to move above Steven's head.

But something was wrong. There was an odd look on Derek's face, and his grip on Steven weakened as he cried out.

Steven pulled free and held onto the edge of the cliff, his feet still perched on the rocks below. Then Derek was flying, flying past him and away from the cave, only now he was no longer flying but falling, falling downward, screaming and moving violently. Steven watched in amazement until Derek met the ground below.

Derek hit the ground with a loud thud. The body bounced once, then settled amongst the rocks with arms and legs twisted at odd angles.

Then there was another strong hand on his.

He had forgotten about Verna.

But when he turned to look it was not Verna he saw, but the man who had just thrown Derek to his death.

"Oh my God." Was all Steven could say as Tim Watkins pulled him to safety.

5

The sounds were quiet at first and built slowly to a crescendo of claps and pops. The two men looked down at the body, which was moving, but more as if caught in the currents of electricity that encompassed it than of its own volition.

Then Verna was looking, fifteen feet to their right, limping from the fall which had come when Tim had thrown her off the first ledge onto this one. Now she was conscious, and watching as her lover left, incomplete, from this world.

"No!" she screamed. "No! No! No!"

Then she leapt.

The two men stood in shock as another body streamed down to the valley. Her arms were outstretched as if she were reaching for Derek, trying to fly to him, but she missed him and bounced on the rocks ten feet away. Soon, as her blood began to wet the stone around her head, her electricity mingled with that of her lost lover's. It popped and crackled, and the smell of ozone filled the air.

"Rebecca," Steven whispered, and he took his eyes from the spectacle below to search for her.

Tim looked at Steven. "She's up there." He pointed.

Steven limped to the southern edge of the ledge and got onto the trail which led to the mouth of the cave. He saw Rebecca leaning against the rock wall where Tim had placed her, her eyes glassy but opened.

"Oh, my god," Steven cried as he rushed to her and knelt before her. He took off his shirt and tore it into pieces which he used to mop the blood from her face. Below he could hear the sounds of departure growing in intensity.

"I'll be okay," Rebecca said. "It hurts, especially my head, but nothing is numb, and nothing's broken. I'll be okay." Then, "Where is Derek?"

At that moment came the loudest clap of all, like a clap of thunder. Something tore through them both as the ground shook and the smell of rotten eggs filled the air. Somewhere below another door had opened, then closed. It shook them to their souls, and they knew that it was over.

"He's gone." Steven said. "Gone forever."

Rebecca tried not to cry, but it was all too much.

Steven sat beside her and held her as she sobbed.

They sat together until Tim came up the path, thinner and older than they remembered him, but with that unquestionable look of curiosity in his eyes. "You okay?"

Rebecca did not know until then who had come to her aide. She thought it had been Steven. She had been knocked unconscious and had awakened sitting where she was, the offending shovel a few feet away as she listened to the sounds of the struggle.

"Thank you." She said to Tim.

"You're welcome," Tim said in his understated way, and he smiled. "Hey, I know a secret way out of here. You guys wanna see it?"

Epilogue

Steven and Rebecca sat across the table from Dean and Julie Curtis at the small steakhouse in Eastland. They had talked some about the things which had happened and speculated about the future. Steven held Rebecca's hand on top of the table, and it was clear they would be doing more than just 'keeping in touch' this time around.

Julie spoke, "This thing that has been running for, what, forty years now? It's finally run its course. But it makes me wonder what unfinished business lingers in this area."

Steven had told Rebecca a little about Dean and Julie, and what they had seen in New Orleans. He had mentioned something about the Cisco area, and the doorways which seemed to populate the area, but they hadn't talked about it much, having had their fill of the unusual.

Nevertheless, Rebecca's curiosity was piqued. "What do you mean by 'unfinished business?'" Rebecca asked.

Julie smiled. Rebecca liked the warmth of Julie's smile, it was inviting, yet unobtrusive.

Julie answered, "I just mean with what happened here a few years back with Frank Sharp, and now with you and your friends. There are many doors here, and it makes me wonder how many of them have opened in the past, if any are opening now, or if that's all over?"

The waitress came with their food and looked at Julie with confusion at her talk of 'doors.' Julie disarmed the girl with a smile and a few kind words, and moments later they had their food and their conversation.

"So," Steven spoke up, "you think there's more to come?"

"I'm just wondering, is all. Maybe we've seen all there is to see. Maybe these things happen over hundreds or thousands of years, or maybe they come through at random, once in five years, again in five thousand. I just wish I knew more."

"Well, I certainly have seen enough," Rebecca offered. "If it weren't for my mother, I would never come back."

"I like it here," Steven responded. "I don't think I could live here again, but I do like this place. It still feels like home to me."

"Amen," Dean chimed in, having been raised an hour away in Albany.

"I certainly consider it home," Julie replied.

It was silent for a few moments while they each began their meals. Then Rebecca spoke again.

"I'm sure glad Tim Watkins showed up when he did. I don't think we'd be here if he hadn't."

Julie nodded her head. "I think Tim's gifts go deeper than his piano playing. He has a special perception that he can't put into words, but it's what saved you all."

Steven agreed. "I hope his life settles down for him now."

They had invited Tim to dinner, but he had declined, saying that he was eating with his mom, but thanked them anyway.

"So," Dean interjected, "what are you two going to do now?"

The question was loaded and meant more than the obvious. Steven and Rebecca had talked some, but the details had not been ironed out.

"I think," Steven replied, "we're going to go to our respective cities and live our respective lives, keeping in touch when we can."

"My work is pretty mobile," Rebecca explained. "What Steven does has him in Southern California for the time being, and he owns his home. I'm just renting, and I've been in San Francisco long enough. I'm ready for a change, something not quite so frantic as San Francisco, but with more to offer than west Texas. Except for the hot weather, I've considered working in southern California."

They had only discussed this some, and Steven did not realize Rebecca was as serious as she apparently was. He squeezed her hand and she smiled at him.

Dean and Julie just smiled.

2

In his own bed at last, Tim Watkins lay awake pondering the days behind him. It had been so lonely at night in the hills, and he had found so little food. His mom had cried when he came home, and didn't want to know where he had been. He thought that was strange, but had agreed not to talk about it.

It was good to be home. The people at the newspaper had found a temporary delivery boy and were not mad at him at all. His mother had spoken to them first, and they had been very nice about the whole thing. He would be starting his route again in the morning, and was looking forward to it with great anticipation.

He had killed someone, and that made him feel bad. He knew they had been monsters inside, and that the woman had not really been a person at all, but that did not seem to matter. He had never thought about really killing someone, and it made him feel even worse because he was so happy they were dead. He remembered the joy he had felt as Derek had left his hands and gone flying over the edge of the cliff. He had saved Steven and Rebecca, and they had thanked him. He had talked to his mom about feeling bad, and she had just told him that sometimes in life there was a big bad and a little bad, and sometimes you had to pick one of them. Tim wished he could have picked even a little good thing, but he knew that he had made the right choice, and he prayed to God to forgive him for breaking one of the commandments.

Then he went to sleep.

3

Frank Sharp sat at his desk, finally out of the hospital, finally back at work. Steven had come by and told him what had happened. The feds had been pushy, but now they were gone, satisfied that there was no foul play. But the word was out. Frank even heard they were going to do a piece on Derek and Verna on one of the many television "news" shows like Primetime or 20/20.

After what remained of the bodies had been removed from the canyon, a search of Verna's house had been conducted. They had found an odd assortment of items which simply attested to her insanity (though Steven had explained that it was something different than that). But something else had been found as well. Inside a shoe box, under the bed, was a note explaining that Derek had, in fact, killed his own sister, as well as Tommy Matson, Pep Barton, and a number of names which were unfamiliar. That piece of information had been a shock even to Frank, and he wished the former sheriff had been alive to hear it. Pritchard had been a good sheriff, but a little overbearing, and always sure of himself. Some of those cases had been closed too quickly for Frank, and this list was a sort of vindication, though an unpleasant one.

Frank finished organizing his desk and he looked once around the small station. It was Saturday, and he was alone except for Sally who took the calls on the weekends for minimum wage. It was a small station, but a good one. Things were getting back to normal, if they ever could here.

That last thought stuck with him. He remembered his earlier discussions with Steven about Eastland, and what Julie Curtis had said about doors and spiritual thresholds. He only hoped that the weird stuff was over for a long time. But if it wasn't, at least he was in a better position to understand it - if it could even be understood.

But perhaps it was all over now. Perhaps there would be no more disturbances like the last two for a hundred years. Maybe this had been a crescendo of sorts, and now the pressure had been released, like just after a big earthquake.

Maybe.

But maybe not.

Frank leaned back in his squeaky chair and closed his eyes, hoping that the things that were best about this place, the friendly people, good hunting, and peaceful surroundings would be what dominated the future of his county.